HIVE

GARIN K. HOVANNISIAN

Copyright © 2025 by Garin K. Hovannisian

All rights reserved. No part of this book may be reproduced, stored in a retrieval system, or transmitted in any form or by any means—electronic, mechanical, photocopying, recording, or otherwise—without the prior written permission of the publisher, except in the case of brief quotations embodied in critical articles and reviews.

First Edition: 2025

ISBN: 979-8-9925903-0-2

Library of Congress Control Number: 2025906795

Published by Avalanche in the United States of America

A V A L A N C H E

For Larisa

Invitation 3
All the Buzz 24
Happy Wife, Happy Life 38
New World Order 51
The Birds & the Bees 67
They Were Goddesses 76

Dance of the Bees 93
The Simulacrum 104
Honey Trap 116
About Jane 126
A Tale of Two Hives 133
Catharsis 144

Dead White Males 154
A Most Terrible Fate 165
An Alternative History 175
The Queen's Gambit 186
The Hive Mind 204
Home 216

INVITATION

On the last day of class, a black envelope arrived in my university mailbox. For months now I'd been receiving death threats and love letters and pictures a professor can get arrested for possessing. This envelope was different. It didn't seem to be the work of a student. It must have been a mature and steady hand that had sealed it down with candle wax and branded it with the letter Q. Against the simplicity of the black envelope, the golden letter snaked intricately. A scent followed. I lifted the envelope to my nose and closed my eyes, trying to remember where I'd smelled that perfume before—a quiet collusion of honey, salt, and ash. It made my body stiffen with a memory my mind could not yet locate. That is when I heard the footsteps.

I slipped the envelope into my back pocket, stepped out of the mailroom, and looked down the hallway. Nothing there. Only the distant dripping of coffee. The flushing of a toilet. The vicious pecking of a keyboard; we were in store for another think piece from Planck. Closer to me, chatter spilled out of Dean Gilbert's open door. He had reeled in his latest victim and was recounting his struggles to get approval for the new coffee bean at the faculty lounge.

Above me fluorescent lights buzzed. They put me on edge.

"Oh, there you are!"

From the other end of the hall, Professor Kieslowska came at me in black dress, pearl earrings, and ruby heels. She had a glamorous stride at seventy.

"I've been looking all over for you!"

I crossed my arms as she closed in.

"Well, you found me now."

"How I'm going to miss you," she said, resting her freshly manicured hands on my forearms. "You're one of the good ones."

"You too, professor."

"Then you plan to make it? To my—well, are you going to make me say it?"

"I'll try."

"It would mean the world to me. I was going to say me and Fred. Old habits."

These native phrases sure sounded sweet in her Eastern Bloc accent.

"He was a good man."

"He certainly was. You remind me of him, you know."

Behind her glasses, the professor's turquoise eyes twinkled with something more. From my early days of teaching, she had misplaced some kind of hope in me.

"Anyway, I'll be expecting you all by my lonesome," she continued. "And you'll bring that gorgeous wife of yours. What was her name? You know I'm so forgetful."

Professor Kieslowska hadn't forgotten. She just wanted me to know that these little tactics weren't beneath her.

"I'll bring her along," I said.

"Good. That's very good. Well, I'll be off then. Oh, and good luck tomorrow. Don't let you-know-who rile you up. He just envies your talent. And he wants to bed you, of course."

Agniezska Kieslowska gave me a wink, like I was some long-lost flame from the dissident underground of her youth. She added as she left—

"You *have* the votes. You just sit there and smile, okay? You haven't forgotten how to smile, have you?"

As I watched her vanish down the hallway, it occurred to me that I was going to miss Kieslowska. After her retirement, the university would finally discontinue her Introduction to the Classics—the survey of "dead white males" which she, having identified herself as a necrophile, had famously defended.

"Aggie," I muttered behind her.

She paused for a moment, but hearing nothing more, continued down the marble hallway. Her ruby heels clattered—her ankles swelling above them. The lights agitated the halls with their buzzing.

The sky opened like a robe of purple and gold. The sun bathed the brick of our buildings, archways, and bell towers in a holy light. The grass sparked at my feet. It was "magic hour" in Los Angeles—that daily hour when the godless city unites in worship, because everything and everyone, down to the last unpaid grip and strung-along actress and transplant student, is imbued with significance and beauty. By this light even a campus such as ours—a set reconstructed from medieval cathedrals and fortresses—can appear real. Even better than the original, some would say, because light is the religion here.

"Fuck you, professor!"

The words came flying out of a black Tesla. A splashing trail of red followed. A slushy drink caught my leather jacket.

"You've got blood on your hands!" the boys called, as they

slipped behind a curve. "Killer! Perv!"

One must not make decisions at magic hour in Los Angeles. One must not fall in love, for example, or take a job. Easiest way home would be to follow that Tesla onto Wyton, hang a right on Hilgard, and walk down Sorority Row. At this time of year, the young women would be sunbathing out on their lawns, as the frat boys raced the street below. I never took that path anymore. Instead I turned left, headed under the CIA-looking building that houses the history department, trailed through the Sculpture Garden, took the higher crossing on Hilgard, and made my slow, brooding descent into the tangle of narrow streets called Holmby Hills.

Ours was a quiet and shady neighborhood, with eucalyptus trees hanging over an elementary school nestled amid Spanish, Colonial, and Provencal exteriors. It was "clean" and "safe," were the code words, and not a single robbery had been reported in years. The only crimes being committed here were the theft of ideas, assassinations of character, and moral burnings at the stake. In other words, it was a good neighborhood to start a family in—and ours was a beautiful two-story Colonial with plenty of room and a lovely lawn on which the sign of the day's political movement, Neve's choice, was perpetually stabbed.

As I walked up the driveway, I noticed the house was dark, which meant that Neve was probably at pilates or at the massage studio. She wouldn't have left the door unlocked, though.

"Hello?"

The door creaked open. I stepped in after it and made my way through a valley of Amazon packages.

"Anybody home?"

There was no answer. Only a faint light coming from upstairs.

"Neve?"

I headed up to the second story. Standing at one end of the hallway, I looked down to the other. Light slipped out from under the bathroom door. My heart picked up.

"This isn't funny."

I walked to the door, turned the knob, and pushed in.

"Neve?"

The woman in the bathtub screamed hysterically, her hands flapping against the bubbles like the wings of a falling angel.

"Oh my God!"

"Sorry. I didn't mean to—"

"Fuck! Fuck! Fuck!"

"I'm sorry."

Neve sat up in the tub and calmed herself.

"I thought you were a rapist or something."

"What? No, it's just me."

"I must have dozed off."

Neve giggled. An empty bottle of Sauvignon Blanc towered over a skyline of scented candles.

"You left the door open."

"That's because I was waiting for you, babe."

"You never leave it open."

"I guess I was feeling a little dangerous."

"Wait—did we have something planned?"

"No! I just thought we'd celebrate. It *is* the last day of class, right?"

Neve got up on her knees in the tub. The bubbly water dripped down her full breasts. I hadn't seen her naked in weeks.

"Hey, what happened here? Babe, is this—blood? You didn't get into another fight, did you? Those fucktards—"

"No. I just spilled some juice."

Neve smiled her relief.

"You're so cute when you're clumsy," she said. "Anyway, I've ordered a bunch of new clothes for you. What? Don't look at me like that. You can return them if you want."

She came in for a kiss. Her lips were soft and her eyes were wandering and sweet.

"I wouldn't mind, you know."

"What?"

"Being raped. By you, I mean."

Neve pushed the jacket off my shoulders, unbuckled my jeans, and brought her hand in.

"Come here, professor."

"It's not official yet."

"It is to me, *professor*," she said, grabbing me with all her strength. "Don't play shy. Come on, don't you want to fuck my brains out?"

So she was in one of these moods—and I was usually suspicious of them. But it was, in fact, the last day of class and Neve was cute-drunk, so I took off my clothes and got in the tub after her.

"Oh my God, babe," she said. "You're hard already."

We entangled awkwardly but managed to settle into a compromise position. She found me among the bubbles and helped me in.

"There we are," she said. "Now fuck me hard, okay?"

"All right," I said.

She was rubbery as I moved in her.

"Fuck, babe," she said quietly. "You feel so good."

She took my hands and put them around her neck. She smiled to say goodbye, closed her eyes, and whispered—

"Fuck me like I'm your little whore."

"Oh yeah?" I said, pushing harder against her.

"I want you so bad, babe."

"I want you too."

"I want you to come inside me."

"What?"

"You can come inside me now. It's summer, remember?"

I tried pushing again, but the friction was too much. The soap was sticky and crusting between her legs.

"Babe, what's wrong?"

Neve opened her eyes. She put her arms around me and pulled herself up for a kiss. Her breath smelled of sour grapes.

"Sorry," I said, with a sigh.

"Really?" she said. "Oh come on! I was just having fun, babe. I'm not even ovulating."

Neve climbed out from under me and we sat across each other in the tub. The water was cool around us. She seemed completely sober now.

"Hey," she said.

"Hey," I said.

"Can you answer honestly? I just want to know. Don't you find me sexy anymore?"

"What?"

"Be honest. I can tell you're not into me. Not like you used to be."

"Of course I'm into you. Don't be crazy."

"I'm *not* crazy. I told you not to say that."

"Okay."

"Do you actually *love* me?"

I sat there, trying to understand how she meant that word.

"Have I gotten too old for you?" she asked, with a self-pitying sniff of her nose. The thinned-out bubbles gathered like a trauma blanket around her pale 32-year-old body. "Maybe you want someone younger."

Neve sniffed again, her eyes squinting and relaxing upon some distant thing, and I could see the fight coming a mile away. It always started with that sniff—which was nothing less than a nuclear threat. That sniff meant that her body was on high alert, the beginnings of "anxiety" could already be felt, and, if things didn't go her way, she could momentarily descend into any manner of fever, rash, or fit that would create a nightmare for everyone around. Today was different, though. Something held Neve back. A shiver passed through her body and the sweetness resurfaced in her eyes.

"You know how much I love you, right?" she said. "I always will."

"We'll see," I said. "Just wait until the baby comes."

"What?"

"Nothing. It was just a joke."

"I don't get it."

"Never mind."

"Okay, well I should rinse off. Meet you on the couch?"

"Sure."

She reached for a towel and rose into it efficiently. There was a time when Neve enjoyed showing me her body. But recently she'd gotten self-conscious about cellulite and taken up pilates. The studio owner, Davide, came well reviewed by the wives of my colleagues. But follow-through wasn't Neve's specialty and it showed. These days she preferred to go in for Tibetan honey massages, which were supposed to work out the cellulite, except they made things worse. The baby would also be helpful in that regard. I thought about staying in the tub, but the water was cold and the bubbles had by now completely dissolved into gray slop.

We sat on the couch watching *The Talented Mr. Morel*, some slick series about a con artist who was seducing women with promises of money, drugs, and jets, robbing them, and leaving them out to dry. I always let Neve pick our shows and she almost always picked true crime. For all her anxiety about such things as being robbed, raped, and murdered herself, she found the genre "strangely comforting." Not that she actually watched. For her it was just a soundtrack to her Instagram-stalking of my students or the buying of more things for the house—these days mostly for the "upstairs room," as she was now calling it. Sometimes, though, when the ominous music swelled, I would feel Neve's hand squeezing mine. In this way, we could hold hands for up to five minutes, creating a temporary bridge between us.

The fact is I wasn't watching either. While my body slumped on that couch, my thoughts were softening with whisky and flowing back to the Corner Bookstore—that day Neve walked into my life with a stunning fur coat and a tall stack of books for me to sign as Christmas gifts. New York was freezing cold and Neve was so warm—not like the usual irony artists and good-time girls who showed up to my readings. Used to show up, I should say, before the climate changed around writers like me. And with Dad having just died and my brother being in rehab and Mom being entangled in another embarrassing romance and, as I said, New York being so cold, what I wanted more than anything was to disappear into that warm fur coat of Neve.

The signing of twenty books bought Neve a lot of time for her to chit-chat in. In the end she asked me if she could buy me a drink next door and I said, "No, but I'll buy you one on the train to my next reading." So Neve ended up traveling with me for three weeks and she gave me delicate little blow jobs and swirled around me at cocktail parties and gave me the biggest hugs in the world, like she'd plucked a good one from the bestseller list and she was never going to let go. I should clarify: My latest novel, the third, didn't actually make the list. And I was mildly annoyed when, in her many retellings of how we met, Neve would claim complete credit for the initiative and leave out my rather swift and effective comeback.

We were married before I knew it. Neve left her family in New York and moved into my place in Hollywood—a two-bedroom rental just off Los Feliz. She made like she was happy and started the redesign, while I figured out what's next. There was some money from the new book, but it wasn't going to last forever, especially now that we were living together and going out all the time. (Neve had a talent for getting reservations nobody else could.) It didn't help that my agent failed to get an advance for my next novel. People weren't into my particular brand of sex, drugs, and murder just now, she said, but not to worry, the climate can change again any minute, keep your head down and don't say anything misogynistic and whatever you do *don't get canceled!*

The university's offer for a Visiting Lecturer position was generous, but I hated the idea for many reasons, such as this was going to be the end of me as a writer, but also I had attended that very university once upon a time and made a college career out of lampooning it. I'd founded its alternative newspaper and published satires, exposés, takedowns, tirades, and literary pranks. I'd even put together a campaign for student government on the promise that I'd dissolve it. The administration tried to kick me out more than once, but by my junior year I was already famous. And on advice of my agent who was styling me into a "literary bad boy," I was actually the one who dropped out, just one quarter short of graduating.

Neve listened to my concerns with incredible patience and care. Then she asked me to keep an open mind and escorted me to a meeting which she had somehow arranged with Dean Gilbert, the same dean who had initiated one of the proceedings to get me expelled. It was magic hour, of course, and the grass was glowing green, the buildings were brick and holy, and Dean Gilbert was saying how secretly proud of me he had always been. I was disarmed by his collegial tone, like we had both grown up and could look back at who we once were—me a spoiled brat with a chip on his shoulder and he a stuffy bureaucrat with a stick up his ass—and just laugh about it.

"As much as you revolted against this place, don't forget you were made here. We gave you the *space* to revolt, see—and wasn't that the point all along?"

Later that night Neve casually reminded me that many great writers had also been professors, including David Foster Wallace. I could only guess she hadn't scrolled down to the part where he committed suicide. But it had been a good day and I even found her manipulation charming. So I took the job and she found this house for us. We couldn't afford it, but she was in love with it because it "reminded her of home and didn't remind her of L.A. at all." Also, there was a room on the second story with big windows overlooking the street and she insisted that this was going to be my office. She was so inspired that I was inspired—and, in fact, it was the perfect place to write my next novel.

I gave myself a month to settle in, but it very quickly became clear that teaching creative writing meant that I would have no time to do it myself. Instead I spent my days coaching a generation of sleepy 19-year-olds as they developed their own novels, which came in exactly two varieties. The first was the "discourse novel," which took on the sins of the white, the crimes of the rich, or the temperature of the world—and read like resumes for the writer's unblemished virtuousness. Its tone of courage, coupled with its complete compliance with accepted politics, staggered into Orwellian proportions. The second, "autofiction," did vie for literary value—but it did so in the relentless narration of authorial anxiety, detachment, or—what was most often the case—boredom, which inevitably led the first-person to suicide. It had the same effect on the reader.

So I had taken the devil's bargain to return to the university. And I realized too late that I had returned to the battleground as the loser, and only as a symbol of the past. I wasn't actually wanted, but would be tolerated so long as I practiced the appropriate cowardly administrative banter, the racial-biological humility, and the teaching of the official line. So I had been institutionalized. And trapped in my office at the end of a long white hallway, I started hearing that buzzing of fluorescent lights. I was by then in my mid-thirties, around when the Romantic poets traditionally died. As a kid, I had always loved the Romantic poets—mostly how they died.

Obviously I kept any such thoughts to myself, so as not to trouble Neve at a time when she was managing the renovation of "our co-working space," as my "office" came to be called. And when the room was ready—my desk against the wall, hers facing the window—Neve had me move in boxes of candles and write copy for her new candle business, since I always "had a knack for words." In moments I began to wonder if Neve actually appreciated my talent or if she just enjoyed the fact that others had. I even doubted if she'd ever read my books—beyond their dedication pages, I mean, where she would go when she wanted to put herself in a bad mood. I'd dedicated each of my novels to the girlfriend I had at the time I wrote it.

Naturally I helped Neve out on her website and newsletters, as a result of which her candles took off for a while. Then some bad customer reviews came in, on account of their catching fire. So Neve rebranded as a "woman-owned social impact enterprise," survived on grants for a few months, and eventually closed up and started a new business. She did this so many times I got sciatica moving all her boxes in and out of the room. Eventually Neve started drinking white wine and broached the idea of having a baby. I deflected for a while before agreeing to a timeline.

Despite my agreement, Neve became increasingly annoyed with me about the little things—the hours I spent at work or the oat milk I forgot to pick up. With all her free time, she also wanted me around more, and proved to be especially horny on Thursday nights, when I'd meet up with my old writer friends at Jones, Lubitsch, or Harlowe on Santa Monica. She lured me into bed for exactly the number of Thursdays required to make my return to the scene fatally awkward. She helped me "set boundaries" with my brother, too—and then my mom—until, before I knew it, Neve and I were the only two citizens of the republic.

And then she took the initiative in organizing dinners with my university colleagues and their husbands and wives. It felt like we were dating for new friends, and I barely mustered up the spirit to attend. I couldn't stand to look at these desperate and lonely normies. I hated their cardigans and how they let their wives put tracking apps on their phones and how all they ever spoke about was that family member who'd gone mad and voted for Trump. Neve would always bring up how my mother was one of them—"must be the pills." Meanwhile she was on pills herself (for anxiety and depression) and got me on them, too (for sciatica and insomnia). She was always on WebMD, curing me of something.

"You can be so arrogant sometimes!" Neve would say after our dinners. "You hardly spoke a word and just sat there drinking, like a psychopath or something. You know you used to be such a great conversationalist!"

"Wonder what happened."

"What happened?"

"Nothing."

"If you have something to say, just say it."

A woman's capacity for suffering is matched only by a man's desire to avoid a headache, and whisky helps a man keep silent. I started drinking heavily. Only I was too much of a pussy to pull a Brando like Dad had. At least he'd erupted in full obscene glory and gotten fat and drunk to the point that he hurled plates across dinner tables and passed out on them. At least Dad never compromised, capitulated, or made a coward of himself. He died in a big intoxicated sleep.

Neve gave up on her quest to civilize me. But I found her getting more and more frustrated—embarrassed even—and then bored. She started sleeping through the movies she used to love when we were dating—emerging only occasionally to ask about the melancholy Swede on screen: "Do you *actually* find that attractive? Would you fuck her?" I think she resented me for even liking these films, as if I was cheating on her just by watching them. "Not my type," I'd say—I'm not an idiot—as I quietly pushed the baby timeline by another semester. I really needed to start "trying" with another book first. So we stopped having sex. We stopped going out, too. We both blamed it on the traffic and Neve said things like "I can't stand a city I can't walk. I miss New York."

Our first real blow-up came when she found me smoking in the backyard and listening to Leonard Cohen. She plucked the earphones out of my ears, snatched the cigarette, and threw such a tantrum that the police showed up at our door. I was ruining my health, she explained, but I think she was more disturbed by the music. I came to understand that she was at war against all the elements of my younger life—or my alone life—which was, of course, my literary life. "I don't think you understand what marriage is," she would say. "Do you even want kids?" So Neve became an enemy of those dark voices in my ear and of that conjuring of cigarette smoke where, she supposed, I kept the dazzling parade of women I'd left behind for her.

> *There is a war between the rich and poor,*
> *A war between the man and the woman.*
> *There is a war between the ones who say there is a war*
> *And the ones who say there isn't.*

I never expected Neve to be my muse. But soon she became the very enemy of my imagination—the nagging goddess of writer's block. She'd never admit it, but I think Neve actually wanted me to stop writing once and for all. So I started spending evenings at my university office, hiding my attempts as if they were crimes or perversions. I would just sit there, staring at the white page, waiting for some muse to come. I'd drink and yearn for that gentle, invisible touch—the one Saint Matthew feels on his shoulder in that glorious Rembrandt hanging at the Louvre. Having drunk myself nearly to death, I'd release a stream of semiconscious sentences on the page.

Without exception, stumbling back to my desk the following morning, I would be ashamed and horrified. Whatever words I'd written were timid, soft, confused. And whatever rough edges did remain were quickly blunted by my agent, who—reading over the pages I sent her—finally came out with: "I think you should consider changing your voice." She'd drunk the Kool-Aid and become a star in the publishing industry, which was by now entirely run by women. Drunk on shame and whisky one night, I tried opening my novel in a woman's voice. She said upon reading: "What made you think you could write from a woman's perspective? Do you *know* that experience?"

While trying to mend things with my agent, I was scheming to get Neve to break up with me—and then scheming to break up with her. But she navigated these moments perfectly. One of her anxiety attacks ended with my holding her hand in an emergency room as some intern with a twitching judgmental nose prescribed a "stress-free home environment." In this way the medical industry was also enlisted in the conspiracy—and I learned never to break up with her again. Instead I ate prolifically and drank copiously. In a matter of months I gained twenty pounds. Neve didn't mind. Fat and unmarketable is the way she liked me. In affectionate moments, she would give me loving pats on the stomach, as I was looking more and more like a dad.

Fortunately I had my teaching. It was a great irony that, after all, teaching was the only thing I took comfort in. I found there was actually value in it, especially now, when everyone in my department except Kieslowska was either refusing to teach the classics or else laying them out as crime scenes for their student-vultures to descend upon in search of clues regarding racism, misogyny, and colonialism. I was happy to read them again and to share them with my class. It turned out I was an inspiring teacher, too, and I really did care for my students.

What followed, naturally, was that my care was misinterpreted. There was a student, Mandy, who'd caught feelings for me. And as gentle as I was in letting her down, her emotions got the best of her. Mandy went public with all sorts of accusations. Then the tidal wave came at me like menstrual blood.

Everybody knew the case was bullshit and Neve, to her credit, never batted an eye. But by now #MeToo was peaking and a lot of students wanted in—and professors, too, especially Planck. Under his influence, Dean Gilbert publicly announced that "all accusations will be taken seriously"—even though, in private, he told me I had nothing to worry about. And so faculty meetings were called, testimonies taken. I was summoned to disciplinary proceedings exactly like the ones I'd endured as a prankster student—more serious this time, of course, but no less ridiculous. It turned out that most of the evidence against me came in the form of excerpts from my own books, where "I" had already committed rape.

The shakedown of my literary work commenced. Previously unnoticed "misogynistic subtexts" were detected by anonymous reviewers, who caused my Amazon ratings to plummet. Then my agent talked me onto some panel to give explanations regarding my work. She was the moderator and her questions were increasingly indignant: *Did I really see women as enemies of men? Why did my protagonists have a habit of murdering their girlfriends?* Despite Kieslowska's moral support, I forced myself to "give all the right answers." Victory wasn't possible and I just wanted to get it over with. The culture of castration was upon us and men like me just had to shut up and take it. In the end, my agent dropped me anyway, like she wasn't the one who fucked me when I was nineteen and then fucked our way to the top of the literary world.

Eventually Mandy's case against me fell apart. Lacking evidence, her testimonies became combative and hysterical, then exploded in a great profession of unrequited love. In the end she suffered a mental breakdown, retracted her story, apologized to me and even Neve, and dropped out of college. The sham of a case was dropped too. But no great victory parade was made in my honor. A week later Mandy posted a Story on Instagram. It was a picture of the Pacific Ocean—clearly a reference to my magician novel—along with the text: "Goodbye, professor." A week later, her purse washed up in Malibu. It contained her wallet, her pills, and her usual supply of Winterfresh gum. So Mandy had committed suicide and I was also guilty of murder.

My agent never asked me back, of course. Neighbors who had already cooled off now froze with contempt. They clung to their suspicions like babies. Neve was holding onto something too. She routinely donated money to Mandy's memorial fund. And from time to time, during our fights, she started saying things like "I know you did *something*." It became the kind of thing she could bring up whenever she felt like punishing me. Just as often she would pull me into bed and play the naughty student and ask me to punish her. In either case, this was a huge injustice in my life. But the greater injustice was that I—the only person who actually cared for Mandy—was not allowed to grieve for her.

The coming of the COVID-19 pandemic was a godsend. First, the virus could help explain the distance our neighbors kept from us and vice versa. Second, as the university had shut down and instruction was virtual, Neve could take comfort in the fact that I was not in proximity to young women. And third, all that wearing of masks and fighting the bug and then racism (this was the summer of Black Lives Matter) really energized Neve with a political conviction that took up a lot of her time. It brought her and all our frightened and spineless white neighbors together again—this time to put BLM signs on their lawns, lest the protesters storm our neighborhood.

The pandemic provided one more unexpected blessing. This was the indefinite postponement of our procreation—at first because of Neve's reading of the blogs that tracked the virus's effect on fetal health and later because of Neve's reading of the blogs that tracked the vaccine's effect on fetal health. I did not attempt to correct her dramatic misinterpretations of the numbers, although I did have some concerns about the state of her mind. I had no choice but to quell a new round of anxiety attacks by consenting to a final timeline. Just as soon as we beat the virus and in-person instruction was reinstated, we could start "our new chapter." I could have a semester to settle back in, but that's it.

So the end of COVID-19 was also the end of my excuse-making. I returned to the university with a sense of dread I had never felt before. I was finished as a writer, of course. No agent would represent me ever again. No publisher would even read my manuscripts. Meanwhile the news that I was up for tenure, presented by Kieslowska as a great triumph for me and a huge redemption, filled me with horror—terrified me even more than the threats and pornography and unmarked envelopes that began to appear in my university mailbox. (The student population had come back from self-isolation with a vengeance, with all manner of mental disturbance.) So I found myself in a perfect nightmare. All that was missing from it was a crying baby.

I waited for Neve to knock out on the couch before grabbing a bottle of whisky and heading to the "upstairs room." I shut the door behind me and flipped on the lights. The room had completely changed since I dropped in last weekend. For starters, our desks were cleared out. Her candles and my papers had been dumped into black trash bags. The walls were bare, except for a few streaks of blue where my Dylan poster used to be. Only now did I understand why she'd been spending so much time in this room and why my "office," which had become our "co-working space," was recently being called the "upstairs room." Neve had been preparing the transition expertly. It was summer, after all, and there was a deal in place, and if I decided to keep my word rather than impose yet another postponement, we would be needing a nursery.

I sat at the foot of my desk, took a long swig of whisky, opened a trash bag, and dived into an ocean of newspaper clippings my mother had saved all through my literary rise. The reviews were coming in hot from the very beginning. One critic compared my debut to *American Psycho* and called me "the next Bret Easton Ellis." An *LA Weekly* cover announced "the New Marlboro Man" and had me posing full-page by the Chateau Marmont, right where the sixty-foot Marlboro Man was recently disassembled amid anti-smoking campaigns. My agent had bought me that leather jacket for the occasion and, as I smoked a Marlboro, I smirked and glared arrogantly off camera.

I took another swig and picked up a tightly folded magazine piece titled "The Harlowe Boys." The author had desperately wanted that coinage to stick to our small group of edgelord L.A. writers who hung out at Harlowe and neighboring bars on Santa Monica. It didn't. But I liked the piece because it glamorized a real friendship I'd developed with those guys, especially the screenwriter Poe Pierce and the comic Skeeze. We were quite the vision, leaning back against that bar, looking so young and stylish and scary. The copy ran—

A generation that grew up on *The Simpsons* and *South Park*, *Pulp Fiction* and *Fight Club*... Tracing a macho literary line back via Mailer, Chandler, and Bukowski to Miller and Hemingway... They come from money, but resent it... Stiff drinks and lines of coke... Orgiastic parties at Jones... They'll fight you if you want, but mostly they want to fuck... Backed by shrewd agents and publicists, they used a window of opportunity (when Obama was elected and the literary establishment was feeling safe) to become the new and possibly final incarnation of that old trope of the "literary bad boys."

A tear dropped onto the newspaper. Ink, decades old, smeared. My hands shook. Self-pity swelled in my throat. I finished off the bottle and headed for the windows. One of them was cracked on account of a "disagreement" Neve had with me. I pushed it open and reached out to the ledge. There was a damp pack of Marlboros—mostly ruined by rainwater—but I flicked it open, caught a dry one with my teeth, and slipped out some paper matches from Lubitsch. It showed a stick figure raising a martini glass, with an exclamation mark on each side, and below it in Soviet design: *Vodka Bar. Cocktails.* I lit up, took a drag, and blew smoke out the window like a real fucking dissident.

The smoke cleared my head. The night air kissed my face. Smoking in L.A. is different from smoking in any other place, because here it is "viscerally connected to all the elements: the winds, the mountains, and—most importantly—the always-present possibility of fire, which can take down the entire city." I'd written something like that in my first novel, featuring an alchemist-arsonist, a messianic and shadowy magician looming in the California mountains. Lonely valley girls were known to make pilgrimages to find him—and to offer up their hearts and bodies to his various appetites. For a few short years, they made similar pilgrimages to me. It must have been quite a sight for my Los Feliz neighbors—those old Armenian ladies cracking sunflower seeds and gossiping on their balconies. Those last witnesses must be dead by now.

It was amid such reveries that I remembered the black envelope. I flicked the cigarette into the night and slipped the envelope out from my back pocket. It was heavy in my hands. And as I moved my fingers over its hexagonal golden seal, with that intricate letter Q branded in, I felt the evil rush of goosebumps on my arms. I tore the envelope open and pulled out the black cardstock paper fitted inside. A note was written on it in golden cursive—

Dear Professor,

Please accept this invitation to a week-long residency on my private island. I am a great admirer of your work and would be honored to play a small role in inspiring your next novel. In these conditions, I believe it will practically write itself. For reasons that will become clear, I ask that you keep this invitation strictly confidential. Should you accept it, please carefully follow the enclosed instructions.

Yours,

Q

Accompanying the letter was a printed travel itinerary and arrival instructions from the Hellenic Travel Agency. It seemed to be a fake, but when I looked into it on my phone, the booking checked out. A non-refundable round-trip business class ticket to Athens had actually been issued to my name, with my birthday and passport number and even my frequent flyer number attached.

ALL THE BUZZ

Who could pull off such an elaborate prank? If not a student, then a colleague? Planck? I wouldn't put it past the vindictive queen, if he weren't also a tightwad. The Harlowe Boys? Had they hatched this as some midlife intervention to get me writing again or to save me from being "whipped by Neve"—Skeeze's famous last words? Did they even meet on Thursdays anymore? Or was the culprit closer to home? No, Neve didn't have the imagination. I knew someone who did. I drank the last of the whisky, sat down against the wall, pulled up my texts, and scrolled down to the unopened voice message from yesterday. I pressed play and brought the phone to my ear.

"Darling! You *have t*o call me back. I've been trying—"

That slurring stream of Oxy and whisky still made me cringe every time I heard it—and I'd heard it a thousand times. I let the voice fall off. A long time ago I had decided not to be drawn into Mom's manipulative labyrinths. The last time she'd visited, after one of her break-ups, she'd brought up my brother again and started blaming me again in her passive-aggressive way to the point that Neve decided to stand up for me. She and Mom had staged such classical Greek theater that I finally had to get her out. With Neve's encouragement, I stopped taking her calls. Anyway, the envelope wasn't Mom's doing. She didn't have the discipline.

I brought the envelope to my nose, shut my eyes, caught the perfume again, and strained to remember its sweet and salty and fiery notes. My bones stiffened. My heart began to race. The scent was becoming familiar—swirling up into a mist of feeling—making an apparition—and hanging in my mind like a ghost in suspense. For a moment I could see within it the hot red buzzing movements and smell the ash-perfumed winds and hear the chewing of gum and the echoing of giggles and glass. Then I opened my eyes and let it spread out into the night.

I trashed the letter and headed to the bathroom and sat on its heated tiles as I scrolled through YouPorn in incognito mode. This ancestral exercise I approached with, I think, the proper attitude of despair. God knows the porn of the nation had been going down the drain, anyway. I'd noticed over the past years how they'd been selling me on stepmom porn, which is strange because I never watched it before. Now it's practically all I watch. One day it will be proven in this way what a sick man I am, whereas the truth is much more miserable. I didn't care enough to scroll down. Mostly I ended up watching women who look like Neve.

Not today, though. The letter having motivated something vaguely deviant in me, I took my time before settling on a POV piece where a guy lures some woman from a bus stop back to his place. I went right up to the 60% mark, which was safely past the unnecessary foreplay and before the degrading finale, and I worked so thoroughly at the squealing brunette that I was finished in a minute. It ended for me with not so much a gasp, but a grunt, after which I slumped back against the wall. In the thirty seconds separating relief from shame, I continued watching as the guy—reflected in the kitchen window, with sunglasses and a backwards red hat—continued to fuck the woman at the sink as he yelled, "Wash the dishes, bitch! Wash the dishes!" So this was already becoming a fetish.

I switched tabs to 4chan. Apparently: the founders of the internet were founding new internets; crypto-democracies would be forming; puppet-masters would not even be human; algorithms were creating social movements on the streets; large language models were being developed; Artificial Intelligence would soon take over everything; it would make most human jobs obsolete; it would make writing obsolete; *homo sapiens* were making way for a new species, the *transhumans*; as people grew increasingly bored and scared of sex (references were made to "incels," "femcels," and other new populations), reproductive processes would be replaced by technology; there was a "paradigm shift" on the horizon—*annusmaximus69* was calling it a "consciousness shift." His latest: "In the war between man and woman, it is robots that will win."

Most urgently, though, the community was convening over the news of a visionary, a Taiwanese billionaire, who was reported missing. He wasn't the first visionary to have vanished. There were speculations of a deep-state conspiracy on one side and a counter-culture resistance on the other. I can't say I believed any of it. I can't say I believed anything. In my thirty-ninth year on this earth, I was neither here nor there—I had already severed my ties with fiction and reality both. Atlas had shrugged, the center would not hold, and the world was spiraling out of control. But at least here, among the deviants and the clowns, I could see the last brilliant flashes of the United States of America. I tore off some toilet paper to wipe away the culture with.

I stood in front of the full-body mirror on the bathroom door and decided to carry out an inventory. I should begin by admitting that I wasn't ugly. I still had my green eyes, although they had dimmed into something more like hazel. The new creases on my forehead and the bags under my eyes had the haunting effect that I was somehow sinking into myself—but a representation of wounded wisdom also resulted. My light beard, initially cultivated to cover my double chin, suited me even better now, with some grays coming in. In my war with time, my most vulnerable front was my hairline. A lost year of squirting Rogaine had not helped—in fact it had caused baby hairs to sprout in all the wrong places—eventually forcing me to accept my defeat. Still, the hair retreated slowly. And, as it did, it was thick and poetic.

My posture was a wreck, and I had nobody to blame for it. My years of philosophical brooding, with all that slant looking-at-the-ground, had slouched me permanently. And the pounds I'd put on had encouraged me to slouch even deeper, in my body's permanent gesture of apology for itself. My chest, once defined, was sagging. My stomach had puffed out. Sucking it in revealed the strong bones buried there, but also caused layers of loose skin to cascade hideously over—like a curtain dropping over the lost and diminished symbol of my manhood. It lingered there between my legs, like a dangling participle left uncorrected, probably because it was considered to be a harmless mistake.

"Fat fuck," I muttered, before turning out the lights.

When I got to the bedroom, Neve was half-asleep—flickering by candlelight—perfectly positioned among the sheets. No sag of arms was observed. No cleavage advantage was unexploited. She had painted herself perfectly into the scene. She was still inviting me in. Even after everything, she would take me without a thought. I had nothing left for her, though. I blew out the bedside candle and, in a swirl of sweet smoke, slipped in and slept on my stomach like a criminal. She snuggled against my arm and breathed heavily. I pretended not to notice. I lay perfectly still. She sniffled once or twice. In another minute, she gave up with a sigh.

I couldn't sleep. All I could think about was the invitation. Had he been alive, I'd be sure my father was behind it. This was exactly the kind of prank he'd pull. He was a loud and exuberant character cut from the Armenian ghettos of Beirut, where he wheeled-and-dealed in his father's car repair shop while also acting in the local theater, his favorite role being Prospero. And even as bombs fell over his childhood and forced his early escape from it, he remained forever a loud and exuberant and theatrical soul—so that, rendered an immigrant and car mechanic in the new world, he still recited Shakespeare from under car hoods.

With his old country charm and tactics, he wooed my valley girl-next-door of a mother into marriage. The daughter of a cantankerous movie producer from his third marriage, she was free of concerns regarding both money and reality, and she had everything and everyone she wanted. She was a party girl with a flair for genius, although she dumbed it down and played it cool in the gossip column she wrote for *Playboy*. Still, those who knew knew—and among her callers were Jack Nicholson, Leonard Cohen, and Steve Martin, with whom she was famously photographed playing chess. He was in a suit. She was naked. It was all a trip until she crashed her classic red 1968 BMW convertible into the Beverly Hills Hotel and ended up at Gary's Auto Collision at La Brea and Olympic, where she heard Shakespeare coming out of a car hood.

Only years later did my father confess that he serviced her car in such a way that caused it to regularly break down—and my mother to come back to complain. Of course he never charged her for this extra service and instead told her great big Middle Eastern stories about "real freedom" and drinking beer from the age of ten and joining the war with BB guns from rooftops. He sent her off each time with trunks full of flowers. She could've married anyone, but she chose Gary (Gostan), the poor, short, broad-shouldered, cheap cigar-smoking immigrant with greasy slick-back hair and a massive mustache curled up at the ends, who made her laugh her heart out and promised to give her many children.

My father was a wizard-like figure for me and my younger brother. He filled our childhood with endless mystery. Inspired by Poirot and Hastings, we the brothers created our own detective agency, as our father sent us out to find clues and solve crimes in the neighborhood. He took us to old movie screenings, too, and embarrassed us with his huge laugh and uncontrollable tears. He was also a physical man. He challenged us to punch his arm and bite his elbows as hard as we could. And in later years he took us to wrestling events and Lakers games, where he once walked right up to Jack Nicholson and teased that he got the girl after all. Jack winked back; they understood each other. My father was proud of my mother—proud of himself for having gotten her—and I saw how he grabbed her waist and gave her big wet smooches when his filthy Armenian mechanic friends were around for cigars and cards.

That was another lifetime, though. A lot happened after that. For example, through a hole in our bedroom wall, my brother and I watched the entire history of cinema disintegrate from screwball to body horror, as our father tore our mother to shreds. And then, when he discovered our looking-hole, he tore us to shreds too. The hell I lived became the fire I learned to control, manipulate, and make into success; I built myself up into a writer. My brother hollowed himself out instead. He became an actor, which meant community theater pieces and clowning and magic on the weekends. But mostly it meant booze and coke. I spent years dropping him off at rehab and going to meetings, but nothing ever worked. The more responsible I was, the more he disintegrated. He bit and tore his nails off. And he scratched the wounds on his arms until they bled again—making his body the canvas of some demented, self-pitying art project. It helped him raise money, too, mostly from me.

Neve saved me from my unhealthy relationship with my brother. "Focus on things you can control," she'd say, "and your brother isn't one of them. You have to cut him loose, babe. For his own good. He'll come back when he's ready. You have to cut him loose." And so I did. I ignored his calls until he showed up one night, begged me to get into his Chevy pickup, and—to show me how serious he was—drove us to our father's grave. The Santa Anas were blowing that night and he was scratching the wounds on his arms and looking at me with those eyes: so crazed, so broken and ready to believe, always in search of salvation. He'd finally found it, he said. He really was going clean this time. There was a teacher—someone who knew "the way out"—and he was planning to leave the country with him. My brother wanted me to join.

I shoved him back, watched him stumble off forever. Turned my head away. Buried my face in the pillow. But only to find that scent again. Maybe it was the trace of detergent in the sheets or maybe the scent had somehow lifted from the letter and followed me into bed. But it was swirling up again, more confidently this time, the perfume rising now to conjure the diseased yellow of her eyes, the chewing of her gum, her voice. "You're better than this," she was saying, her voice echoing out as it did during those hearings. "Be a man for once, professor. Tell the truth!" It had always been, in its twisted twang of innocence and desire, a terrifying voice. Except it was now also dead.

"Remember the window."

"What?"

A hand on my arm.

"There's still that crack in it. A man could break in if you don't fix it."

"A man?"

"I don't know. I'm just saying. Goodnight, babe."

"Goodnight."

Neve finally rolled over into her sleeping position. I turned my back to her and slipped a hand under my pillow. I imagined Mandy rotting at the bottom of the Pacific Ocean—her jaundiced eyes—her cold blue lips parting for one last plea—

"Come on, professor. Tell the truth. Free yourself of this."

I woke up exhausted and hungover and the morning didn't feel very real. I entered the kitchen like I was on the set of a multi-cam and Neve was waiting with the coffee and breakfast. She could cook when she wanted to and this was her most extravagant breakfast ever: delicious poached eggs, crispy bacon, and banana pancakes. She sat on the other side of it gracefully and made easy conversation. Afterwards she said she had a surprise in the bedroom. I was relieved to find it wasn't a blowjob or anything. She just had some new clothes laid out on the bed. I still got to wear jeans, apparently, but my black t-shirt had been upgraded to a button-down and a gray cardigan was to go over it.

"Sexy professor," she said at the door, sending me off with a kiss on the cheek, like the first day of school.

It was the third time the tenure board had called me back and this was supposed to be the last. The delays had to do with Professor Planck. He'd had it out for me ever since I began teaching here. When Dean Gilbert had promoted me from Visiting Lecturer to Assistant Professor on the tenure track, Planck had objected on grounds I didn't have a bachelor's degree, let alone a PhD. And after that issue had been resolved by issuing me several honorary degrees, he started to hate me properly. Meanwhile that scandalous incident of mine, debunked though it was, gave him the excuse to look upon me as the enemy of all women, whose protector he—feeling no enchantment by their mysteries—was posturing to be.

Planck had spent the better part of a decade developing "an alternative history of the Western Canon"—an embittered and envious retaliation against his East Coast rival Camille Paglia, who hadn't heard of him. He had made a minor name for himself at academic conferences for arguing that *Frankenstein* was actually a parable about "motherless man"—the monster being created by a man and raised by a single white heterosexual cisgender father, without female influence. He had also discovered in a recent 23andMe test a 1% "Indigenous American" lineage, and this had exacerbated his personality issues. Not having taken one myself, I was presumed white until proven innocent.

The tenure board consisted of Professor Planck, Dean Gilbert, and Professor Kieslowska.

"The question is simple, really," Planck said, rubbing his gray eyes under his glasses. "Do you even want to be a professor?"

"Have I done something to cast that into doubt?" I replied.

"See, this is exactly what I've been telling you," Planck said, glancing over to his colleagues. A diamond stud twinkled in his ear. "You always deflect. You never want to take responsibility, even to answer a question. Do. You. Want. The. Job?"

"Why else would I be here?" I said. "Obviously I do."

"Really? Perhaps you'd prefer to retire early and write another one of your buzzy little novels?"

I accepted the question as rhetorical and looked over to the dean. He was on my side, but he was a coward and would never take on Planck directly. He was always sucking on a lozenge and rubbing his hands together and comforting himself in such ways. He wouldn't even look at me. He only lifted his styrofoam cup to his tiny nose and took a quick whiff of his coffee. Above me, the fluorescent lights buzzed.

"I'm not sure you are aware," Planck continued, "but you are a straight white man vying to fill a vacancy at a very delicate time in our history. How do you feel about this?"

"Well, I'm not ashamed," I said. "Should I be?"

Planck tilted his head in amusement at my response. The fact is I had surprised myself too. But really the lights were very aggressive.

"No, no. But perhaps motivated, then. To do your part. Can you tell us, for example, what female authors you intend to teach. What are your thoughts about Mary Shelley, for example."

"I like *Frankenstein*," I said.

"So then you do accept she wrote it."

I glared at Planck. I knew he was baiting me, but all that buzzing was getting in my head. I had to raise my voice to speak over all that buzzing.

"I'm sure she wrote most of it."

Planck gasped. The dean quickly followed with a gasp of his own.

"Perhaps we can change the subject," Kieslowska intervened.

But Planck wouldn't let go.

"Because a woman couldn't have done it all on her own, right? Without her brilliant poet of a husband! I understand this theory is all the rage in far-right chat rooms these days."

"Well, her husband *was* brilliant," I said, slumping now into an indifferent pose. "And she was nineteen. Maybe she took some notes. I don't know."

"And yet I seem to remember that you believe nineteen is a viable age for a woman."

"Professor Planck!" Kieslowska shouted.

"Professor Kieslowska, with respect, please manage your tone," Planck said calmly. "This young white man has a lot to answer for."

"Perhaps you'd like to take a moment," Kieslowska said to me. "Go on, step outside. Clear your head."

"Be honest," Planck persisted. "Do you actually want this job?"

Kieslowska turned her sparkling eyes to mine. A lozenge clicked against the dean's teeth. On the wall, the clock took its famous one step back, before stepping twice toward the hour. The fluorescent lights buzzed insanely.

"Come on then!"

They must have caught a special wavelength and were vibrating right through the center of my mind.

"Come on then, answer me!"

Suddenly the bell rang. All the buzzing cleared.

"You're right," I said. "This job *isn't* for me."

Kieslowska deflated in her chair. The dean planted his face into his hands. Planck pointed his nose at me.

"Well, you've certainly given us a lot to consider here," he said.

"I'm glad I could help," I said, as I got up to leave.

"Wait! Don't go! Wait! What's gotten into you?"

Professor Kieslowska ran after me in the hallway.

"Don't leave the war, man! Come back and fight!"

I turned around and let her catch up.

"Fight!" she said, breathlessly. "Fight!"

For the first time in years, I believe, I looked directly into those turquoise eyes. There was so much love in them—but now also fear. I grabbed her arms and made for her lips. Kieslowska was ready. She let herself faint a little in my arms, then smeared her lips on mine, left and right. It was like a first kiss, before you learn how to suck or bite or slip a tongue. I understood only later that she must have seen this kiss in old movies. And the only man she ever kissed must have learned it the same way. And neither of them had had any reason to believe there was anything to improve on.

I walked right down Sorority Row, took the straight path home with all the bikinis flying off, and didn't question the good luck of Neve not being there. Alone in the nursery, I fished the black envelope out of the trash. I sat on the floor and held it in my trembling hands, gazing upon the golden hexagon of wax, with that letter Q branded it. And I wondered, finally: *Could the invitation be real?* There had been a Mrs. Palmer up Mulholland Drive who used to host lavish book club meetings and throw *Eyes Wide Shut* parties with her personally curated "collections of interesting people." Surely there must have been others like her. *Was it impossible that someone out there still remembered me, believed in my talent, wanted me to write again?*

I slipped out the invitation from the envelope and confirmed that the cursive was practiced, glamorous, superfluous—definitely a woman's. And it was a woman's perfume, too, that was rising from it. I shut my eyes and took it in again. The scent was sophisticated, mature, complex—its sweetness balanced by the salt and ash. It aroused me and inspired me in personal and intimate ways. And then it began to pursue me. Later that day I picked it up in the laundry room, then in the coffee shop, then at the supermarket. Of course this did not diffuse its effect. It only helped assert its omnipresence—its total domination of my life.

For the next week I read the letter again and again, to the point that I could hold it and see it in my mind. I chased its full-bodied curves. I fell into its splashes of gold. I spent my days in a lull of wakeful dreaming. And I spent my nights in sleepless wonderment of that distant island to which I was being called. And the island was Treasure Island. The island was Avalon. The island was Christie's Soldier Island and Rand's Galt's Gulch. The island was Homer's Ithaca, where Calypso held Odysseus hostage and singing sirens led boys like me to shipwreck. So the island grew large and bright in my mind—it became a unity of all islands I'd ever known or read about.

And presiding over it was Q—a hot and luminous figure, not quite real. *Who could she possibly be? And why was she summoning me now to Greece—the birthplace of the Western imagination? Was she the muse I had been waiting for all along?* For the first time in years, I started spending evenings at my university office, drinking and staring at my computer screen again. I didn't dare write anything yet. I needed an idea and I didn't have one. But before the idea there had always been this feeling. It's what Saint Matthew feels that moment the angel touches his shoulder. And his eyes fill with doubt and thrill.

After the debacle at the tenure hearing, Kieslowska kept calling me, but I wouldn't be talked sense into. My mother kept leaving her messages, but I wasn't about to engage. Over a cup of breakfast coffee with Neve, I found myself mentioning "that conference I've been talking about."

"Right," she said, barely lifting her glance from her phone. "How long is it again? Remember I peak on the fourteenth. I sent you a calendar invite."

"I'll be back by then," I said. "If I even go."

I hadn't decided to accept the invitation yet. The madness of the idea wasn't lost on me and, truth is, I was looking for any reason to shake it off. But Neve wasn't giving me any.

"And when do we get news from the tenure board?"

"Who knows? You know how bureaucrats can be."

"Well I think you should go."

"Yeah?"

"I just want you to be happy, babe."

And that was it. Neve was playing it cool and my rosy account of the tenure hearing would hold her over until the impending ovulation. She continued being warm and flirtatious, promising me a life of regular sexual favors and good motherhood. She did not know how much she was boring me—how far my thoughts had drifted from home. She could not see that, even as I kept my slant and brooding glance to the ground, I was living a great exhilaration of the spirit.

HAPPY WIFE, HAPPY LIFE

The day before the scheduled ticket, one of Neve's girlfriends was throwing a surprise fortieth for her husband "all the way in East Hollywood." But I was happy to get out, even if it meant witnessing one of the great tragedies of the modern American world, which is the bagging of a homie by a hipster in his own neighborhood. I didn't mind Manny at all. He was a registrar at the university and his friends came from the admin side, which was preferable to faculty. After the surprise and the cake and the toast the birthday boy drank to his wife for throwing such an amazing party, the guys got together on the couch to watch the Dodgers.

From the backyard, their wives kept watch on them. Kids ran in and out. I got myself a buzz and scanned the small library not far from the TV. It was a predictable arrangement of mental disorder—pining for social acceptance (the editor's picks from *The Times*), screaming for help (17 steps to this, 12 rules for that), and of course searching for "the secret" (some new formula or

Happy Wife, Happy Life 39

ancient concept that was going to help you fuck or not give a fuck or not get fucked in the game of life). So I was surprised to find in this collection a stark book I recognized. I hadn't looked at it in years.

I pulled out the book, broke it open, and understood it wasn't Manny's. It must have been his wife who had annotated it cover to cover—marked up almost every sentence in it. My heart raced as I flipped through her highlights—"Behind every great man is a woman backstabbing him"—the golden words flashing before me—"Every first kiss worth the price of its lipstick is an act of violence perpetrated outside the rules of consent"—lushious, opulent, bloody—"It is better to be raped than murdered, if you cannot be both"—and she'd even put a heart next to this last one: "Sex is not a game of strength, but endurance, and in this game, the woman always wins."

That was when the birthday boy, drunk on two Coronas, erupted at the events unfolding on screen. It appeared to be a completely normal celebration, but it sent his wife Claudia running in.

"Manuel!" she called. "Keep it down! You're scaring the children."

"Babe, come see this! Bases loaded and he fucking cracked it!"

"Language, babe!" she said, taking the third beer from his hand. "That was the last one, okay?"

"Agh," Manny said. "I'm not even drunk!"

Then, unexpectedly, Claudia glared right at me.

"What would a professor think, looking at you like that? Why don't you just try to be a little more like him!"

I peered into her hopeless eyes, trying to grasp what she meant.

"Be careful what you wish for!" Neve interrupted, storming onto the scene. She looked at the book in my hand, then my drink. "Don't be such a loner, babe. Now come over here and give me a kiss."

This stupid game Neve played, delighting in petty exertions of power over me in the company of others—I was fed up with it.

"I'm fine, thanks," I said.

Neve knew I wasn't into PDA, but she found a way to be disappointed each time I withheld such affection. She chalked this up to my "intimacy issues," which also explained why I didn't like holding hands, why I was the one who said "I love you too," why I didn't wear my wedding band. On account of this, she regularly tried getting me into couple's therapy, from which at least three men I knew had emerged suddenly "vulnerable," having divulged information their wives would use against them for the rest of their lives.

"I need another drink," Neve said, rolling her eyes. "See you outside, Claudia."

Neve left. Claudia lingered back. She seemed to smile at me, then floated off into some den. "Vulnerability"—that's what women say they want out of men these days, according to *The Bachelor*. But it's not vulnerable men they end up fucking on their washing machines.

"Just let it go," Manny said, still gazing at the TV. "It's better that way. Let it go."

"What?" I said.

"Happy wife, happy life," another guy added.

"Right," I said. Neither Claudia's moves nor my humiliation had registered. Manny grabbed another beer, deposited a handful of pretzels into his gaping mouth, sank into the sofa, and watched the game through the cracks of his closing eyes. He appeared stoned in his surrender, and deliriously happy.

"Grab one, bro," Manny said. "Join us. Dodgers about to make a comeback."

"Thanks," I said. "I'm good."

"Suit yourself," he slurred, from what appeared to be a trance-like state of tribal wisdom. "Sooner you join the better."

"Maybe later," I said. This time next year, I'd finally be neutered into the Dad in the Great American Sitcom.

Finally I let the back cover fall. The young author looked back with a reluctant smile and a sly squint of his green eyes. He was so full of himself in that leather jacket it was unbearable—he thought he was going to be the next B.E.E. I returned the book to the shelf, then headed quietly into the corridor Claudia had gone down. I could hear the rumbling of a machine from the far dim end of it. I stood there a moment, then turned back with a sigh. She was probably just doing the laundry.

Fireworks exploded behind us—the Dodgers had won after all and not all Mexicans had been cucked yet—and Neve quickly made her way to a boulevard she recognized, even if it was Hollywood Boulevard. I was drunk so she drove and I rested my cheek against the window and watched the lights race by. The air was tense and thick with unsaid words. By now we had more unsaid words between us than said ones. But I could easily understand her language of long breaths and plunging sighs and quiet sneers of contempt—contempt for me, our life, our car (still my dad's gray 1980 Mercedes 450SL), and this backwards city I had brought her to, where we laid out our stars on filthy ground. I could practically hear her rolling her eyes at Michael Jackson at Madame Tussauds and the plastic miracles at Ripley's Believe It or Not!

I knew what she was thinking—*dirty, grimy, fake tourist trap* is what she was thinking. And I was thinking back: "Only L.A. would build a tourist trap specifically to keep people like you away—so that the real people of L.A. can slip into Broadner's or Musso & Frank and drink delicious Blood Marys and, yes, mingle with the wide-eyed tourists who are their true collaborators in the creation of the greatest dream ever dreamed—and none of this is fucking tacky." And right there—where that wig shop is now—*that* was the magic shop from my novel!

"I've decided to give you a hall pass."

I came back to myself, as though from a hallucination, wondering if I'd let one of my thoughts be heard.

"What?"

"If it'll help, I mean. You can have a hall pass. You know, if you meet someone at that conference, you should—you know—feel free."

"Feel free?"

"If you need to get it out of your system, I mean. It could be good for us—before we start this new chapter. Anyway, I'm just saying I wouldn't mind. Babe, we all know what these conferences are for."

I stirred into form and tried to understand what was happening. Was this Neve's way of confessing she fucked that pilates teacher after all? Or had she been click-baited into some article on "how to spice up your sex life"? Had she *actually* gotten a sense of my condition—and was trying, in her own way, to help? No. It was probably just a trap. I was supposed to decline the gesture. Instead I said—

"Whatever."

"And you don't need to tell me about it either. If you find some grad student slut, you should definitely go for her."

And then she put her hand cheerfully on my stomach and gave it a little slap.

"I mean, you can *try* anyway. You can definitely *try*."

Then, throwing her glance all over me, Neve just started laughing.

"What are you saying?"

I looked to her for a reply, but found her in the grips of her own hysterical laughter. She was laughing so hard she was about to cry.

"Nothing," she said, gasping for air. "Nothing. I didn't mean anything by it. I bet there are women who would still be interested. I mean, they *must* be out there."

I looked out the window again: Elvis at the Oscars. Spiderman vs. the Terminator at the Chinese. We were coming up on Orange and my glance swerved right from the Hollywood Roosevelt to the Magic Castle up on that hill. A memory caught. It was the night my brother first invited me to that glowing mansion above Franklin. He was so proud to have become a member and he beamed with delight as he showed me the trap door and trick piano and that table where Dai Vernon held court with cards. But there was another memory, too—and not long after—that night my brother was kicked out of that very place and all the magic of our lives finally began to unravel.

Still, the laughter did not relent. It only grew deeper, stronger, louder. It was hideous laughter—hateful laughter—fanatical.

"Stop the car."

"What?"

"Stop."

Neve pulled over quietly. I said, as I got out—

"I'll walk from here."

"Babe, what the fuck! Hey, get back in. You can't walk home from here!"

"Yes I *can*. And I'll take that hall pass, by the way."

I slammed the door and walked off. Neve waited a moment, then blasted away, almost crashing into a lamppost.

"Whoever says L.A. isn't a walking city is full of shit. It's a longer and harder walk from Yankee Stadium in the Bronx to Coney Island in Brooklyn than it is from Dodger Stadium downtown to the Pacific Ocean where Los Angeles ends. And when you get there, by way of a single majestic boulevard, it's not hot dogs or pawn shops you find. It's the conclusion of *manifest destiny*, the last sunset of civilization, and the beginning of a new project: the creation of the sounds and images that make up the imagination of the world. America was invented in L.A. Love was invented in L.A. In L.A. we created the stars for you to worship, but back here on this boulevard we trample over them because they're one of us. The fakest city in the world is actually the realest, because everybody here is allowed to be fake, which is what they are—real. The illusion becomes real in Los Angeles, but you don't really care for magic, do you?"

Did I care for magic anymore? Douglas Fairbanks Sr.—King of Hollywood. *Did I believe my own words?* Charles Buttersworth. *Was that voice even mine—so strange and daring and dark?* Ernst Lubitsch. *And how had I lost it—my own voice—through compromise, capitulation, cowardice?* I stopped at Sophia Loren. Beyond her, the boulevard darkened into the night. *Could I get it back?* I turned around. *Could I possibly go back?* I could still see it, of course—just barely, but I could—the past clinging to the palm trees—the neon lights making minor mirages in the heat—and a familiar wind growing at my back.

I staggered toward the lights again. Tears filled my eyes. My vision blurred. And then I was back in Los Angeles—lost in its maze of violence and madness. Whoever says L.A. isn't a walking city is full of shit, I thought. Those who say L.A. isn't a walking city only mean they don't like walking it, not that they can't. They don't like it because we don't have a skyline—we have a sky instead. And hot winds. And mountains. And valleys that erupt in wildfires. And smog. They don't like L.A. because it hasn't denied nature—because it is *too* real—because it actually has no tricks or charms—because it refuses to protect them from the catastrophe of being alone with themselves on long dirty blocks.

In L.A. there is nothing to distract you from the smog of your own soul and the ghosts that haunt you.

The wind found me again as I crossed Sunset southward—and this time I knew it was real. The Santa Anas are scheduled to blow in the fall, but once or twice a year they come out to play unexpectedly and this was one of those nights. Almost every L.A. writer feels the need to make something literary out of these hot winds. Most of them say they are evil and others say they are warm and kind. And others try finding a clever third way out. It really doesn't matter. Whether the winds take you to the place you need to go or you use the winds as your excuse to go to the same place, you're still going down seedy alleys, brother—you're still headed for the gates of Hollywood Forever.

Judy Garland and Joe Dassin are buried on these pristine lawns neighboring Paramount Studios, so naturally I had buried my father here, too. I had witnessed at his grave my mother's breakdown. My brother and I had met and drunk there for years after that—until the last time we'd met—that night I turned my back on him and he vanished forever. I gripped the gates and looked in. Tonight a "screening under the stars" had brought the community in to watch *Bullitt* on the big screen. Boozed up and reclined on beach chairs among the dead, the people of Los Angeles were whistling and cheering for Steve McQueen.

I was drying up and the winds were lashing. Coming up on La Brea, I thought about making that left and heading down to Olympic to see if Gary's Auto Collision was still around. Instead I crossed La Brea and closed in on the red brick building with the bright red letters lighting up:

JONES

"Do you have an invitation?"

"Oh. No, I don't."

The man in the cowboy hat and Aviators glared at me.

"Just kidding, sir! You get inside, okay? Enjoy yourself."

Jones hadn't changed: Red brick walls, red hot booths, golden lamps. Between wooden dividers, across red-white checkered tablecloths, only the people had changed. There was a time when I'd know every last one of them—they'd know me, anyway—and for the past few years I'd feared coming in, thinking they'd all still be here and they'd tease and laugh at me. Or maybe that's what I was hoping rather than fearing. Anyway, I didn't recognize anybody. But the place was popping and a hall pass has a way of being revoked unless it's used immediately.

I found a woman at the bar and headed for her. She had damp curly hair and pock marks on her face and her waist-high baggy jeans did no favors to her body-positive. But it was better this way. It took the edge off and somehow made the affair less reprehensible. I took the stool next to her and ordered a vodka martini from a fresh-faced bartender who, nevertheless, served the drink exactly as I remembered it. It was bitter and strong, and came with an extra helping in the shaker. I quickly got my buzz back and started looking more intentionally at the girl. She seemed to smile back, then slid a rubber band down her hairy forearm, wrestled it from her thick wrist, and brought her hair up into a bun.

"Now why would you do that?" I said.

"What?"

"Your hair. Why did you bring it up?"

Her eyes darted over. I could now see they were cold and black.

"Uhh, because I'm *logical*," she said. "I don't want it to get in my food."

The bartender appeared, sliding over a plate of artichoke.

"I just meant—your hair is beautiful."

"Oh," she said, with a quick smile. Then added, "I guess I still don't like being objectified."

Another woman materialized on the seat between us. A rash of piercings spread across her eyebrows.

"Hey bitch."

The two women hugged and drank and chatted to no end—and I could hear their suck and grate, as they devoured the artichoke like gargoyles. The ugliness of the second one really brought out the hideousness of the first, and when I saw the clump of hair under her arms I was truly relieved it hadn't played out. Then I remembered my kiss with Kieslowska and wondered if I might as well use my hall pass retroactively. So I was being pathetic. I took a long drink, tried cynical instead. *Who were these ghoulish women anyway? Did they not want to be fucked? Had they given up on being women?*

Across the bar, a man in his fifties was following the events. He was chubby and bald, but carefully groomed and with a set of horn-rimmed glasses that made an intellect of his round face. He held a guidebook with one hand and with the other made small perfect spoonfuls of crumbling apple pie and vanilla ice cream, right out of its blazing pan. He was obviously from out of town and probably on some lonely sojourn having to do with the movies. He might have recognized me as the writer, or simply as a fellow sojourner, but in either case the threat of conversation was too great. I chugged the martini and made for the restroom in the back.

My hand flat on the wall, I let the events of the night stream out of mind, as the images flashed around me. One photograph in particular was making a presence in the corner of my eye. Captured within it is a smiling blonde with a stuck-out tongue. She lifts her bra, but two hands cover her breasts. It can't be proven—because the men are half hidden on either side of her—but one hand belongs to me and the other to my brother. In any case, the new ownership of Jones maintains that these are only recreations—no such debauchery actually happened here.

I felt a strong bout of nausea coming on (I shouldn't have mixed drinks) and headed out for air. I'd always liked this particular strip of Santa Monica Boulevard because it represented my own psychological location—somewhere east of the insufferable rich kids of Beverly Hills but safely west of the reeking ethnic strip malls and K-town booking clubs—close enough to the gays, where the culture was, but also not too close. Yet I could now clearly see that the strip had changed its own location. A low white Cadillac teeming with brothers passed ever-so-slowly by, revealing a small community of tents trembling violently behind it. A few feet away, some golden-haired beauty was sprawled: face to the asphalt, arms all shot up, long black legs emerging from a sequin dress.

"Can I bum a cigarette?" I asked, stepping toward her.

"Yeah," the woman bawled. "Of course you can."

But it was a man's hand reaching out to me. It was a powerful, veiny black hand, manicured red, shaking under the weight of a pack of Marlboros.

My heart dropped.

"Poe?" I said.

The hand suddenly fell. The woman turned to face me.

"I'm not Poe," she said. "I'm *not* Poe."

Her hair was different. Her nose was different. Her cheeks were different. Her chin was different. Her voice was different. Her eyes were different.

"No," I said. "Sorry. I thought you were someone else."

"Got me?" she said again, growing violent and mad. "I'm *not* Poe!"

"Sorry, sorry."

I stumbled off. My stomach turned. Tears flooded my eyes. I needed another drink and Harlowe was coming up. The place was packed with Persian Jews and a spillover of Armenians on the street, their hairy ape-like arms around each other, laughing and speaking their dark language. There was a brief moment, at the height of my fame, when I'd ended up in their horrible newspapers—I'd made some Armenian-American culture listicle together with Kim Kardashian and Cher—but they were the first to turn against me when my fame ran out. Not because of the murder and misogyny in my work, to clarify—but because I never wrote a book about the Armenian Genocide. They groaned to learn I couldn't utter a single phrase of Armenian and never attended their marches.

A TikToker snapped at me like a snake, asking something about a million dollars, and I crossed the street from Astro Burger to Lubitsch. It was dead and perfect for a few shots. I reemerged completely drunk and light-headed. As I floated west, I felt myself growing angry and desperate. Everything appalled me. In West Hollywood, the gays were bored and bickering like old straight married couples. In Beverly Hills, the shops of Rodeo Drive were boarded up and the winds had blown out all kinds of miscreants to the street. Policemen watched as protesters lit trash cans. I kicked one over and earned a solemn nod from a bum. I quickly turned away, stepping off to avoid a puddle of urine on the path.

Have the dreams of L.A. finally run dry? Has the imagination mechanism broken? Where the fuck is Kobe Bryant?

So I was shivering mad as I loitered, lurked, and haunted the streets—watching the bright framed broken sleeping families hanging like museum pieces in the night. Finally I reached the familiar elementary school. I was almost home. The chartered, orderly sequence of long houses was in view. At the end of it, Neve was waiting for me. She was going to give me shelter again. She was going to give me pills to numb my pain. She was going to cure me of the cancer of my dreams. She was going to return me to the perfect pleasure of the biological state. She was going to bless me with children, whom I would love with a kind of love that makes everything better—heals a wild one like me of his vanity, his addiction to affirmation, his ridiculous need-to-write.

And yet, across distant seas, the possibility of an island was still glowing in the night. Q wasn't just an idea anymore. She was real. I knew she was, because I'd known her so many times—lost her—found her again—and killed her, I believed, once and for all. But as I headed up the driveway, those hot ghostly winds were musing and raging and lashing at me like never before. They were ravishing my body and kissing my face like a dead lover. And they were stirring up that scent again—taking me under its spell of honey and ash—and inviting me into a dream I would never wake up from.

NEW WORLD ORDER

The landing into Athens had been turbulent and the bender of business class booze and Xanax wasn't helping. I glanced deliriously over the instructions and headed for Baggage Storage & Wrapping. Behind the counter, a heavily perfumed middle-aged lady perked up at the sight of me.

"Professor, this is you?" she said, plump and rose-cheeked, a silver bob of hair on her head, her black eyes glinting through thick lenses. "With Hellenic Travel Agency?"

"Yeah," I said. "Should have my passport here somewhere."

I set my backpack on the counter, unzipped the pouch, and slid out my passport from behind the napkin-wrapped PB&J Neve had handed through my Uber window twenty-four hours earlier. She took it from my hand, then pushed forward a document.

"The locker is ready for you," she said, her pearl ballerinas clattering on a keyboard. "Is your phone in the bag?"

"Right," I said. "You know, I'd rather keep my phone, if you don't mind. My wife might want to reach me."

"Exactly, professor," she said, with a polite but insistent smile. "It's best not to take our burdens to the retreat, Q believes."

And only then did I understand that the woman wasn't here for the graveyard shift of Baggage Storage & Wrapping. I noticed the hexagon pinned to her lapel. I recognized her perfume too.

"You may list an emergency number below the signature line if you'd like."

I tried rubbing the grog from my eyes as I glared at the document—a blurry litany of clauses, waivers, and warnings I was clearly meant to ignore.

"That's all right," I said, slipping my phone out. "So about Q—"

"All questions will be answered soon," she interjected. "For now, please enjoy the mystery. You still remember how to enjoy a mystery, don't you?"

Her smile was playful, suddenly intimate. I smiled back.

"Yeah. It's been a minute."

"I do hope you will write another one, you know. We all do."

I dropped the phone in her palm and signed before the flattery wore off.

"Good, very good. Now, professor, you must go. Your car is waiting for you outside."

Under the flapping flag of the European Union, a line of yellow taxis ended upon a black Lincoln, its back door held open by a young woman in slender suit and skinny tie, her ginger hair weaved into a chauffeur's cap. She held a smile of burgundy lipstick but kept her gaze away as I got in—a courtesy I didn't understand, which made me nervous instead. She shut the door behind me, then got into the driver's seat behind the partition, where a black screen was lit with the symbol of a golden hexagon. From its simple form, it folded out in complex maze-like patterns, suggesting something expansive and conspiratorial.

I couldn't remember the last time I was sober and this was no time to start. As we made our way out of the airport, I threw back some salted cashews from the minibar and washed them down with Gold Label. In these early morning hours, Athens was dead, so we moved quickly through the desolate streets of this ceramic city, cracking up around me—its silence broken by the occasional chime of church bells and the grate of roll-up gates—the morning's first shopkeepers arriving with gnarled and grotesque faces. Then they slipped off the tint. A vista of olive trees opened out. Fountains burst up. Through a tangle of tram lines, I caught a glimpse of the Mediterranean. I downed a third bottle as we pulled into Piraeus Harbor.

The door opened. I stepped out. Once again the driver kept her glance away. This time I tracked it down a promenade of bobbing yachts. I saw the one she was looking at. Shimmering in the fresh morning sun was a black and sleek affair, with a gold-trimmed lounging area and an upper deck for the captain. Seagulls circled above. Six silhouettes twitched on board.

"Hey dude, get in here. Will's my name."

I walked onto the boat and straight into the firm grip of a shirtless kid, early twenties, tightly muscled, tatted, and topped by a backwards red hat. He was surging with energy—pumping up and down in place, like he was hyping himself up for something, probably being taller. I sized him up to 5'6".

"Adam," I said. "Didn't realize there would be anyone else."

"Word," Will said, before turning to call up to the bridge. "Yo, cap! We got the sixth man in. That makes all of us, yeah?"

No answer came from the captain's deck, however.

"You a writer too?" I asked. "You here for the—I guess—the retreat?"

Will turned back, flashed a smile of silver-braced teeth, and pulled down his Ray-Bans. His eyes were wired up, electric green.

"Nah, man," he said. "I'm not a writer. I'm a personality. Get called to these things all the time. And usually decline, too, but the appearance fee was generous."

"Appearance fee?"

"50k in Bitcoin. Right into my wallet. My lifestyle brand's pretty big, so I guess they want to cross-promote or something. You've heard of Manifest, yeah?"

I shook my head.

"Then I bet you've come across my content. Life hacks. Power moves. Motivations. All of it for men who want to get made, get paid, and get laid."

He turned to show off the calligraphy on his back.

"*Man*ifest, get it?"

I grinned over this puffed up self-promotion of a man—a fuckboy troll-philosopher invented out of podcasts and protein powder—the remnants of his original self preserved only in his thin ankles and wrists.

"Yeah, you get it," he said, patting my back vigorously—probably one of those power moves. "You get it."

"Yeah," I said. "Cool. So—why are you here again?"

"I just said, dude," Will replied. "I'm here to party."

I winced, had a look around. The strangeness of my situation was slowly dawning.

"We all got different invitations," added a voice, very quiet, belonging to the tall man at the bar. He must have been in his forties, silk scarf tucked into an Oxford shirt, luxurious finely-combed brown hair, thin lips, and circular orange-and-black glasses. He might have been an Arab or a Jew once, but wealth had washed him of his race completely. "My name is Camillio. I manage wealth—for high net-worth individuals. This Q has invited me to talk business."

"So you haven't met her either," I said.

"None of us has," Camillio replied, making his way over with two whiskies. "From what we can tell, she's hosting some kind of gathering. Even got the legend himself to come out and run kundalini sessions. Isn't that right, Hari?"

I followed his glance to the dark man in the lavender robe, reclined on a lounging chair, his feet resting comfortably on an Ottoman.

"Must've taken a vow of silence or something," Camillio said. "He hasn't said a word since I got here."

I recognized Hari Rajneesh from my L.A. childhood, when he was known around town as "the guru to the stars." He'd set up a studio in Beverly Hills, where he drew in adoring crowds full of wash-outs and has-beens, including my mother. He was by now an ancient artifact—a guru in decay, with sleepy eyes, heavily bagged, and the last of his hair dyed black, oiled up, and tied tightly behind his head. He was looking intently to the far end of the boat, where a young man with curly blond hair was hunched over a guitar, his feet dangling over the sea.

"Hey," Camillio said, pushing a glass into my chest. "Did you not want one?"

Apparently one of the whiskies was for me.

"To Q," Camillio said, clicking his glass against mine. "Whoever she is."

I took a big long gulp, letting the alcohol pour into my system and drown any possibility of sobriety. At the end of it, sunlight caught the glass and sparked out in radiant colors. Then the brightness dimmed. A dark voice followed.

"So you believe, then, that Q is a woman?"

When I lowered the glass, my view opened to the sixth and final passenger, looming on the other side of the hexagonal glass table. He was an impressive man, with broad Greco-Roman shoulders and a disheveled gray beard that grew thick and dark at the mustache, before thinning at the hair to military grade. His eyes were black, although the left was restless and searching, while the right was motionless and seemed to be made of glass. A many-pocketed dark green fisherman's vest hung loosely over matching corduroys, which bunched over distressed white Reeboks. A rolled-up newspaper was clenched in his hand.

"Do you have another theory, Maxim?" Camillio replied, in a tone of playful amusement. "Are you saying Q is a man?"

"I *have* no theo*r*ies," Maxim said, with a rasp of his *h* and a roll of his *r*. He had a bombastic Slavic accent, but spoke English with academic formality—and with a kind of elegance available only to those who speak it with contempt. "I only observe the design. The *modus operandi*, as it were. The money spent. The secrecy."

"Most of my clients are quite rich," Camillio countered. "And discreet."

"So you are invited often, then, to such private islands?" Maxim said. As he spoke, his right hand, the one with the newspaper, waved out in great gestures—while the left satisfied nervous tics by tugging at his shirt and wiping the sweat off is forehead and pinching his nose, which gave moments of nasal reprieve to his baritone. "Confidential information gathered. Non-refundable tickets purchased. Invitations delivered without footprint? No, my friend. I maintain this Q is not a woman—or a man. This can only be the work of a—" Here Maxim paused. He took a step toward us, stopped just short of the glass table, and only then—lowering his voice to a whisper—concluded his thought: "—a highly effective clandestine organization."

"I see," Camillio said, humoring him. "Like the CIA?"

"*Fu!*" Maxim exclaimed. "This vile institution is also the most incompetent in the world! I refer, of course, to a much more serious arrangement."

For the first time Maxim's wandering eye crossed mine. I took my cue to exit the conversation. I retreated to the bar, poured myself another whisky, and followed from a drunk distance. I knew Maxim's type well—the members of the defunct Soviet intelligentsia who were enjoying their retirement on subreddits and 4chan message boards. Maxim might have been a serious man once. But the iron curtain had fallen in his mind, too—caused all kinds of truths and lies to mix. It had infected his mind with the disease of post-Soviet madness. Yes, standing in our midst was one of the hard-working practitioners of the last living artform: the conspiracy theory. And I was all for it. The best ideas, I found, are the ones you don't actually need to believe.

"But it is in the name itself, is it not?" Maxim said. "Well—Q."

"Q? Surely you don't mean—" Camillio's tiny eyes shot up behind his circular glasses. "Maxim, you're talking about QAnon, aren't you?"

"Whoah, whoah, whoah," Will said, making a bee-line back into the conversation. "The right wing group—from online? What would they want to do with us?"

"Think, my good Chad," Maxim said. "Think."

"To recruit us?" Camillio inquired. "Into some—New World Order?"

"Well," Maxim said, assuredly, "we would not be the first ones."

With that, Maxim lifted the newspaper above his head and slapped it down like a trump card on the table. I squinted—watched the headline unfurl:

> *Two more men reported missing: Tech mogul and Nobel Laureate now among the twenty-seven men vanished.*

"Holy fuck," Will said, with a dunk of his red hat. "Are you saying what I think you're saying?"

"He's saying they're on the island," Camillio explained, in a rising tone of indignation, which Maxim noticed this time. "He's saying we're about to disappear too."

"And why not, Cami*ll*io?" Maxim replied, slipping an accusation himself through that softened *l*. "Are they not very much like us? All of them—men. And precisely the *type* of men one would gather. I mean, for an experiment."

This was getting good. I finished my drink, took another. By now the golden liquid was having a real effect—pouring like a warm waterfall over me—softening the reality all around—reducing the men to their gestures, their energies, the tones of their voice. As I continued with the whisky, glimpsing over the glass, they were becoming somehow familiar to me, like friends I knew from a glowing childhood—or characters from a scene I'd read. I smiled to recognize it. How many times had I encountered this very scene at the beginning of a mystery, when a group of strangers gathers on a boat, preparing to set out to an island from which there is no return?

"Experiment?" Will said, anxiously.

"What experiment?" Camillio sneered.

"I can say only this," Maxim replied. "In a former life, in the late great Federal Republic of Yugoslavia, I was not a minor figure at the Ministry of Defense. Psychological Operations Division."

And there would be a character just like Maxim, wouldn't there, holding court with his grand stories and theories? Such a character is fundamental to this scene, actually, as he serves at least three important functions. The first is to create a sense of danger in the journey ahead. (A mysterious guru in the background and the soundtrack of a lonesome guitarist is also helpful in this.) The sense of danger, in turn, helps reveal the character of the other passengers on board. Rich boy Camillio might reinterpret his fear as contempt. Young Will might just crack. Maxim's third and most important function, however, is to eventually take his own theories too far—in doing so to subject them to mockery—and so to take the edge off that very sense of danger they first created, lest the characters quit the story before it even begins.

"But I see you do not believe any of this."

A silence followed. In another moment, I realized Maxim was addressing me.

"Your name is—"

"Oh. Hey. I'm—Adam."

"You were smiling, Adam. Perhaps you have another theory?"

I winced. Then dropped my glance to the bottom of the glass. I gave my whisky a little swirl, tried to conjure something up.

"About what awaits us," Maxim said. "On the island."

"Well I think it's pretty obvious, isn't it?" I replied. "I mean—I'm pretty sure we're going to be murdered."

"Murdered?"

"That's what happens, right? At the end of the mystery."

For a moment there was silence. Then Camillio got it.

"That's right!" he said. "*And Then There Were None*, wasn't it? They *do* all die in the end."

"Is that a novel?" Will said. "I don't really get fiction."

"Agatha Christie," Camillio said. "And this is exactly how it begins, too—with some mysterious invitations going around. Well that explains everything, doesn't it Maxim?"

So I had served my role, too, apparently—I had pulled the rug out from under Maxim—I had restored calm and order to the scene. And I had done so in a brilliant stroke, I should add, by simultaneously implementing another important literary strategy. Very often, at the beginning of a mystery, the detective articulates the correct theory of the crime, only to dismiss it—or arrests the real criminal, only to let him go. In the reader's eyes, this rules out the truth definitively, so when it returns again in the revelation, it not only guarantees a surprise, but also leaves the reader with the wonderful feeling that he has been duped. Of course I wasn't entirely conscious of this role just then. For starters I was too drunk. And then I was also too impressed by my comeback to Maxim. He'd put me on the spot and I'd put him in his place—his arms folded like a misunderstood child—grumbling: "You make fun of me now. But you will see. You will see."

"Attention! Attention!"

We jolted back, looked up to the bridge, and caught our first glimpse of the captain—a short, bald, and fat spectacle of a man, bursting through the seams of his white uniform.

"Mister Elders of Zion!" he called, in a heavy Greek accent. On his swollen face, the expression of a tyrannical anger was sustained. "Pioneers of, eh, New World Order! Are you ready to be murdered now?"

Then the expression broke. The captain started laughing his face off. It was a huge, full-bodied, painful-looking laugh—like an insurgency from the inside—and it took a real effort for the man to suppress it. Only through a serious battle, and after a few false victories, did the captain emerge from its grip.

"*O po po po po!*" he rattled. "You are too much! Too much!"

Eventually the captain caught his breath. With a checkered pocket handkerchief, he wiped the sweat off his bald head.

"Please, guys," he announced. "This is going to be very long journey if you continue this way. Now make yourself, eh, comfortable. We embark now, just! River—bowline please!"

When the captain vanished out of sight, we had a good laugh ourselves. The young man at the stern set down his guitar, leaned out over deck, and worked at the rope. Then the engine growled. In another minute the boat was loose.

I stood on deck, watching the port recede before me. Behind it the vast white sun-baked city was leavening in the summer heat, making a mere geography of the place. I glanced to the other end of the deck. The young man in faded baggy jeans, wrinkled white t-shirt, and curly blond hair had returned to his original position on the rails, hunched over his guitar, strumming a melancholy tune. The morning sun was coming in hot against him now, glowing him up, almost making a hallucination out of him. For some time I watched him bathing in that light. Then I moved in.

"Hey," I said.

"Oh, hey man," he said, turning gradually. "Didn't see you there."

He was a thin young man, no more than twenty-five—with a long, uneven nose, sensitive white skin burned in odd patches around it, and a faint mustache under. His eyes were a pale and opaque blue, although they were concealed behind a deep squint, like they were hiding from the sun.

"You a musician?" I asked.

"Guess you could say that," he replied. He spoke slowly, as though from the heat. "Although I'm not famous or anything like that. I was working the boardwalk when I got the invite. Someone dropped it right into my guitar case, funny as that sounds."

"But you accepted."

"Always up for an adventure," he said, picking up his tune where he'd left off. "I've been on the move since I can remember—just going with the flow. Nominative determinism, I suppose. You know—my name being River."

"Right," I said, like I recognized him. "River."

What I'd recognized, I think, was that phrase "nominative determinism" and the tone of Salvation Army wisdom in which he'd said it. And then I also recognized that slow smile of his—the smile of the stranger, the man-off-grid, the addict who had found his way out of the matrix and was now living in the real world—the world of "truth" and "feeling"—where my brother had also lived.

"Heard you say you were a writer. Adam, right?"

"Yeah. I'm hoping to get started on a novel."

"Good luck on that," River said, with a glance over to the other guys. "I mean—doesn't seem like we're going to get much peace and quiet, does it?"

"No, it doesn't," I said, with a grin. "No, it doesn't."

"Well, you never know when inspiration strikes."

As his fingers twisted upon the strings, I could see the emotions passing like clouds across River's blue eyes, hanging from his lower lip, making every limb of his body yearn for something. And by the familiar swell of my own emotions, I knew better than to trust his effect on me. I had lived it too many times. I could see all of it plotted right there on his arms. The cuts, tears, and injection points weren't fresh, but they also hadn't faded completely—and they created a map of a personal tragedy I had sworn I would never again be drawn into.

"That does it for me," River said suddenly, his hand falling off the guitar. This time his smile was quick, maybe embarrassed, like his music had revealed too much. "You know, Adam. I think I'll get some shut-eye. Best way to avoid seasickness is to sleep through it, I find. It's going to get choppy."

"Oh, okay," I said. "Sounds right. Nice to meet you, River."

"My thankfulness to the band," River said, raising his guitar with a sneaky smile, like he was in some inside joke with himself.

I looked out to sea again, watching the last of the city sinking into the horizon, until a solitary structure remained. On the summit of that distant hill lay the ruins of the Parthenon, with its roof blown out and its pillars propped up by scaffolding, transfigured beyond recognition over time—first into a Catholic church, then an Ottoman mosque, and now a cemetery for a civilization, where the godless came to feast like maggots on their dead. Just below it, at the Theater of Dionysus, men had once put on masks to stage our first plays.

I felt a sense of a drunken, exhausted, poetic doom coming up—and I decided to go lie down with it a while. My best creative ideas always came to me in such conditions, and there was something to those masks. River had already found a spot on deck. He was dozing off, hugging his guitar like a life raft. Sitting on an armchair, Camillio had one foot bouncing over the other, watching the swirling pattern the sun left in his empty glass. Across him, Hari was reclined, fresh as a manicured corpse, his dark feet quietly rubbing against each other. Maxim was fast asleep under the fold of his newspaper. Will was restless—flopping on deck like a dying fish. The boat was bobbing intensely now, splashed by rising waves of gold.

I stepped among the bodies, found a spot near the stern, lay on my back, and shut my eyes. I kept thinking about those Greek masks—each mask engraved with a single expression and called a *persona*. I recalled that Jung had suggested that this persona represented the outer self, as opposed to the inner self, which was truer. Jung had been a romantic, however. The age of social media had obliterated the myth of the inner self. Genes were replaced by memes. Our inner selves rushed to the extremes. We were already being digitized—subjected to competition, selection, then duplication—until each of us was left with one of six or so masks he could wear. These avatars would surely be helpful in our final transition.

As the waves lapped against the boat, washing me into sleep, I could see a new world opening up to me—the primary colors and themes of a novel. Yes, there was something to this idea of masks. And I began to imagine that the characters on this boat were wearing such masks. And I imagined that this boat was a specially chartered boat, carrying these masks from the theater of a fallen civilization to a new one—to the *event horizon*. A long time ago, in the seventh grade, when my mind had bent into black holes and other cosmic phenomena, I had learned about this concept and always wanted to write about it. The event horizon is a boundary, beyond which events cannot affect the observer. This means that if six men travel beyond that boundary, they will vanish into another plane of existence, but they will leave behind a set of final images of themselves. The men will disappear, but their personas will be permanently stamped on the event horizon.

When I opened my eyes next, the sky had dimmed. A gray layer of smoke had swept in under the sun. I thought nothing of it at first, but then Will started coughing in his sleep and I got up to have a look. An atmosphere was forming around the boat. Ash was flying around.

I crossed the deck and headed upstairs to the bridge.

"Hey, man."

Our captain was unconscious, his face smashed among a scattering of chocolate wrappers on the dash.

"Captain," I said, on the approach. "Hey, are you okay?"

I poked at him. Still no response.

"Wake up man. Hey, wake u—"

"Agh! What? What!" he shouted, snapping upright. "I not sleep! I not sleep!"

His eyes broke open. They were soft and watery, vulnerable from their dreaming, even as his eyebrows gathered like thunderclouds over them.

"What you want!"

I glared to the ashen sea.

"Something's burning out there."

"Eh? Oh, *that*? Don't worry about *that*. Just big fires in Rhodes today. Very normal."

"Global warming?"

"Global—what? No, man. Turks! Turks!"

"Oh," I said, studying the vulgar exaggerations of the man's face, which I guess passes for native charm or bravado in these parts.

"Call me Stavros," he said. "And I tell you this. I am not actually captain. I am beekeeper, just. On island."

"Really? I've been reading it's a tough time for you guys."

"Eh?"

"I mean—the bees are vanishing, right? Without cross-pollination—"

"Bah!" Stavros erupted. "That's just big bee lobby trying to get grants from EU. Bees have not vanish. You will see soon, you will, populations of bees I have! Even new bees I have."

"New bees?"

"Yes. They make not honey, but make milk."

"The bees make milk?"

"In fact. I show them to you, just. I call them—boobies."

"What?"

"They make milk. They are *boob-bees!*"

And with that, Stavros slapped his thigh and started laughing his uproarious laugh again—his body shaking, his expressions twisting, his bald head breaking out in sweat. He had come very far, it seemed, from that other captain, pictured and taped to the windshield. He was a handsome young man with a full head of hair. A little girl was thrown on his shoulder. A busty beauty beamed at his side.

"Hey!" someone called from below. "What's going on?"

We looked down. Standing among the guys, Will was shouting—

"What the fuck is this?"

"*Opa!*" Stavros called back, just as a gust of ashen wind swept onto the boat. "We will be on other side soon! Do not breathe, just!"

"Stavros!"

The air was so dense with ash I couldn't see the guys anymore. I buried my face in my arm, muffling the noise.

"It's no problem! No problem! Wait! Wait, just! Wait!"

And then, very slowly, the air thinned out. Rays of sun pierced through. The atmosphere cleared. We emerged as though from a religious experience.

"What the fuck was that, Stavros! I almost died, man!"

"Pussies!" Stavros yelled. "No problem, I say! See yourself!"

We looked out. And, with the smoke parting, we saw. In fact it was a pristine sandy cove we were headed for, and beyond the cove a cliff, and on the cliff a town, and above the town a hill, and on the hill hundreds of cave houses from the very bottom to the very top, swirled up in a latticework of black iron stairs and ladders.

"Look!" Stavros said. "Ladies are out!"

"The ladies?" Will said.

"*What* ladies?" Maxim said.

As we pulled into the island, we began to notice them, too—on the balconies of their cave houses: the figures of women. There were hundreds of women waving to us from their balconies.

"*O po po po po!*" Stavros exclaimed, crossing himself in sync with the syllables. Then he slid out a cigar from behind his ear. He lit it with a golden lighter and thundered through a cloud of his own smoke—

"You were almost right! Almost! I present you—New World *Orgasm!*"

THE BIRDS & THE BEES

"Hello, gentlemen! My name is Penelope!"

We were on the dock, gathered around a bubbly little sea creature with a sunny smile and honey eyes and a wreath of golden hair unraveling into the breeze. A long white dress was hanging by threads from her clavicles, clinging to her small, mermaid-like breasts, and blowing out behind her.

"This is special woman!" Stavros announced, bowing to kiss the woman's hand. "You are very lucky, understand."

"Oh stop it, Stavros," Penelope said, with a flirty wave and a Greek accent sweetening her voice. "You're such a charmer."

"Treat her well, yes?" Stavros added, as he retreated to the boat. "We catch up soon. Enjoy, my friends. Enjoy, just. Bye!"

"Bye, Stavros," Penelope said, before turning her attention to us. "Hi Will! Camillio. Hari, so honored. The ladies have been dying to meet you."

She pressed her palms together and bowed for Hari, which seemed to cause a slight smile in the guru.

"River, I see you brought your guitar. Is that you, Maxim? We didn't know what you look like, to be honest."

"In fact," Maxim said. "I'd like to keep it this way."

"Of course," Penelope said. "And you're not the only one. We've hosted presidents here. Movie stars. Famous writers too. Adam, we are such big fans of you."

Against her freckled, make-up free face, her eyes were warm and kind—although they rested on mine too long in some New Age practice of "presence" or "mindfulness" that gave me the creeps. I pegged her to her forties, overeducated, proud—an heiress on the run—like she'd left her dad's house with a copy of *Eat, Pray, Love* when she was sixteen and never went back. Beyond her, the city on the hill appeared as one of those old movie backdrops, painted against the sky.

"Naturally the women of this island are no less important," Penelope continued. "Some of them are celebrities themselves. That is why anonymity is so important here. We did leave all our phones and cameras behind, right Will?"

"Most definitely," Will said, with a grin. "Could use the detox, honestly."

"Well that was pretty silly of you!" Penelope exclaimed. "I mean, the recklessness of men *is* mind-boggling. But—that's why we love you, I guess. The fact that you're here, despite all the questions you must have, proves that we have not been mistaken. More on that soon. Oh you are all so perfect!"

Penelope turned around, lifted her dress, and hopped onto the sand. Will and Camillio exchanged some glance of perverse solidarity and set out behind her. River took Hari's arm and followed. Maxim stumbled after. As he gazed up at the population of women stirring on the balconies, his eyes were filled with abject horror.

The cove opened like a crescent to the cliffs. To the left a stage was covered by a golden curtain. To the right high stools proceeded along a bamboo bar. Nearby some hammocks were strung between pine trees. Farther up the beach a pile of wood was prepared for a bonfire.

"This is the cove," Penelope continued, "where we will spend our evenings. We have music every night and the most amazing cocktails. Our bartender Oriana is a wizard with her drinks—you don't want to miss them. And we're set for a bonfire per your tradition, Hari. So many of our ladies are eager for your sessions."

Hari was able to produce a nod this time.

"Daytime, though, we usually hang by the pool," Penelope said. "That's right above the cliffs there—on the road leading up to the Hive."

"The Hive?" Maxim muttered.

"You mean you didn't catch the clues?" Penelope said. "The black and gold? The hexagons everywhere?"

We followed Penelope's glance above the cliffs and beyond the strip of town. I could now see that the cave houses punctured the hill like the honeycombs of a beehive.

"The bee's symbol, right? Maxim, we thought at least you would recognize a code when you saw one!"

"A hive?" Maxim said. "A *hive?*"

I could actually see the new theory landing on Maxim: tensing his shoulders, gathering his eyebrows in, tightening his gaze into a squint. His entire body was resisting the theory.

"It turns out that the greatest society in the world was actually created by bees, millions of years ago," Penelope explained. "Productive, beautiful, harmonious. And run exclusively by women, of course. So you'll find our community is entirely self-governed, self-sustaining. Here we have a medical clinic and dry-cleaning services, concerts and sports. Naturally we have a spelling bee, too. I jest, I jest. Everything on the island is actually *made* of honey. Literally. There is at least some honey in everything we wear, everything we eat and drink, everything we produce. As our founder likes to say: Honey is the glue that binds us together."

"Your founder," Maxim said. "You mean—Q."

"Well, do we have to spell everything out?" Penelope said, her gaze rising above the cave houses and to the glass house at the very top of the hill. "That's where your host lives. Come on, guys—the Queen!"

For some time Penelope did not blink, her eyes spellbound to that sparkling, diamond-like creation. As she spoke, her smile quivered eerily on her face—and her voice softened with musing—

"She has created this civilization for all of us. And she rules with such grace you have to see to believe. And you will see. You will. I promise you that."

Slowly the spell broke. Penelope's eyelids fluttered. She returned to us with a new serenity and the dew of a true believer in her eyes.

"It is a rare honor, you know," she said. "The Queen invites men to her island very selectively—and only as guests. Six at a time, she finds best."

"So to clarify," Maxim said, "we *are* the only men here?"

But it was clear he was already surrendering to the truth: his shoulders humbling, his squint easing, his scowl breaking down into a sigh.

"Well don't be so disappointed, Maxim! Our guests typically welcome the news. I believe this qualifies as 'good ratio'—am I right, Will?"

"Wait, what?" Will said.

"The Queen is a great admirer of your work too, of course. She understands the value of strong, virile men. The truth is she must have found something very special in each of you, to ask you here. At some point during your stay, she will want a meeting. In the meantime, though, the Queen wants you to enjoy her island. And for her ladies to enjoy you too, of course. They're all at home now—getting ready for the party. Now follow me, my beautiful little drones. Come! I'll take you to your residences."

As we headed for the cliffs, I sent one more glance up to the Hive. The women had in fact retreated from their balconies. But through the swelling slits of curtains, their strange and curious glances descended upon us.

Where the cove ended, the cliffs tackled the hill and forced an opening. We followed Penelope up the narrow stairway. At the top of it, a trail forked. To the left a path headed up to town and then the cave houses of the Hive. Instead we took the right path into a circular garden—a labyrinth of hyacinth, oleander, and rose. We passed a pond. Then a little gray chapel came into view. It was surrounded by pine trees that parted in the breeze to offer spectacular views of the sea. But the entire project was centered around a miniature fortress, built of black and gray brick, with stained glass windows.

"This is where the history of the island began," Penelope explained. "It was founded by the Knights of St. John, during the Crusades. The Order was stationed in Rhodes. But the Grand Master built this outpost for himself—and his guests. Hint: They were women! From the north, the aristocrats of Constantinople. From the east, the beauties of Beirut, the truth-seers of Jerusalem. From the south, the intellectual belles of Cairo. From the west, the nymphs of Athens. History has recast these women as some kind of feeble creatures. But long before their so-called liberation, these women were free, beautiful, powerful. On this island, we see ourselves in their tradition."

The black iron door of the manor was guarded by a silver knight. He was fully armored, with a helmet and the insignia of the cross on his chest. Penelope put her hand on the knight's shoulder and gazed into the rectangle of his mask, where a man's eyes used to be.

"And we see you in their tradition," she said. "Exciting. Brave. Adventurous. We may be a matriarchy, but we do enjoy our boys around here."

"Even you?" Will asked.

The move was sudden, but it didn't seem to trouble Penelope.

"Who, me?" she replied, with a coy smile. "I'm sure you'll forget all about me when you see the fangirls waiting for you. Now, I'll have to say goodbye. You'll find your rooms upstairs and some very lovely attire—tailor-made for you, of course, by one of our more famous members. So please enjoy yourselves, gentlemen. The ladies and I will be waiting for you at sunset—at the cove. Goodbye for now!"

We stood at the door of the manor, watching Penelope cross the garden in sprightly twirling performances of some great personal freedom, which looked very stressful to me.

"*Chyort!*" Maxim exclaimed, when she was out of earshot. "I must leave this godforsaken hippie commune!"

"Commune?" Camillio said, as he examined the silver knight. "This place rather reeks of old money, don't you think?"

"Some bored rich lady's fantasy then," Maxim grumbled.

"My favorite kind of client," Camillio said. "Look, Maxim. You don't have to be embarrassed because your theory didn't pan out."

Maxim shook his head, mostly at himself, and this got his shifting left eye to shift even faster.

"Come on, dude!" Will said. "I mean—isn't this better? We're absolutely swimming in pussy! And they don't seem to be closed for business, either."

"Hmm?" Maxim said.

"You saw how Penelope was coming onto me."

"Coming on?" Maxim said. "I believe she declined."

"What? No, man. She didn't *decline*. That was just ASD."

Will glanced around for affirmation, but found only a circle of blank glares.

"Come on, guys!" he said. "You haven't heard of Anti-Slut Defense? Women don't want to appear to be easy, so they say no even when they don't mean it. It's just a defense mechanism. Trust me, it's my job to read body language. And her body was saying yes. It's all in *The Manifesto*. You guys really need to follow me when we get our phones back."

"I admit, I am usually the mad one," Maxim said, scratching his beard irritably. "But now, my friend, I must congratulate you."

"Thanks, dude," Will said. "Now let's go get ready for the party, yeah?"

He pulled open the iron door and invited us in with that intense smile of his, which life had not yet found the opportunity to correct.

"It's too good to be true," Will said, seemingly unaware of the meaning of his words. "It's too good to be true."

As the guys headed upstairs, I hung back to have a look around the manor. Antique candelabras swayed above the corridor. Lacquered floors creaked below. From the walls, square-jawed men looked on. A sitting room led to a parlor, then a living room, which was surrounded on all sides by stained glass windows and vast shelves of books. I couldn't remember the last time I'd been in a library like this—a proper one, I mean, composed of the dead white males who had actually created the Western Canon—not the "inclusive" collections the university library had installed after systematically dismantling its permanent holdings.

I poured myself a whisky from the bar and walked along that golden procession. Those books had shone so bright for me once.

As a kid, they'd drawn me into dreams and journeys to islands very much like this one, where muses inspired art, sirens lured captains to shipwreck, and nymphs conquered even the most powerful men with promises of immortality. As a young writer, I had believed I would achieve it, too—my own books would find their place in the collection. Then the culture changed. I became an embarrassment, then a coward, then hardly anything at all. And yet, as they passed along the books now, my fingers were tingling once again to their touch.

I threw back my drink, set the glass on the coffee table, and only with a passing interest noticed the slim golden volume which had been placed there. The title read: *Catharsis*.

The bedrooms were on the second story and mine was a windowless little number with a Moroccan mosaic lamp that spread a dim soft light upon its appointments: a Persian rug, a carved walnut desk, a mosquito net bed. I took off my clothes and put on the new ones laid out: white silk pants, a button-down with black-and-gold Versace stitchwork at the sleeves, and a pair of beach shoes with the golden letter Q embroidered into the toecap. The uniform fit perfectly, as expected. By now I was accustomed to the idea that my host, whoever she was, knew me intimately. And she had, in fact, created the ideal conditions for me to write in.

I made for the desk at the far end of the room. Under the lamp, surrounded by stationery, was a typewriter. I stretched my arms and took a seat before it—a Remington Home Portable, 1930s vintage, with a sheet of paper already rolled in. Quaint, I thought, that Q should want me to write on a typewriter. But the amusement didn't last. As I leaned in for the page, a slow chill was already working its way up my spine. Because rising from the ribbons of the machine, the page in front of me was not actually blank. A single sentence had already been written on it:

On the last day of class, a black envelope arrived in my university mailbox.

My heart twisted up inside me. My body snapped back. A thrill took me over. I read that line again, then again up close, before I understood what it suggested. Already on the boat I'd heard the first whispers of this idea. I had dismissed it as a joke—a playful insinuation of my subconscious. But now it was announcing itself clearly and forcefully. *Had I actually found myself in the very story I had come here to write? Was this Q's way of inspiring me? In her invitation, she'd said that the novel would "practically write itself"—why?—because it would be happening to me?—is that what she meant?—because the novel had actually begun the moment I received that black envelope?*

A surge of energy sent me to my feet—got me pacing. If this was a joke, I didn't find it funny at all. Who did Q think she was, I thought, to write this sentence in my name—to believe she could open my book for me? And was this the best idea she had for it—some vacation read you leave behind at the beach when the summer ends? How many times had it already been written, anyway—usually by some "female author" who, incapable of writing an original, opted for an "homage"—a tribute to that original dame who first invited her guests to an island and slaughtered them dead? How insulting, I thought. I'd rather meet that fate than write this book again.

I tore the paper out of the typewriter and trashed it. Then I headed out to meet the guys downstairs, amusing myself with the thought that I had some pride left after all. So it was a promising start to my residency. My plan was to check out the party, then return to start the novel myself.

THEY WERE GODDESSES

The moon was bright in the sky, the sand warm under our feet. Will almost fell, but Maxim caught him and held him up. Hari grabbed my shoulder. River pushed against me. Camillio followed. We moved together, like a rugby team in white, pushing into the darkness—following the woman's voice. They first appeared to us as gold-dipped silhouettes—a sea of swaying figures in the moonlight—ebbing and flowing like the waves. Their eyes closed and tilted to the sky, the women waved their hands in the air, as though to welcome a great cosmic event. Beyond them, a golden curtain covered the stage like an altar. Above it, on the cliffs, a strip of town was illuminated. Then the cave houses of the Hive ascended as a shining city on a hill.

It wasn't the first time I'd seen a party open like this. In college days, my friends from the Burner crowd had lured me into exactly such raves. But I was more into powder than pills in those days—and I liked going home with a girl, not sand and salvation in my shoes. I got out of the desert scene quick. Still I did appreciate its artistic intent, its pagan symbolic order, its play on theme. In this case the theme was being set by the woman's voice—at first ethereal, but already gaining reality—still very far, but slowly echoing into embryonic form—even tangling into harmonies—even, at times, coalescing into words. The simultaneous formation of language and life was being insinuated—the fleshing out of words and bodies waiting to be released.

Suddenly a scream tore through the dark.

It echoed against the cliffs.

It vanished into the sea.

Then a beat dropped.

A second beat.

A third.

And the voice returned, but now with intelligence—

Let there be light.

The stage lights beamed. A flood of gold came for the women. It caught their curves and filled their bodies and lit up their flesh. Then their eyes opened—one after another—like airport departure signs flipping open in bright blues and greens, blacks and browns, grays and glowing turquoises. The women screamed and whistled and cheered. They came tall and glamorous, petite and athletic, black and white. They came as belles and barbies and big bad bitches. They came in every kind and color, and swept the cove with all the accents of the world.

"Gentlemen!"

From the depths of the spectacle, Penelope burst out with a huge smile, beige crochet dress, and long seashell necklace. A fleet of women followed.

"You all look so handsome in your whites!"

Maxim had on linen pants and a button-down, which he kept open over his graying chest. River came in white jeans and a t-shirt. Hari donned a lush silk robe. Camillio was fitted to a nautical suit. Will was zipped up in a silly jumpsuit. He still wore his Ray-Bans and backwards red hat.

"Penelope," Will called, reaching out. "Looking good tonight."

He took her hand and attempted a twirl. But she stumbled awkwardly—slipped out of his move.

"Ahh, you're so sweet," she replied. "As promised, though, I've brought some ladies you should meet. Monica and Lucia are big fans."

Penelope pushed forward two done-up Italian babes. They had plush lips and frazzled hair and ample breasts bursting out of tight leopard prints, torn at the midriff and the back, like they'd just escaped a mauling. I watched with amusement as Will looked them over with a slobbering grin.

"You know, Penelope," he said. "I actually think that's a good idea. I prefer women who take care of themselves anyway."

"What?" Penelope said, her smile bewildered among her freckles.

"You didn't have to be such a bitch about it, that's all."

It was all very excruciating, to everyone except Will. As Penelope stood in shock, he swiftly moved on to the Italians, who took him into a dream of sweet-nothing kisses and *ciao bambinos* and that great empty magnificent carnival unrivaled in Western Civilization. Then the swarm came for the rest of us. In another moment we were all lost in their giggles and perfume—caught up in their chains, clutches, and gold-letter buckles—surrounded by their endless buzzing.

"Hello, Adam."

She was a stiff and pale beauty in a dark green dress, her black hair pulled back tight to accentuate the cruel slant of her eyebrows. Above high cheekbones, her eyes were also dark green, intensely focused yet enigmatic. Black and purple eyeliner had been applied, a gothic revolt against her bourgeois breeding.

"Imogen," she said, her voice cold, lush, and rainy—she was English. "I'm an admirer of your work."

"Oh?" I said. "I didn't realize I had many left."

"No, you don't," she said. "I intend to use that to my advantage."

I grinned. I couldn't remember the last time I was angled by a fan—and with such intent. It was flattering, for sure, and I was up for some cheeky banter.

"So you like a man when he's down," I said.

"I have all the materials we might need for that."

"Maybe we use them on you instead."

"I was hoping you'd say that."

A smile extended out as a serpent on Imogen's lips. She bit down on it. Her gaze eased. Her entire seduction was made through such suggestions of the control she was ready to lose, if only a man came along who could make her. Her hair, collected back, could be snapped and unraveled in an instant.

"So what materials are we working with?" I said.

"Nothing out of the ordinary. Ropes. Rings. Saws."

"Saws?"

"Well, you remember the scene, don't you darling? You wrote it after all. When he tied her down in rope and sawed her in half and had the whole trick done on her."

"So you've read my books?"

"The sex scenes, mostly. I've been wanting to meet you since I was fourteen."

"That's a lot of rape and murder for fourteen."

"Yet something about that magician of yours made it all okay, didn't it? Such a dark figure, half-shadow half-man. That was a smart move, of course, not giving him a physical description, letting him stay a mystery until the end. That was how you got into the heads of girls like me, I suppose. Every night, I'd watch the shadows on my bedroom curtain, waiting for him. He never came, of course. But—I did. In a way, Adam, I guess you could say you groomed me."

"Groomed you?"

"Oh don't get excited. I mean, metaphorically. Anyway, those sex scenes ruined other men for me. You know you had a real talent for those scenes. Apologies—did I say *had*?"

"You did."

"Well, maybe you still do. I wouldn't know."

At the end of her line, a hook dangled. I could see it there, shining—there wasn't even any bait on it. I was supposed to take that hook into my mouth because I liked the cold violent taste of a hook. *I guess we'll have to find out*, is all I had to say, or something like that. And from there would begin the hours of tug and pull—the continuous tensing of that line between us, which could only be resolved, suddenly and brutally, by a single act for which I would bear sole responsibility. So I would be performing against her fantasies—propelling myself against the strain in my back and the quickening of my breath on a deranged mission to prove myself and maybe even the validity of literature itself. Then the line would snap. I'd be off the hook. And as I fell into the abyss, I would look up desperately in search of the only possible reward—the reassurance of a woman who, only then would I realize, was a stranger.

"Those sex scenes ruined me too," I said, emerging from thought. "Every girl I dated expected me to tie her up or beat her up or something."

"And didn't you?"

"No."

Imogen blinked. And by the flush of her expressions I understood I'd fucked up—tipped my hand somehow.

"Never?"

"Never."

After that Imogen's shoulders relaxed. Finally she gave out a sigh and for a moment appeared to be an ordinary woman and very pretty, but probably too tall. The tension between us evaporated completely, leaving two cold bodies on the sand. We had already become strangers.

"Yo!"

Will swept in from nowhere, grabbed my arm, and started pulling at me.

"Hey man," I said, shaking him off.

"Good, good! I like that. There is hope for you."

I tried looking into his eyes—caught my reflection instead—dwarfed and doubled in his Ray-Bans.

"I mean—what the fuck were you doing back there? She was just shit-testing you, dude. You just had to meet her challenge."

"Yeah, well. I wasn't into her. I mean—I'm not looking for anything."

"Come *on*, dude. At least be honest with yourself. Of course you're looking. Fact is you fucked up, which is why you're making up excuses now."

I shook my head, realized there was no point trying with Will. Clearly the fact that I was once the most eligible bachelor of the literary world was lost on him.

"Don't look at me like that," Will said. "I'm not your enemy here, okay? Walk-and-talk. This place is lit and we should probably find the bar."

I took a breath, glanced over my shoulder. The party was picking up and I wasn't going to survive it sober.

"Yeah, all right," I said. "Let's go."

"Fucking gurus do it right, don't they?" Will said, as we set out past Hari, circled by a group of adoring women. "Not my game, though, to be honest—putting in all that time to build trust, emotional connection, and all that. Besides, between me and you, the truth-seeking types are never really seeking beauty, are they? I just can't do bad hygiene. And I need at least an eight to get a semi going. Even then I go straight for the kill. Will doesn't fuck around."

"How's that going for you tonight?"

"Great, man. Great. You liked my neg, yeah?"

"Your neg?"

"When I called her a bitch. The look on Penelope's face was priceless."

"She was definitely pissed off."

"Pretty strong Phase 1. *Put her in her place*, am I right?"

"So you're not going for the Italians."

"The Italians? No, man. Fuck the Italians. They do have some good fucking tusi, though. Gotta love doing bumps out of those long-ass fingernails. That was Phase 2. *Build social capital among the competition.* After that—hey baby."

Mid-sentence, Will caught a hand and spun up a tornado of glitter.

"Tomorrowland bitches, man," he said. "Hot as hell. But it's all druggy-druggy, no fucky-fucky with them. What were we talking about?"

"Penelope."

"Oh, yeah. I'll give her about ten minutes before she comes back."

"To kill you, maybe."

"Hope so. Aggression-to-sex is the easiest workflow, actually. Look, I usually charge for this stuff. But I like you, Adam. So I'm going to tell you some things that will last a lifetime."

I hung back a moment, watched Will head for the long bamboo bar lost in a sea of women. He pressed into an opening, pushed some women around, and made space. He plopped himself on a stool, swiveled around childishly, and waved me onto the seat next to his. Something horribly motivational was coming up in him.

"Look at me and tell me what you see," Will said, when I'd settled.

"What do I see?"

"You see a put-together guy, right? Calm. Cool. Confident, yeah?"

"Sure, Will. Sure I do."

"But let me tell you. Just fourteen months and three days ago, I was addicted to video games and living in my mom's basement. I was practically an incel. Hadn't slept with anyone except my girlfriend, and she dumped me for some fucking cellist. And he was tall, man. *So* fucking tall. That's my real Achilles Heel, if you ask me. All I did during the pandemic was get high and google 'short famous guys.' Houdini 5'4"; Bruce Lee 5'7"; Napoleon— well, actually he was super tall, that's a myth. Hence why I started wearing this hat, to give me those extra inches, but then it started working in a magic way almost, like a peacocking thing, and one day I *accidentally* turned it backwards. I swear to you, dude, on that day, I was reborn—I became like a new man! This is why I say: It's not how you're born—it's how you're *re*born. Hey, can we get a drink over here!"

Will followed that up with a whistle down the bar.

"A moment! A moment!" the bartender called back.

As he returned his attention to me, Will's glance crossed another conversation happening at the bar. With a martini poised in his hand, Camillio was deep into it with Penelope.

"Case in point right there! Case in point! Look at that guy, right? Good old Camillio—always talking himself up—always pitching himself—never not pitching, right?—always pitching, but not pitching. Leaning back, speaking quietly, forcing *her* to lean in—God forbid she misses something he says. You see how he's crossed his legs? Classic! Look how he's putting his drink down, too—his fingers circling around the glass. That's called sexual suggestion. And sales is just sex by another word, isn't it? But let me tell you, and mark my words, nobody is born with this technique. That dude must have spent years learning the book—rehearsing—practicing—to the point that... *Wait* a minute!"

"What?"

Will's lesson came to a screeching halt.

"That—that mother fucker! I *knew* I recognized him!"

I leaned in for a look.

"He has his back to us," I said.

"Exactly, man. Exactly! That's how he is in his Stories. Always on yachts and planes, looking off in the distance so you can't see his face. That's Morel!"

"Morel?"

"Yeah! They made a doc about him."

"Wait," I said, recalling something on TV. "I think I watched it. Isn't he a—"

"—con artist! Yes! Only money he has is from the girls he's catfished. They've never found the dude either. Oh my God, he's a genius. Case study. Maestro right there. And just look at him pitch! Decommissioned island, bla bla. Sovereign wealth, bla bla. Tax incentive, bla bla. It's just words, right? And in this case, lies. But it doesn't matter, does it? So long as *he* believes it. And then *everyone* believes it. And then it's *actually real.* That's why they call it a confidence game. And *that's* what you need, my brother—confidence. The red hat! Once you find it, you'll start loving yourself. And then, the ladies will love you. That's really what women want—a man who loves himself—ideally a total narcissist. After that it's just a script. Phase 1. *Put her in her place.* Phase 2. *Build social capital among the competition.* Phase 3—"

"What's Phase 3?"

"*This* is Phase 3," Will said, grabbing my shoulders. "*Demon-*

stration of alpha status. Remember, a woman is always watching, even when she's not watching. So every second counts. You don't mind my hands being here, right?"

"Happy to help," I said. "I guess this means—you're still going for her?"

"What?"

"Penelope."

"Ugh! No, Adam. You're not *listening*. You never go after a girl, okay? You make her come to you. I really have to get you a subscription to my content. A lot of it is practical advice for men—*exactly* like you. It's so fucking easy to get women when you get the hang of it. And I actually *show* you how to do it, step by step, with *real* women. How to open. When to close. Honestly, you've probably jerked off to me without even knowing. My POV-work is always trending on YouPorn. You don't see me, technically, but even better: You see what *I* see—"

Suddenly a memory struck. I'd been watching a video recently—an amateur kitchen scene, pretty sure—where I'd caught a reflection of a red hat.

"Oh shit," I said. "I think I *have* seen you."

"Really?"

"Some girl in the kitchen, right? You were yelling at her to wash the dishes or something. That was you?"

"Yes!" Will erupted. "Hell yeah! Told you you've seen my stuff. Literally! I guess that means we're kind of eskimo brothers. Tell me, tell me, tell me. Did you like it? You saw how I pulled her from the street, yeah?"

"Very realistic," I said.

"Not realistic," Will said. "*Real.* I mean—they don't even know I'm recording."

"What?" I said, perplexed.

"I'm *always* recording," he said, pulling his sunglasses an inch down his nose. "Say hi if you'd like."

For a moment I looked into Will's eyes. They were even more amped up than before—shocked-open, almost—surging with a powerful, electric optimism.

"No, dude. Right here."

I followed the tapping of Will's index to the bridge of his sunglasses. Finally I noticed the tiny camera embedded there.

"Are you—" I began. "Are you serious? Hey man. You can't just—"

"Dude! Don't be an NPC, okay? This isn't for me, obviously. I do this all for you. And millions of guys like you."

Will grabbed my shoulders again—shook me hard. He needed the point to sink in.

"I want you to believe in yourself, okay? I want you to *be* yourself. It's the hardest thing in the world, but once you accept who you are—once you *love* who you are—there'll be no fucking stopping you."

I stood in silence, gazing into Will's blinding eyes and that horrible silver-braced million-follower smile. And yet I found myself surrendering to them. If he hadn't been persuasive, then Will definitely was exhausting.

"Will!"

It was Penelope coming up behind us and she wasn't herself. Her smile had cooled. Her eyes had dimmed.

"I need to talk to you," she said.

"What's up?" Will replied, without turning. He winked over to me instead, then pushed his sunglasses up.

"I didn't appreciate what you said. Calling me ugly."

"That's not what I said."

"You called me a bitch, too."

"No. I said you were *acting* like a bitch."

"Will, turn around when I talk to you. How was I—"

"Hey," Will said, turning for Penelope. "Listen to me."

For the first time since I met him, I detected a kindness in Will's voice.

"*I* know you're not a bitch, okay?" he said. "Deep down, you're obviously such a great person. That's the part of you I like."

"Huh?" Penelope said. "You do?"

"Of course," Will replied, in a reassuring tone. "Look, we clearly got off on the wrong foot. What say we get out of here and correct?"

I could now see all the anger dissipating from Penelope's eyes. That smile of hers was warming up again.

"Oh, I'd love that," she said, sweetly. "I really would. Except—"

"Except?"

"The Queen wants to see you."

"The Queen?"

"Yeah, she's waiting for you at her place. I've come to take you up."

"Oh? Oh! Well that's—" For a moment Will grew quiet and ponderous. Then he exclaimed, "That's amazing!"

"Good!" Penelope said. "Well, she's looking forward to it too."

"Yeah. Fuck yeah! Let's go!"

Penelope nodded to me, then headed off. Will slipped off the stool behind her. He was shaking with excitement.

"I'm actually going to do it," he said, before setting out after her. "Imagine that, dude! I'm actually going to fuck the Queen. See you, man. Or at least you'll be seeing me. This shit's going viral when I post!"

Long after we've outgrown all of life's illusions and stopped believing in everything including love and God, we keep the faith that, somehow, the young know something we do not. This is, in hindsight, the most ridiculous faith of all. But as I watched him leave—bouncing between his feet, pumping himself up, taking his red hat for a victory lap around his head—I couldn't help but smile. At least Will believed in something, I thought, even if it was only in himself.

"Crisis! Crisis! Crisis!"

The words emerged from a cloud of smoke.

"Catastrophe! Liberation creates psychological disorder, understand. Great confusion. But seduction has been made. Equilibrium must result."

When the smoke cleared, I caught sight of a cigarette dangling from the lips of an emaciated woman in the twilight of her beauty—coarse black hair falling along the mountainous erosions of her face—with caved-in cheeks and bent-in nose and a black gaze afflicted with some obscene truth.

"Oriana," she said, with a smoky, working-class voice. "I am therapist here. Also bartender, which is how I do therapy. I make you something, eh, special for writer."

Oriana clicked her tongue and tipped a smile of crooked, coffee-stained teeth. She adjusted the black lace shawl draped over her thin bare arms, then cast her hand over a private garden of flowers, fruits, and mixers. She picked up an apricot, a jar of dark honey, and some sugar cane, before starting on a drink.

"So you know who I am," I said.

"We all have read your novels, of course," she replied. "Official selection of our book club. Well don't look so surprised! You have many fans here."

"I'm starting to see that," I said. "It's just hard to believe. I mean, don't you find my work a little—"

"Yes?"

"I don't know. Misogynistic?"

"Bah!" Oriana exclaimed. "Don't bring academic jargon here, boy! It is only natural to hate women you love. I certainly do not blame you for killing them!"

I grinned at Oriana. I'd always been into women who had lost all hope and embraced their madness. They knew how to hang with the boys—and spar without being offended—only I thought they'd gone extinct.

"Maybe you're right," I said. "But I think you mean my characters."

"Yes, yes, okay!" Oriana replied, impatiently. "Your *characters*. How very disappointing, Adam! Writer without, eh, conviction—always hiding behind his characters. I can see why you became professor. And then they cancel you anyway!"

It was a hard hit and Oriana knew it.

"Look," she said, softening her voice. "This is safe space we have made, okay? You do not have to worry about woke police here. Or feminazis. Or #MeToo witches! That entire business was great crime. Against women, most of all!"

I let down my guard a little—leaned in.

"Against women?" I asked. "You really think so?"

"Of course!" Oriana replied, her neck bending to the next provocation. "It made KGB informers of us. Branded us victims for life! Yet long before so-called 'feminism,' did women not rule over men?"

"I don't know," I said, playfully now. "Pretty sure you were our property."

"So you owned debt. Congratulations."

"We beat you without consequence."

"*Opa!* Only to cry like babies and beg to be taken back."

"We threw money at you as you danced on stages."

"Yes, this is my point."

"Your fathers sold you off with dowries."

"Just method for fat ugly girls to be married without doing anything. And you know who sweat and worked for mine?"

She jabbed a finger in some liquid, tasted it, and grimaced as she said—

"My poor father!"

I just started laughing.

"Well according to God, your only function is to obey and serve men. That's what you've been made to say at the altar for thousands of years."

"Words. Just words! Really, sentimentality of man is wonder of modern world. I tell you this, Adam, Christiantity was invented by women to stop men from fucking around! Church is run by castrated men, yes?"

"You know," I said, "you really should write a book about this."

"And give up all our secrets? Never!"

Oriana took one last hit and smashed her cigarette in an ashtray full of them. She spun a spoon among her fingers, dropped it into a shaker, and began to stir. In another moment, she jabbed her finger in again, then sucked on it, then smiled. The last of her femininity was in a smile that could be made to rise on such an occasion.

"Aha! This is not bad!"

I watched her dark thin lips as they took in another cigarette.

"Come," she said, tilting her pack of Presidents. "Join me."

"Sure," I replied, catching one with my teeth.

I leaned for a light. The flame brought us into a new intimacy. I could now see the beauty of Oriana's past radiating into her face—the moon catching her black eyes.

"We believe in freedom here, Adam," she said, when the flame had passed. "Your mind must be free in order to create, yes?"

Then, pushing a tall glass of golden liquid toward me, she added—

"Mead. In Norse mythology, one sip of this fermented honey turns you into poet. And I have direct orders from Queen to make you one again."

"Queen's orders, huh?" I said, taking a drag.

"Nothing short of masterpiece she expects from you," Oriana

said. "And I believe you already have your idea?"

Oriana smiled curiously and dropped a wink after. Before I could say anything more, she'd vanished down the bar, mumbling to herself—

"Crisis! Crisis! Crisis! They were goddesses once. Then they wanted jobs!"

I grinned Oriana off, took another hit, then a first sip of the bittersweet mead. Such an odd woman, I thought. In this theoretical novel I was again reminded of, she'd fit naturally into the role of the "mad bartender." An evolution from the "butler" figure of older mysteries, this updated version is meant to provide the detective with some much-needed comic relief from the A-story. Even a dick needs a diversion, is the pretext, except of course she isn't really a diversion. Disguised in the bartender's madness— and dismissed for that reason, too—a phrase or clue might well be recalled, much later, in the solving of the mystery. I thought, as I put out my cigarette: *Oriana might even be the mastermind criminal herself.*

It was upon this thought that I was startled—suddenly chilled to the bone—at the sound of an explosion rocking the cove, followed by the screams of women. I braced myself as I turned for the view. But they were screams of joy, it turned out, and those were only fireworks blasting in the sky—soaring above the cove, beyond the cliffs, and toward that distant road swirling up the cave houses on the hill. I quickly understood what they were celebrating. For I could see, by their golden glare, those unmistakable silhouettes—the first pulsating and orbiting the second as they made their ascent. I witnessed that boy in his pure atomic excitement, with his huge and innocent and inefficient movements, as he circled around the girl leading him calmly into the Hive—and toward the Queen's house.

I took a long sip and shook my head at the scene. In fact I was becoming pretty annoyed with these signs from Agatha everywhere—in this case, a reminder of the poem she had set at the heart of her most famous mystery:

> *Six little Indian boys playing with a hive,*
> *A bumblebee stung one, and then there were five.*

DANCE OF THE BEES

As I swiveled back to the bar, my glance crossed a woman in a short red dress. She was sitting a few seats away, her face hidden behind chin-length platinum blonde hair. The thrill of the fireworks and mead must have been collaborating, because I found myself strangely vulnerable to her effects: her spine, running like stitchwork down her open back; her legs, crossed and caught tightly in fishnets; her shiny red doll shoes, dangling at her tipsy feet. More than anything, I was drawn to that look of despairing boredom-at-the-world, as she poked at an olive at the bottom of her red lipstick-stained martini. I could see her getting impatient with it, too, getting aggressive with that olive, until she finally stabbed it through.

"So you gonna wait 'til I pass out to talk to me?"

She hadn't even looked up. But the bar having emptied out—the fireworks had sent the women dancing—there was only one man she could be talking to. I downed the last of my mead and went for it—

"That's usually my move."

The young woman turned slightly. Her cheeks were white and plump and her downturned eyebrows gathered like a schoolgirl above running-away-from-home eyes. Her voice was sweetly rasping, like she had a cold.

"So you like a woman who hates herself, huh?"

"I like a woman who trusts herself."

The gambit worked, apparently. She let a smile go, like a thin layer of despair peeling off.

"Oh yeah?"

"Yeah. Also, you're cute."

"So you're objectifying me now."

"What? No. I was just—"

"That's too bad. I like being objectified."

She turned a playful glance this time. Her eyes were still, but bursting with internal motion, like a cosmic explosion of scarlet from amber. Her slight smile left dimples on her cheeks, which calmed the effect of her troubled beauty. She had the kind of easy sensuality you can only get in California or on pills.

"Is that true?" I said.

"Every girl does, I guess," she replied. "To be worshipped and desecrated—to be treated like a goddess or whatever."

"Didn't realize you were a goddess."

"No? Well, next best thing. An actress. Used to be, anyway."

"Used to be? But you're so young. I'm sure you—"

"Stop, okay? I know all about life's disappointments already."

I smiled. She couldn't have been more than twenty-five. Oriana came by, swapped in another mead and martini, then vanished again.

"I get it," I said. "I don't like being inspired either. I'm Adam, by the way."

I picked up my drink and moved to sit next to her.

"Jane," she said. "I know who you are."

"So you've read my books, too?"

"I didn't say *that*," Jane replied. "Honestly, I was never into you L.A. writers. Always brooding and dark. Yet always romanticizing your seedy shithole of a city, with your palm trees and jacarandas and those fucking Santa Anas! You guys really should be sued for writing about those winds so much, like they're magical or something. You know I moved halfway across the country for a feel of those winds!"

Jane took a huge courageous gulp of her martini, then continued—

"That first night I finally felt them coming on, I thought my life was about to change—like there was gonna be a huge revelation or something. But then they came in hot and disgusting like sewage and with no trace of magic at all! Such a fraud! I ended up following a couple midgets to some seance in the hills and got into a three-way I was so fucking bored."

I started laughing. Jane smiled back. Another layer peeled off. Some red blush rushed into her cheeks. And I saw the game ahead of me—the night of peeling away at her. Against my patient and gentle efforts, Jane was going to become warmer and softer. She would shed her bitterness, then her irony, like they were clothes she no longer needed. In time she would be naked completely, her white body in my hands, and even then I would continue to peel—even more fanatically—because each layer of an onion reveals something warmer, softer, and sweeter—a secret moistening at her core.

"Anyway," Jane said. "It just wasn't for me. L.A. chewed me up and spat me out before I got there. But everything happens for a reason, I guess."

Of course everyone knows there is no secret at the core of the onion. With girls like Jane, the end is always empty and bitter and full of tears. I was into it.

"And what reason is that?" I said.

"Well, it's how I ended up here, right?"

"Right. Right. So—what is *here*, exactly?"

"Fuck if I know," Jane replied. "Pretty damn weird, yeah?"

"Yeah," I said, with relief.

"I'm only now figuring it out," Jane said, "and I've already been here three months. All the *kumbaya* bullshit can be a little much, I confess. Plus some of these girls are absolutely fucking insane. But—I don't know—the longer I stay, the more I belong, I guess. The more I'm impressed by what she's built."

"The Queen," I said.

"Yeah," she said. "The Queen."

"So maybe you can tell me who the hell she is?"

"I would if I could."

"You mean it's a secret."

"No. I mean—I wouldn't know."

"What?"

I sat in bewildered silence, watching Jane as her eyebrows spread earnestly over her eyes.

"Nobody knows," she said.

"You're being serious."

"But that's the point, right? Her entire power is in her mystery."

"Wait. So what are you saying exactly? That you left everything behind and came to this island for some woman you don't even know?"

"Isn't that what you did?"

I chuckled back in my seat.

"I guess I did. But I don't plan to stay forever."

"Maybe you'll change your mind."

Jane slipped a mysterious smile and hid her scarlet gaze behind her curtain of platinum blonde. Then she came back with a vengeance.

"Take me to dance!" she exclaimed.

"What?" I said.

"To dance," she repeated, in a cutesy-bossy tone. "Now! I haven't danced in forever."

"I don't really dance."

"Of course you do! Everybody dances!"

Jane threw back her drink, grabbed my hand, and pulled.

"Easy," I said. "Wait."

I downed my mead and followed her to my feet. I found them shaky under me. So I was wasted, apparently.

Tell me what you want, what you really really want,
I'll tell you what I want, what I really really want.

"I can't do this," I said, when it was too late.

We were now completely surrounded by jumping bodies and stuck-out tongues—the music having inspired a collective tantrum among the women.

"It's the Spice Girls! You don't like the oldies?"

"For me it's not the oldies."

"What are you talking about? You're not old!"

I knew she meant it. All night she'd been looking at me like she had no clue how old I was—like we were the same age. I started to move.

"There you go!" Jane shouted. "You're a natural! Now look. This is the waggle."

Around me, the women danced in a zigzag pattern.

"It's how the honey bee informs the hive that a source of nectar has been found. Here, do it with me."

And I did—following her as she threw her hips around and let her hair fly, like a girl jumping on her bed and singing—

I wanna, I wanna, I wanna, I wanna,
I wanna really, really, really, wanna zig-a-zig, ah.

"The bees are the coolest," Jane said. "Their language is all dance."

She took my hand and gave herself a spin and, one by one, showed me the dances of the bees. There was the "shake," there was the "tremble," and then there was one that seemed to take her away but then, with a secret turn, brought her right to my lips.

"Is that another one of the bee's moves?" I said, the lights swirling around.

"No," she said. "That's one of mine."

Her eyes came at me from a low angle. She stood there, just a breath away, her lips full and moist.

"You're so handsome," she said, taking her hands through my hair. "You have gorgeous hair. What color is it?"

"Brown."

"And your eyes?"

"Green, I think. You tell me what color they are."

"Well I can't, obviously! Or else I wouldn't ask. I'm colorblind."

"Colorblind?"

"Yeah, I know. Crazy, right? You're just light and shadow to me, baby."

When she said that, Jane changed right before my eyes—I could see the layers of her peeling away all at once—unraveling like film—and Jane falling through all the decades of the movies—falling right into the smoky screwball cutting rooms of Paramount Pictures—leaving behind only the blonde of her hair and the red of her dress, shoes, nails, and lips. I pulled her close, like I'd just caught her on her fall.

"Baby," she said, breathlessly. "This is something, huh?"

"Yeah."

"Come with me."

"Where?"

"With me!"

She took my hand and I followed her out of the party, as Britney Spears came in with "Oops, I did it again."

The music slipped behind us. The waves clapped at our feet. The moon hung like an ornament in the sky. Jane stumbled beside me, her shoes in her hands.

"Adam, Adam, Adam."

"Jane."

"You're not like the usual guys who come here."

"Oh yeah?"

"Yeah. You're different. Not the Queen's usual type."

"It did seem strange, honestly. When I got the invitation, I was sure it was a mistake. Or a prank."

"Maybe you shouldn't have accepted then."

"Well, I *was* intrigued. And, truthfully, I really needed some time away. I mean—it's been a minute since I wrote anything."

"So that's why you're here."

"To write a novel. Or try, anyway."

"Is that *all* you're here for?"

I tripped over those words—tried grasping what they meant.

"How often do you cheat on your wife?" Jane said.

"My wife?"

"Oh come on, obviously I know you're married. How often do you cheat?"

I was too drunk for this. Thankfully, Jane burst up in smiles and ran off ahead of me and twirled and called back from the darkness.

"How often? I don't care! I'm just wondering! How often?"

"I don't cheat on her," I said.

"What!" she called.

"I don't ch—"

I stumbled back into her.

"I don't cheat on her."

"Agh! Lying is worse than cheating if you ask me. There is no biological reason to lie. Even animals cheat, but they don't lie."

"I'm not lying," I said.

"So you want me to believe you've never looked beyond the holy bonds of marriage?"

Jane slipped into my arm and pulled me into a cozy walk.

"I *have* looked," I said. "But I don't know—it's just so—exhausting. To actually go through with it. All that talking and being nice to a girl and pretending to be interested in who she is."

"Well that's fucking sad, Adam."

"Yeah, I guess it is."

"Good thing I don't believe you."

Jane let her hand drop into mine, slid her fingers in. We staggered through the sands together, getting even more drunk off each other.

"It's probably better this way," she said. "If we don't believe each other, we can't hurt each other. Besides, there is a first time for everything. And the first step to cheating on your wife is talking about her, I find."

"So *you* have experience, then."

"I won't lie. I've been the other girl before. Actually that's mostly what I end up being. I'm not good at relationships."

"No?"

"It's the most heartbreaking thing in the world, isn't it? To feel love so intensely, like a fire in your soul—and then to watch it burn up and engulf you in flames and become your personal hell?"

"Or just to watch it die," I said.

"*Exactly*," she said. "Or just to watch it die. I'd rather skip that part, thank you very much. I'd rather live at the beginning of things."

Jane broke from my grip and ran off giggling again. A wave

crashed in and twisted out.

"Catch me if you can! I bet you can't catch me!"

The moon caught my eye. Something buzzed inside. A figure twirled ahead. I started for her.

"Agh!" Jane screamed. "No, no, no!"

In darkness I was fast. I closed in quickly.

"No!"

I tackled her to the ground.

"Ohhh," she sighed, as we sank into the sand. "I love being caught."

"Oh yeah?"

"I always wanted to play that girl in the slashers. Just running away and being caught and stabbed to death. But all they ever cast me in was Brecht and Arthur Miller. Such old bores!"

I laughed. The sand was soft and wet where the water met the land.

"How drunk are you?"

"Very, very drunk."

"Beyond the point of consent?"

"Fuck consent. I don't know what all the rage is about consent. *As if any first kiss worth the price of its lipstick doesn't come out of nowhere, suddenly, violently—*"

I caught her lips with my teeth. The tide touched our feet.

"So you haven't read my books, but you can quote them."

"I love your books," Jane said, quietly. Then she closed her eyes, offering up her lips to be tasted, parted, entered.

"You're sweet," she said. "I know everything about a man from the way he kisses."

Then she opened her eyes and escaped from under me and shoved me onto my back. She lowered herself to taste my lips again, slowly now, like she was extracting nectar. Under her dress, my hand played among her fishnets.

"So maybe you *do* like being inspired."

A thread broke between my fingers.

Then another.

"Fuck," she said.

I slid my hand through the opening and grabbed her flesh. I brought her in closer.

"You want to fuck me," she said.

"Yeah?" I said.

I flipped her around again. The moon blew up her eyes. They were exploding with scarlet passion.

"You want to fuck me," she said again. "You want to fuck me like that little whore."

I peered into her ravishing eyes.

"Come on, professor. I know the rumors are true."

When I heard those words, my breath left me completely. My heart crashed.

"Baby, what?" Jane said.

Then it ignited again. I could feel it like an engine, working now with propulsive force to pump fresh blood into my head—to clear it of the buzzing—to get me thinking straight. I spun off and sat next to Jane on the sand.

"It's just something I read," she said, regretfully. "Adam, look at me, please. I mean—it was *all* over the news in L.A."

"Well, it *isn't* fucking true," I said.

"Okay," she said. "I'm sorry."

"What the fuck is wrong with you?"

We just sat there. The tides nagged at our feet. A cold wind whipped at our backs. Jane started shivering and then I did.

"Sorry," Jane said. "It was just my stupid fantasy, okay? You don't have to be so *angry* with me."

I glanced over to Jane. And at the sight of her doomed and wounded eyes, I understood I'd overreacted.

"We better head in," Jane said. "We're both gonna get sick otherwise."

My clothes clung to me as I got up and headed inland.

"It's just something I've had to deal with for a long time," I explained. "Being on the defensive, not being understood—I guess it's taken a toll—made me suspicious of everything and every—"

I realized then that Jane wasn't walking beside me. When I turned around, I saw she'd stayed back. In another moment her dress fell to her ankles. She stepped out of it. Jane cut a stunning figure in the night—her body silhouetted by the sea—like a siren in the mirage of moonlight.

"Jane?"

She dived into the waves and vanished in a trail of giggles.

"Jane!" I called again.

I thought I saw her in the distance, but it could have been the waves. I wasn't about to go in. I was shivering from the wind. And my back was aching from the false exertions of my youth.

THE SIMULACRUM

I was cold and coming down to a lousy mood when I noticed the bonfire upshore. As I approached, I saw Hari there, his legs crossed under him, surrounded by a dozen women. The truth is I never trusted these guys, with their false serenity and sick unblinking wet eyes. My brother had been drawn to them and they'd always bled him dry and sent him back more broken than before. But Hari was old, almost baby-like in the winter of his life. And in his voice, now that I heard it for the first time, was preserved the sweetness of a child: "As we have a physical body, so we have an energy body. *Prana* is the life force, which comes to us from the universe, brings us love, joy, pleasure. But on this journey of our existence, these channels are gradually blocked. Today we begin to unblock these channels."

From a dark distance, I followed the scene with interest. Right before my eyes, the guru was coming to life: his dyed hair glistening, his posture straightening, his Indian voice growing rich and enchanted. As for the women, I could tell they weren't like the others. While the party was picking up, they had followed Hari on this exodus for a reason. They flickered around the fire with sick eyes riddled with questions and haunted eyes begging to be calmed and questing eyes that were ready for the truth: "Most people who walk this earth do not reach this awareness. They do not even know about this journey. And yet you are already living, whereas they are the living dead."

This was as much enlightenment as I could take. As I walked away, Hari's voice faded behind me. The music pulsed ahead. At the stage, still covered by that golden curtain, the party was peaking. The bougie crowd had quit and only the party girls remained—fans clapping, sunglasses coming on, hair twirling around. And among them was River, with that curly blond hair resting as a halo on his head. I watched him as he wandered through the crowd—moving casually from a little chat here to a little dance there—never threatening or wanting anything, but sweetly accepting the offer of a hug or a kiss on the cheek—making everyone feel good, but never quite finding his place—flashing his dimples and then moving on like the music itself—searching for something more. He was so familiar to me in that ghostly dance of his—so much like my brother.

"Adam! My friend, over here!"

I turned for the voice and saw Maxim waving me down from the bar. From that slurring, Slavic bombast, I could tell the man was drunk. This was in contrast to the woman sitting next to him. She was poised and elegant, as she sipped at a tall glass of champagne.

"Come, come!" Maxim said, as I neared. "You must chat with us. You have met Imogen, yes?"

"Imogen?" I said, recognizing her now by the cold enigma of her eyes. "Yes, I have. How's your night going?"

"Better now that you're here," Imogen replied. "Your friend has been absolutely torturing me with his theories."

"Only they aren't theories!" Maxim shouted, before correcting tone—sweetening his voice with a sentimentality I've encountered only in Russian novels. "You know, my dear, sometimes I believe you actually enjoy abusing me."

"But that's what you want," Imogen replied. "I know your type, Maxie."

Maxim slumped in his seat and threw up his hands.

"You are probably right. Yes, sadly you are."

I could now see Maxim was a total wreck. His gray beard was messy. Sweat was dripping down his face. He seemed utterly enslaved to the woman.

"Please, Adam," Imogen said. "Do take my seat."

"Oh, don't get up for me. I was actually going to call it a night."

"And I was going to freshen up. He could use a break from me, besides. See you soon, Maxie boy. Don't miss me too much."

That softly-slapping graze of her hand on his cheek stirred Maxim—he rose to its touch. Then, resting his chin on his palm, and with a gaze of boyish adoration that showed even in his glass eye, he saw her off into the crowd. Only when Imogen had vanished did Maxim turn to me suddenly and exclaim—with a look of total terror—

"*Blyat!* Save me from this vampiric creature!"

I chuckled, supposing he was joking.

"You seem to be getting along well," I said, taking Imogen's place.

"Yes!" Maxim groaned. "This is in fact the problem. No woman gets along with me like this! Now, Adam. You must drink with me. We have much to discuss. Perhaps this lovely bartendress will deliver something for us!"

"I think you've had enough, Maxim!" Oriana shouted from the far end of the bar.

"You are a Nietzschean, but I still love you!" Maxim called after her. "Please, darling, one more!"

"But the last one, yes?"

"Yes. Yes!"

"And one more mead for our writer?"

Obviously I couldn't leave Maxim like this. And I should probably get my buzz back before returning to my room to write.

"Yeah," I said. "Sure. I'll have a drink."

At this news a great sense of relief came over Maxim. His shoulders relaxed. Then he hunched over the bar and started rubbing his dead glass eye, like it was a credential.

"Belgrade," he began. "April 4, 1999. Tomahawk missile, like straight from a Hollywood blockbuster. And into my face. We were the first target. Ministry of Defense. Group 69. You have heard of us?"

"Group 69?" I said. "No. I don't think—"

"Very good, then," Maxim interrupted. "So we succeeded after all."

"Right," I grinned, pleased to accept my role in this conversation—that of the captive listener who blindly walks into every new trap being set for him, is flabbergasted at every turn, and continually rewards the grand storyteller with the gasps and laughs he so hungers for.

"But you *have* heard of Tesla's Weapon."

"Tesla's Weapon. Rings a bell, I think."

"Teleforce could accelerate pellets to high velocity via electrostatic repulsion. The most powerful weapon ever invented, yes?"

"Yeah," I replied, actually recalling something from the radio of my childhood. "But the bomb didn't actually exist, right?"

"The bomb? No, of course not. That wasn't the weapon, however. The real weapon was the *idea* of the weapon, simply. Fear, you understand! Transmitted by brainwaves, with frequency of below 32 Hz, traveling faster than light. Tesla called this 'scalar waves.' This is how we win the *parapsychological* war. But of course there was one weapon even more powerful than fear."

"And what's that?"

"Love, obviously. Love! Well, forgive me, I am Orthodox after all, but in fact love shall rule the world. And a greater inventor than Tesla was responsible for this."

"You mean God."

"What? No. I just said—Group 69. Except to weaponize love was not so easy, when we tried. Nor was the radio or television the ideal transmission device. You will now ask me what *is* the ideal transmission device."

"Yes."

"And so I obediently answer: But of course—a woman! And perhaps, might I suggest, a woman very much like the lady-friend to whom we have been speaking. Am I correct to assume you noticed her eyes?"

"Imogen's? They're pretty striking, yeah."

"Precisely! Just as you say: Striking! So aggressive, cold, intentional—and something *unnatural* about them, yes? Oh, do not look at me like I am mad. Before I became the resident clown and 4chan vulgarian pervert, I was a scientist. A *most* important one. And I tell you this gaze is not natural. It is not normal. It is, in fact, *programming*."

Oriana came by with our drinks, glared over us like a couple of boys up to no good, shook her head, then left us again.

"Thank you, my dear!" Maxim shouted after her, before raising a tinted vodka cocktail and gulping it down in one go. I could practically see the alcohol pouring in—irrigating the various systems of his body and mind.

"Fantasmatic!" Maxim exclaimed, slamming the glass down. "I do believe that oracle-witch puts something in these drinks! Where were we?"

I took a sip of my mead, waiting for Maxim to find his

own plot.

"Sleeper agents—yes!" he continued, surging with intoxicated energy. "Specifically programmed for psychological operations. In old school KGB days, theory was the seductress was agreeable and flirtatious. CIA model, by contrast, was inert, kind of—with inverted, almost medicated gaze—one layer removed from reality. Male target in this case prefers woman who is aloof, without will, almost unconscious. So you see the appeal of Kim Kardashian, for example."

"Kim Kardashian is a sleeper agent?"

"In more ways than one, my friend! But this Imogen—she is something else! Cruel, judgmental, uninterested. Her contempt is her greatest weapon, yes? Oh, but I would recognize her anywhere, for she is my own creation! Well, perhaps not her exactly. But this model! I tell you, Adam, the numbers of NATO libtards this model was able to seduce is staggering, simply. They walked right into the honey trap!"

"Honey trap," I repeated, perking up.

The coincidence somehow made the idea more plausible—or at least interesting, literarily. The mead was helping, too. I took another sip and followed Maxim's theories with the new goal of actually believing them.

"And we are surely walking into one now, are we not?" Maxim said. "Just as those twenty-seven men did before us. Now do not ask me what happened to them—for this, I do not know yet! It could be they were recruited, trained, and sent back into the field. Or that they are still here, being tortured for information. Or it could be they are already dead! Well this is what happens in your book, yes?"

"My book?" I said, perplexed.

"This mystery novel," Maxim clarified. "Of Dame Agatha Christie. You spoke about this on the boat. The guests are murdered in the end, correct?"

"Yeah," I said. "They sure are. But—not by sleeper agents, right? Look, Maxim. I'm trying to follow here, but you're mixing theories. Which do you actually believe?"

"But I believe all of them!" Maxim pronounced, with a big wave of his hands. "I believe all theories! In fact all theories can be true... in the Simulacrum."

"What the fuck is the Simulacrum?"

"The most sophisticated psychological operation ever designed!" Maxim announced. And from the spray of saliva on my face and the increasing frenzy of his left eye, I understood we were closing in on the finale. "A multi-dimensional game, as it were—in this case, six games—or, if you prefer, six plays—happening all at once! Each play is designed by the Queen, yes? Tailored to each of her guests' distinct psychological condition. We had the clues to this from the various invitations we received, but this was only the beginning. By now, I assure you, we are very much living in different realities—we can hardly communicate! So you listen to me about sleeper agents and honey traps and such—you believe I am mad. But you do not see the play *I* have been drawn into! Just as I cannot see the play you're in!"

It was like watching sparks fly out from a self-destructing nuclear power plant—I couldn't keep my eyes off it. And it was amid this smoke and chaos, and really for the first time, that I began to appreciate the beauty of Maxim's outlandish ideas—and possibly, even, their truth. From the moment I'd received the black envelope, I wondered, had the Queen not been fucking with me too—luring me into a play which seemed too real to believe?

"Now you understand," Maxim said, with a cryptic smile. "I can see it in your eyes too. You understand at last."

And upon those words, a bell tolled across the island.

Darkness fell upon the cove.

Then the women started whistling and screaming.

Just as they had at the beginning of the night, they faced

the golden curtain. Except now the curtain was parting, ever so slowly, to reveal the figure on the other side—her breasts bound by leather, her hair pouring down like honey, her eyes hidden behind a mask of gold—a lascivious insect—a monarch—a god. And she was being received by the women with outstretched hands—her name screamed, cried, and worshipped—

Queen!
Queen!
Queen!

Rising from her throne, the Queen pressed her palms together and bowed before the women. Then she raised a hand and held it there—like a guillotine in the air. Only when total silence had been achieved did she let it drop.

A series of frantic fluttering notes was released.

Laughter followed.

In another moment, I got the joke. The new track was "Flight of the Bumblebee." I started laughing, too. But Maxim was serious as ever.

"So she exists," he mumbled. "Q exists."

I could now see that the search was over in Maxim's left eye. Its restless gaze had settled, at long last, and—unified with the right—was fixed with singular interest upon the woman on stage. And yet its intention was not the same. The right eye was cold, sterile, and scientific in its curiosity. It was dead. The left, now that it had stopped moving, betrayed a virility and a passion that touched upon the perverse.

"Maxim!" a woman's voice called. "Maxim!"

I looked into the crowd, supposing it was Imogen. Actually it was Penelope buzzing in. She rested one hand on Maxim's shoulder and pointed the other to the stage.

"Just look at her!" Penelope said. "She's beautiful, isn't she?"

"Yes," Maxim said, still glaring at the Queen.

"So you'll be pleased to know—she wants to see you next."

"Me?"

"Confidentially, there have been some issues," Penelope said, lowering her voice. "And you're the only one who can help, Maxim. You *can* help her, right?"

"Right. Of course. Yes."

"Good. Very good! I'll be happy to take you, then. Just after the Queen's Dance. Now come on, Maxim. Let's dance it together!"

Penelope grabbed Maxim by the hands and tugged him out of his reverie.

"In fact," he said, suddenly. "Let's dance, Penelope! Goodbye, Adam. It was a very nice chat, indeed."

"So you will be going, then?" I asked. With Penelope standing by, it was the best I could do.

"Naturally," Maxim replied, a beautiful smile surfacing from the depths of his beard. "After all, she is my child too."

Then Maxim pushed himself off, patted me on my back, and gave me a double-wink—a kind of signal of affection, I supposed, which a Serbian grandfather might make for his grandson.

"I doubt you will see me again," he said, softly. "This is how it ends for me. But you must come to your own conclusions, yes? Goodbye, Adam. Goodbye."

After that Maxim stepped up to Penelope and raised his elbow for her to slip into. Together they moved into the party. In another moment, Maxim was swinging his arms and snapping and doing the disco finger like *Saturday Night Fever*. Meanwhile the women around them were jumping and twisting and screaming in joy. Some made cute buzzing sounds. Others flapped their imaginary wings and ran around in delirious dance—crying in rapturous adoration—hailing the one on stage—hidden behind that terrifying mask—

Queen!
Queen!
Queen!

It was an exhilarating spectacle, but I couldn't enjoy it anymore. The mead must not have been sitting well, I thought, or else it was those theories sickening my stomach. I needed to walk this off. Without another thought, I got up, hastened across the cove, and took the opening in the cliffs. I climbed the stairway, crossed the garden, passed the knight, and entered the manor. Once upstairs, I stopped at the only open door of a long and dark corridor. I looked in: Wearing nothing but white boxer briefs and his circular glasses, Camillio was standing before a mirror, rehearsing a speech.

I felt even more sick than before. A spell of nausea was coming up. I stumbled down the corridor, pushed into my room, and shut the door behind me. I leaned back against it, closed my eyes, and took a deep breath. Was I really so drunk? Had I caught some bug, which was now working at me from the inside—spreading its disease in my stomach, kidneys, lungs? I couldn't hold it down anymore. I opened my eyes again. I staggered across the room, flung myself at the typewriter, slipped a blank page in, rolled it up, and let it out:

> On the last day of class, a black envelope arrived in my university mailbox.

When I saw what I'd written, I gasped in horror. I could barely breathe. Because those were, of course, the opening words of the novel the Queen had wanted me to write all along—the novel I had laughed off, then rejected, and was now returning to as some scorned lover begging to be taken back. Suspended above the keys, my hands trembled. Was I really going to release them, I thought, into this journey from which there was no return? But before the answer could form, my hands had taken off—they were already long gone into the next sentence: "For months now I'd been receiving death threats and love letters and pictures a professor can get arrested for possessing." Then the third: "This envelope was different." Then entire paragraphs materialized—page after page of a story so familiar to me.

But the story was also surprising. And what surprised me most, in those opening chapters, was the narrator and protagonist himself. I hardly recognized myself in that bitter, defeated man. I had not considered, until I'd written those scenes with Neve, how loveless he actually was—how petty, cowardly, and lame. I had such pity and contempt for him now—this scapegoat of a writer and man. I was so angry with him. But this anger was good. This anger had always been the poetic pulse of my novels. I had been famous for this anger. So my eyes misted up as I began to hear it again—rising from the clamor of that typewriter—the resounding voice of a writer long presumed dead.

Against such exhilarations, any misgivings I had about writing another island mystery vanished. I was sure my work would be original. That I was writing in the first-person was the key to this. It meant that I would be telling the mystery from a unique perspective—from the inside. I wouldn't need or care to follow all the characters, or to resolve all the plotlines. I had only to follow my own story—to do so in the voice I wanted—and along the way to engage the ideas that interested me. I would be writing the book I wanted after all, reflecting to my heart's content on those masks, for example, that we wear at the end of civilizations. So the mystery was itself a disguise—a mask, very much like the Queen's.

As I wrote furiously into the night, I did not pause to question what I was doing. Or the nature of the contract I had entered into. Or the fate of the role I had assumed. For the time being, I was spellbound and thrilled: to be writing again—to be feeling again—to be feeling that touch on my shoulder. I didn't look back, of course, just as Saint Matthew doesn't look back when the angel touches him. But unlike Saint Matthew, it isn't out of fear that I won't find a woman there. It's out of certainty that I will. I can feel her even now—massaging my shoulders, caressing the back of my head, guiding every movement of my hands. No, the new muse standing behind me isn't like the muses who stood there before. She is something else entirely—this masked creature who is luring me, deeper and deeper, into the Simulacrum.

HONEY TRAP

"So he was drunk," Camillio said.
"No," I said. "That wasn't it. He was just acting—strange."
"Strange how?"

I took another sip of coffee and shut my eyes. The events of the previous night were lost in throbbing pain and swirling mist.

"Like he'd finally found the truth," I said. "Like he was at the end of his journey. He knew he wasn't coming back."

Under the pine trees, on a long table overlooking the sea, breakfast had been set: bowls of yogurt; platters of berries and watermelon; sesame bread rings; feta cheese; jars of honey; plates stacked with baklava; tall glasses of orange juice; and miniature porcelain cups of coffee, which was the only thing I could keep down. It must've been an hour since I'd woken up with a major hangover and my face smashed against the keys of the typewriter, but I still couldn't pull myself together. I knew it wasn't the mead I was coming down from, either. Those hours of intoxicated creation had drained the life out of me—transferred it onto those hundred or so pages currently stacked on my desk.

"Well that's Maxim for you, isn't it?" Camillio said—fresh as ever, skin moisturized, hair finely combed back, as he tossed a blueberry into his mouth. Sitting between us, River wasn't showing interest, either. As he played among the strings of his guitar, he was following the drama unfolding on the plate in front of him, where an island of baklava was floating on a sea of honey. For several minutes a bee had been buzzing around it—swooping in and circling out again—driving itself crazy in its moment of existential crisis. The honey-soaked plate promised paradise and almost certain death. Farther out, at the pond, Hari was bathing himself. Wearing only black speedos, he was vigorously washing out his armpits.

"Oh no," River said, his chords making a minor sigh. "Why would you do that?"

I'd missed the move, apparently. The bee had gone in for the honey after all—and the landing was problematic. Its little legs were now steeped in the golden trap.

"Hang tight, amigo," River said. "We'll get you out of there."

"Oh just let it die," Camillio said. "His fucking fault for being so stupid."

There was, in fact, something very mean and petty revealing itself in Camillio. But this did not deter River, who had already put down his guitar and was organizing the rescue operation. In no time he got the bee crawling onto the tip of his thumb.

"There we are. Come on then."

It was a stunning creature River brought up to eye level—a stitchwork of gold and black, with long drooping eyes and a pair of miserable antennae on its head. The honey had glued its wings shut. The bee was straining helplessly to unstick itself. Exhausted and delirious, it was preparing to die.

"Couldn't resist the temptation, could you?" River said. "I know how that goes."

"It's hopeless," Camillio insisted. "Put it out of its misery."

"Don't listen to him, you. I don't give up on my friends."

We watched as River bathed the bee in droplets of water, made a breeze for it, hummed some native healing song. His refusal to give up on the creature was touching upon something very dumb and holy. Even Camillio gave up his pose and leaned in to witness the miracle. Under River's care, the bee was struggling against death. It was vying for life instead—bumbling around drunkenly like a newborn.

"Come on then," River said, his blue eyes opening above sunburned cheeks. "Come on, little guy. You can do it."

Finally the bee was free. Its translucent, plastic-like wings broke away and began to flap. The bee had not yet taken off from River's thumb, but its life force was restored, and it filled the air with its joyous buzzing.

"There you go!" River shouted, drawing a huge smile. "I knew you could do it! I knew—"

Then River stopped. He jolted back. His eyes sealed shut.

"Agh!" he cried.

"What happened?" I said.

"What?" Camillio followed. "Did it sting? It stang, didn't it?"

"Fuck, man," River said. "That hurt like a motherfucker."

"Hah!" Camillio said, some half-suppressed laughter leaking out of him. "I told you! Serves you right, River, for being so trusting."

River slumped back into his seat and took his thumb to his lips. He seemed hurt, emotionally. Meanwhile Camillio slumped the other way, returning to his careless recline, as though he had never believed any of it.

"Yeah, I can be a sucker that way," River said, despairingly.

"You sure can, man."

"I'm always falling into these traps."

I winced. The phrase pierced my mind, cleared the mist,

startled a sleeping memory awake.

"A trap," I muttered.

"What?" Camillio said.

"A *honey* trap," I said, recovering the memory. "*That's* what Maxim was talking about."

"Huh?"

"Apparently he was involved in something called Group 69, in Belgrade, in the nineties."

"Group 69, huh? Sounds like another one of his fantasies."

"Except I don't think it was," I said, riding a fresh burst of energy. "He was telling me about these psy-ops he used to design, where male subjects would be lured by women into honey traps. Maxim said the same thing was happening to us."

"And is that what *you* believe?" Camillio said, with a look of indictment.

"I believe what I see," I cut back. "And what I don't see is Maxim. And Will."

"So they were seduced back to some secret laboratory—is that it? I suppose you'll tell us they're being brainwashed or tortured or something."

"Maybe something else."

I tripped over my own words—took a beat to regroup. Of course this same thought had occurred a few times already: first, on the boat, in the form of a joke; second, in my chat with Maxim, as a theory; and third, during that night shift of creation, as a literary idea. But now, by the harsh morning sun, it was being reborn in a new light entirely. It was asking, finally, to be taken literally.

"Wait a second," Camillio said, stiffening in his seat. "You think they were—my God, man—are you... I thought you were only messing around! You *actually* think they were murdered, don't you? You think we've ended up in that mystery novel!"

With that, Camillio burst out in laughter. I had heard that

sneering, contemptuous laugh before, when it had been directed at Maxim. But now I could feel it on my own skin. And I could also see, behind those spectacles, the disdain in Camillio's tiny eyes. It was under such tiny eyes that Maxim had lived out his entire intellectual life. So it was out of solidarity rather than conviction that I made my reply.

"That's exactly what I think, Camillio," I said. "And actually I wouldn't be surprised if you're next. After all, you're a lot like those characters in the novel."

"And how is that exactly?" was his retort.

"Well, they were criminals, if you recall. Only they'd escaped their punishment. That's why they were invited to the island. To finally face justice."

When I said that, Camillio fell silent. At the pond, Hari stopped his bathing. River lifted a curious glance from his sting—gazed at me with a detached, incredulous amusement.

"What are you even saying?" Camillio asked, his eyes getting smaller by the moment—as though under stress of intense calculation.

"You know what I'm saying," I replied. "Will recognized you before he left. And then I remembered you too—from that documentary. You're Morel, aren't you? You're the con artist."

"Con artist?"

"Yeah. The charlatan who catfished all those girls."

And here any humanity left in Camillio's expressions collapsed. His thin lips quivered with malice.

"That is *not* true," Camillio snapped back. "Those are *vile* rumors. *Vile.*"

"I can't say I'm surprised to hear that," I said. "That's exactly what you say in the novel too."

Camillio scoffed. Then shook his head. But then, slowly, his expressions relaxed again. A cool smile returned, as he asked—

"So what about you?"

"Me?"

"Yeah, you. If your theory is right, then tell us: What crime are *you* in for?"

The question was obvious but unexpected. It hit me hard—got my heart going—my thoughts racing to the previous night: the sand, the wind, the waves at our feet. We'd been making out on the beach when Jane had lifted her lips from mine and said those horrifying words.

"Go on then, tell us," Camillio said. "Are the rumors true? About the rape."

I cringed at those words—glared into Camillio's scheming eyes. *Were the rumors about me any different from his?* I studied Hari at the pond. *He didn't look like a criminal now—but in younger days?* Really, in that moment, it was only the sight of River that calmed me. With his golden curls and slow, cherubic smile, he was still biting at his thumb—trying to catch the bee's stinger with his teeth. I took a deep breath, for I could recognize the plain truth in front of me: River was the furthest thing from a criminal. He hadn't even hurt the fly. And, as discussed, I hadn't either. Those accusations against me had been lies—mendacious lies.

"That's what I thought," Camillio said, with a triumphant toss of one last blueberry into his mouth. "Now can we please enjoy this epic day?"

"Hey guys!" Penelope called, as she crossed the garden. "Am I walking into something?"

"No," Camillio replied. "River just had an accident."

"Only a bee sting," River said, with a wave of his hand.

Penelope kissed Hari's head at the pond, before making her way to us. She had on gladiator sandals, high-waisted denim shorts, and a white crop top.

"Oh those darn bees!" Penelope said. "They know they're supposed to stay on the other side of the island, but once in a while there's a defector. Don't take it personally, River."

"All good," River said. "Got the stinger out already."

"Good. Good! Now if you're finished with breakfast, I can take you to town. Everyone's waiting for you at the pool."

"The guys too, right?" Camillio inquired.

"The guys?" Penelope answered. "Oh, no. The guys had quite the wild night. I'm guessing they'll want to sleep in."

"Sleep in?" I asked, perking up to the news.

"The Queen *does* have plenty of spare rooms up there, you know," Penelope replied. "And it's a tradition for her guests to spend the night."

"Right," Camillio said, with a glance-over to me. "Makes sense. And I'm very much looking forward to it myself."

"Then you won't have to look far!" Penelope said, setting her hands on his shoulders. "She wants to see you next, Camillio."

"Really?" Camillio said, twisting for a look at her.

"Really," Penelope said, giving him a little massage. "I do hope you have your pitch ready."

"Oh I wouldn't call it a pitch," Camillio said. "I rather want to hear what the Queen has to say. I take up clients selectively—and first we should make sure our visions align."

For a moment, I believe, I saw Penelope's eyes begin to roll. But they rolled back just as quick.

"The Queen expects nothing less," she said, "given your reputation. I'll take you up just as soon as we drop off these gents by the pool. Well, come on then!"

Camillio rose to his feet and escorted Penelope into the garden. River flung his guitar over his shoulder and followed. Along the way, he picked up Hari from the pond. Alone at the table, I poured myself another coffee. The birds were chirping all around, the pine trees swaying in the breeze, the waves of the sea rushing to shore and making a great campaign to bring in good feelings. And yet only new anxieties were washing up. Hovering over that plate, as a god watching over an ancient amphitheater, I was witnessing the tragedy conclude: Having committed its crime, the bee had lost its stinger and, consequently, fallen dead. The beautiful creature was now being embalmed in its own honey.

I jolted to my feet and fled the crime scene at once. The truth is I had always been vulnerable to such scenes. As a novelist, I was known and sometimes dismissed for my obsession with synchronicities and signs—for the rigid symbolic order in which I placed my works. My magician novel, for example, is designed as a sequence of illusions—the plot of each chapter reflecting the mechanics of the magic trick it features, while the novel as a whole investigates the overarching illusion, which is of course love, and what happens when you figure out how it works. Same with my billionaire novel, which is organized around the lessons of the guru. And my chimpanzee novel, which explores man's primal self. Real life isn't so symbolic, obviously. A dead bee in a puddle of honey is just that. But in fiction, that dead bee is called to be much more. It can be a pronouncement, a premonition, even a prophecy of the nightmare ahead.

As much as I tried leaving them behind, my suspicions swarmed after me. On the curving cobblestone road along the cliffs, I followed the black-and-gold pattern of its shops and galleries. Through their hexagonal windows, I glimpsed into secret meetings and whispered conversations. And everywhere I looked, I found the clues of a great conspiracy and the insinuations of its elusive mastermind. The Queen was not only the authority here, but also the author. And she enforced exactly the kind of tightly-designed symbolic order that can be found in my books.

"Almost there!" Penelope called, as the strip unraveled into a lawn upon the cliffs. "And you seem to be up first, Hari. I believe those are your students waiting for you!"

A dozen women, who had been lying in wait on yoga mats, now jumped to their feet. Their bodies blacked against the glistening sea.

"Guru!" they called, as they circled around their teacher. "We've missed you."

Beyond them, more women bubbled up from a jacuzzi. Hiding under the deep brims of their sun hats, the pack of cougars cooed—

"River! Over here, babe!"

Beyond the jacuzzi, more women surfaced from a swimming pool, sat up on sunbeds, and swiveled toward us from bar stools. *No*—I thought—*something isn't right here*—*this isn't how reality works*. And suddenly I felt very weak, out of breath. Fresh waves of anxiety were coming on: *What had I done last night? What game had I entered into when I began to write the words of a novel which I was living, but did not create? And who, after all, was the one who did?* Ahead of me the road snaked through town and up into the cave houses, before concluding upon that crown of glass. The Queen's house sparked in the sun, winking to me with a horrible mystery.

"Hey, Adam—you okay?"

I came back quickly, caught my breath, and turned to Penelope. She was looking at me with genuine concern.

"You don't look so well."

"Sorry," I said, putting on a smile. "I'm just—exhausted, I think. I had a very long night."

"Oh *did* you?" Penelope said.

"Yeah," I said. "I've been writing."

"Well isn't that wonderful!" Penelope exclaimed. "Her system works, I guess."

"Yeah," I grinned. "Her system works."

"Sure you're all right, Adam?"

"Of course. I'll have a look around. You guys go ahead."

"All right then," Penelope said, taking Camillio's arm. "Shall we?"

"We shall," Camillio replied. "See you, Adam."

"See you," I said, although I knew I'd never see him again.

ABOUT JANE

"Adam, hey! Over here!"

It was Jane waving me down from the sunbeds, lined up on one side of an infinity pool which poured down the cliff on the other. Her supple body was strung up in a black bikini. Her platinum blonde hair flashed in the sun.

"Hey," I said, making my way over. I needed to play this cool. "Got room for me?"

"I tried to save a bed for you, but I must've fallen asleep and these women are ruthless! What happened to you last night?"

"Yeah, about that. I just wanted to say—"

"Oh God, don't do that."

"What?"

"Apologize. Isn't that what you were about to do?"

Jane stretched out her arms and took me into a long, yawning hug. Then she pulled her legs back to make a nook for me to sit in.

"Your apology is no good for me, okay?" she said, in a tone of sweet chiding. "A lot of us are addicted to apologies, apparently.

Instead of cutting off a bad relationship, we prefer to stay in it—just to see a man get down on his knees."

"Is that so?"

"Yeah, that's so. And it's one of the patterns we've come here to break. Anyway, last night I was just being rude. Bringing up some stupid scandal I know nothing about! Truth is I haven't been good with guys ever since the first one left when I was two. Fuck, I can't do this sober!"

Jane stretched for a martini, took a big gulp, and made a huge sour face. Ravished by the sun, her lips were dry and her face was spread with freckles. I relaxed a bit, as I gazed into her drunken, hopeless doom.

"I'm probably not supposed to talk about it," Jane said. "But—what the hell! The least I owe you is an explanation."

"No worries," I said. "You don't owe me anything."

"I do," Jane insisted. "Let's go for a walk. I know the perfect place for a chat."

It had been only a minute, and yet Jane was already dispelling that entire swarm of suspicions which had been following me all morning. She threw a white tunic over her bikini, gulped the last of her martini, jumped to her feet, and pulled me up.

As we walked the road along the cliffs, the wind blew out Jane's hair and the sun bathed her body in warm hues of orange and red.

"My dad left when I was two and it was all over before it started," she said, her voice rasping and dreamy. "That's why I became an actor, I guess. Such an attention whore I was and looking for daddy everywhere and all that. Looking for him in dark rooms full of spectators. In the glare of bright lights. And in that lens, most of all. I didn't care about money or fame. But looking into that lens—man, I became addicted to that feeling. Kind of like all the burden of living was lifted from me. Like I was finally relieved—of being myself.

"The guys used that, obviously. Mostly one guy. So suave with slicked-back hair and a baby face and all kinds of hand gestures. Typical agent-type, was my guess, moving a mile a minute—that kind—always making you feel that if you didn't catch up he was just gonna disappear around the corner. Deep down I knew from the beginning he wasn't going to help me, but there was always another audition at the end of the hall—another door opening just when the one before it closed. And in between, you know, I just—let him have it. He was so casual about it, too, like this was all part of the custom, and I even liked it sometimes. Or maybe I liked how good I was playing into it, so long as he got me into that next audition."

Jane's voice cracked. The road took an incline, curved up ahead, and hit a set of black iron gates. That's where the public strip of town ended—and the private hillside community of cave houses began.

"But they weren't auditions," Jane continued. "Not really. Homeboy wasn't even an agent, apparently. He had some crapola indies to his name as an executive producer, but mostly his talent was 'putting movies together' that never happened. And then I began to wonder if he even wanted them to happen. And then I started looking at the other girls going in and out of those rooms, with their bright hopeful smiles. And I knew what was happening."

Jane glanced over, like she wanted me to ask.

"What was happening?"

"The horror, Adam. The horror. Although my pride wouldn't let me admit it for a long time. So I kept following him down those hallways. I still sat in front of those cameras. But what I saw in that lens didn't bring me comfort anymore. I saw my image flipping and warping, until I couldn't recognize myself anymore—until I didn't know who I was anymore. So now you know. That's my story—Act 1, anyway. That's how I became Jane."

She stopped suddenly—just short of the black gates, plated with that familiar golden letter: Q.

"What do you mean?" I asked. "You changed your name?"

When I looked into Jane's eyes, a mist of shame had passed over them.

"No," she replied. "They did. To Jane Doe."

"Jane D—" I stuttered. "Oh my God. You mean..."

"I should *not* be telling you this, Adam," Jane interrupted, lest she be forced to endure some sympathy. "You can't tell anyone about this, okay?"

"I won't," I said. "You can trust me."

Jane smiled, tenderly. Then she slipped her hand into my arm and led me away from the gates.

We sat on a bench at the edge of the cliffs. Below us, on the cove, teams of women were criss-crossing the sand, preparing for the new night's party.

"I never wanted to go to court, is the truth," Jane said, resting her head on my shoulder. "I never believed in the courts since they took me away from my mom and sent me on the foster home circuit. But a case was being made, apparently, and my testimony was going to make a difference. So I agreed. Made a new career for myself, too, crying in court and on TV—God, those fucking #MeToo panels!—just crying my eyes out as those moderators told me how 'brave' I was. That was more humiliating than anything. Looking into those 'understanding' eyes and watching them press their lips. Anyway, that's not the point. The point is—my performance was adequate."

"So he was convicted?" I asked.

"Yeah," Jane replied. "He lost everything. His wife and kids, too, which I never knew he had, by the way. He's still in prison for another year."

"Good," I said. "Good! Well, he got justice, didn't he?"

"Justice?" Jane said, tearing away from me. "That's exactly what everyone said! But what justice was that for me—when nobody would work with a snitch like me again. And any guy who dated me had that same 'understanding' look about him. Always tip-toeing around and making extra sure that a kiss would be well-received rather than send me into a psychotic episode. So they'd made me into a victim. That's the role they wanted me to play. I was all fucked up sexually, too. After I'd given up all my fantasies in life, the one that remained was of *him*. Fuck, I can't believe I'm telling you all this. It's disgusting!"

"It's not disgusting," I said. "Hey. Hey. It wasn't your fault."

"No, I know," Jane said. "It *wasn't* my fault. But it took meeting Penelope to find that out. She's the one who told me about the Hive—how it had changed her life. You can't tell looking at her, but her story is even more fucked up than mine. Her dad—man, hearing about her dad makes me feel lucky I never knew mine. But anyway, that was all behind her. And my past could be behind me too. Here was a community of women who *actually* supported each other, beyond all the politics and moralizing..."

As Jane spoke, I started breathing for the first time all day. I had been wrong about her—I had been wrong about all the women here. On the cove below me, the choreography of their movements no longer suggested a conspiracy, but a communion. Just now a new team of them was entering the cove, carrying two long wooden crates toward the boat. Wearing a wife-beater, with a cigar stuffed into his mouth, Stavros was waiting for them there—waving his hands like a mad conductor.

"And not just a community," Jane continued, her voice softening now. "But a leader who could actually help us—save us from our past. The Queen taught me that I couldn't be a victim all my life. I couldn't overcome my trauma by running away from it. Or blaming others. I had to face it. As hard as it is, I still do."

"And how is that exactly?"

"For starters, by not pushing men away. By continuing to live and love—to dance and play and flirt. That's what I was trying to do with you—before I ruined it again!"

Tears streamed down Jane's cheeks. I moved closer, rested my hand on hers.

"But you didn't ruin it," I said.

"What?"

"I think you're great."

I touched Jane's cheeks, wiped her tears off.

"Really?"

"Really."

I closed my eyes and moved for her lips.

"You're a good guy," Jane said, taking me into a kiss.

But this wasn't the drunk, passionate kissing from the previous night. It was slow, soft, bittersweet.

"I mean," Jane whispered, between kisses, "except for this."

"This?" I said.

"Yeah," she said. "It's a little naughty, don't you think?"

I opened my eyes.

"I mean—what would your wife think?"

The question startled me. But I was happy to be patient with Jane.

"Honestly, I'm not sure she'd care," I explained. "Things haven't been so great between us."

"Really?"

"Yeah. She actually gave me a hall pass, if you can believe it."

"She gave you a hall pass?"

Jane's hand slipped off mine. A shadow crossed her scarlet eyes. And by that suspicious arch of her eyebrows, I understood something was wrong.

"Yeah," I said. "Before I left. She said if I met a girl I liked, I should go for it."

I moved for Jane again. This time her body snapped back.

"No," she said, coldly. "She didn't *actually* give you a hall pass."

"She did," I said. "Jane, I wouldn't—"

"You're lying," Jane interrupted, her breath quickening. "Fuck, man. Why are you manipulating me? She said you'd try to do that and now you are!"

"*Who* said that? Jane, I'm not manipulating you, okay? I wouldn't just—"

But my words were cut by a slap to my face.

"Fuck you," Jane said. "Fuck you!"

Her body was shaking now—her cheeks scared red—madness rupturing in her eyes.

"I can't do this," she said. And then louder—"I can't do this!"

Before I could say anything more, Jane had jumped to her feet. She burst into tears again, ran for the black iron gates, buzzed herself in, and raced up the hill.

"I can't fucking do this!" she kept shouting. "Sorry! I just can't do this!"

I realized only then that she wasn't talking to me. High above the Hive, on the balcony of the glass house, that chilling figure had emerged. From behind her mask, the Queen was keeping watch over all her children—she was watching me, too. Suspicion had stung me earlier that day, but now I felt the mad rush of paranoia in every vessel of my body—pumping in my heart—tingling at my fingers—filling my mind with dread. When my glance fell back to the cove, it no longer seemed to be a coincidence that, currently being loaded onto Stavros's boat, those two wooden crates were exactly the size of coffins.

A TALE OF TWO HIVES

The world swerved around me. The wind lashed at my back. As I descended breathlessly through town, I could see the angles folding down—the cobblestones slipping under—the colors blowing out in bright dizzying patterns. It was an electric spectacle—a kind of cosmic collision I hadn't experienced even under the influence of a hallucinogen or love. In the moment it felt most like *déjà vu*—a staggering sensation that I'd walked these steps before—except that *déjà vu* comes in a dim haze—the dead reality passing as a dark ghost over the living one—whereas the overlap here was luminous and living. I was not being pulled back, but propelled forward, and with a calm I could not yet account for, and with my entire essence clarified down to a single curiosity: I needed to see what was inside those crates.

It was a stroke of good luck that Stavros and the women had cleared the scene. I made my dash confidently, crossed the cove, headed down the dock, and jumped onto the boat. The sea was uneasy, and I stumbled once as I made a half-circle around. I paused upon a set of open double doors at my feet. Then I hopped in. With only a square of sunlight coming through, the compartment was dim. But a deathly reek of sea salt, mold, and honey took me in. My body cringed in recognition. This was the scent from the black envelope—the scent which had started this story.

The boat made a violent shake—some waves must've crashed in—and I stumbled into the thick dark air. It took a moment for my eyes to decipher the darkness. But soon, at the far end of the compartment, the two rectangular crates came into shape. I headed for them quickly. Something caught, though. I tripped to the ground. Above me footsteps spread across the deck. Chills ran up my spine. I locked my gaze onto one of the crates. This was my best chance. I pushed myself to my feet and lunged into the darkness. I reached out. Finally I held the lid in my hands. I lifted it off.

"*O po po!*"

The voice echoed through the dark.

"Well hello, my friend!"

When I turned to it, light flooded my eyes.

"It is I—Stavros! Remember? Or have you forgot your old friend in much abundant pussy? Haha!"

Behind the beam of his flashlight, the captain appeared as a cycloptic mass of darkness. My grip loosened from the lid.

"Hey, Stavros," I said, out of breath. "Fuck, man."

"Yes, fuck man. Yes."

"What?"

"What you do here, Adam?"

I gasped for air, inhaled the odor instead. My head was spinning out of control.

"Want to know what is inside, eh?"

"Oh, the box? I mean—I don't know. Is it a secret?"

Stavros's expressions remained hidden behind the light, but I could hear that disgruntled wet click of his tongue.

"You are problem one, Adam. I knew this from start. I told her too! I told her! But she did not believe me. Anyway, I do not think Queen would like me to show you."

"Right," I said. "That's fine. We can just—"

"Still, I show you, of course! Stavros is no over-push!"

Stavros stampeded toward me. He stepped up to the crate, swung his foot back, and kicked off its lid with gusto.

"One day," he said, casting his flashlight in, "we all go to prison for this!"

I glared into the crate, trying to make sense of what I saw. And I could already feel that other process under way—those sensational chemicals retreating—making room in my mind for the disappointing truth: The crate carried no corpse. Neatly packed in were a variety of glass jars, candles, and bottles.

"So much branding, so little quality," Stavros continued, shoving a jar into my stomach. "Read stupid label, just—you will see!"

"Exfoliant," I read, following the light to the label. "*A drop of honey makes the world a sweeter place.*"

"Arts, crafts, feminine products," Stavros explained. "For women by women social entrepreneurship bullshit. Exports of Hive. We have factory on other side of hill. Nectar of gods this. Busy bee's wax that. Like true communists, they are most capitalist of all. But please let's go out before I vomit. Even smell is disgusting, yes? Like fucking dead body! Wait—is *this* what you believe you find? It is, yes? It is!"

I couldn't get myself to answer. The idea I'd been fanatically pursuing had evaporated from my mind, left me feeling empty and stupid.

"Anyway," Stavros said, "this crime is *much* worse than murder."

I followed Stavros back to the double doors overhead. He climbed out first, then helped me up after. Once on deck, the cool air swirled around my face. I took deep fresh breaths of it. Stavros, meanwhile, slipped his thumbs behind the rows of his wife-beater and sent a soft, watery gaze up to the Hive.

"This is, eh, big business happening here," he said. "Production and distribution network. Not only for products, you see. But ideas. Girl power, etcetera. But I tell you, Adam, let them have it—it is their choice! They were goddesses once. Then they wanted jobs!"

"Right," I chuckled. "Actually Oriana said that exact same thing."

"Bah! She stole this phrase from me, that cunt—God forgive me," Stavros said, crossing himself vigorously. "Sometimes I think to kill her, but big boss would not like this very much."

"You mean the Queen."

Stavros exhaled so much air, he immediately appeared to lose ten pounds.

"You know, Adam. Most boys come here to enjoy. And here you ask all boring questions of universe!"

"I guess I just want to—you know—understand."

"Oh fuck me!" Stavros said. "Understand? What is to understand? This is hive, just! You were told this is hive and this is what it is. Hive! Bah, you are impossible! But if you insist, you come with me to valley. Yes, okay, you twist my arm, so I take you to other side of hill now and answer all your boring questions of universe! I have not spoke to man in ages and we are still both men, thanks God!"

I followed Stavros across the cove, up the cliffs, around the manor, and onto a trail of thought including: a detailed recounting of the Panathinaikos overtime; a tirade about Turkey's latest machinations at the NATO summit; and an ode to the juicy Greek pussy (a protruding clitoris, he maintained, is the sign of a woman with high orgasm potential—which is desired). He crossed himself upon each vulgarity, swiftly absolved himself, then took the next bend in the trail. Eventually we ended up at the foot of a hill. We paused there for a few minutes so that Stavros, sweating and panting profusely, could mop his bald head with his handkerchief and catch his breath.

"You are intellectual," he said. "You know about world. Geopolitics."

"Just what I read in the news."

"Tell me this. Do you think if Armenia invade Turkey from behind..."

"If Armenia invades Turkey? Well, I don't think Armenia has the military to—"

"But *if* it did. From *behind*. If Armenia invade Turkey from *behind*—you think Greece would help?"

Stavros glared at me inquisitively.

"From behind, professor. From *behind*. Do you think *grease* would help?"

And here Stavros's eyes cracked. He slapped his knee, rattling some keys in his pocket. Then he exploded in laughter.

"From *behind*... *Grease!* Hah! This is good joke. This is very good joke."

And just like that, Stavros was up and running again, and I was following him up the hot dry passage through the twisting hills. I had to pay close attention to his every word, because a joke could be in the making, and at any moment he might glance over his shoulder and expect to find me laughing. It was an exhausting task—although he didn't seem to mind when he once caught me zoning out at the punchline. He looked back at me affectionately, as though to a kid in a car seat.

"Almost there," he said, with a wink almost wise. "Almost there."

The valley washed down in spectacular waves of gold. These were sunflowers, thousands of them, sticking their necks out over each other. Their bright blooms were eyelids and their black disks were eyes staring at us. It was a stunning sight, and even Stavros had the good sense to shut up and let me take in the view. My glance dropped down the hill, flew across the golden fields, and landed upon a vast collection of boxes, stacked like baklava on the flatland. Behind the stacks stood a massive factory, with smoke rising from various pipes and chimneys. And beyond the factory was the sea with huge rock formations surfacing from it.

"The other side of Hive," Stavros said. "My side. Come, come."

The population of sunflowers was dense and tall, reaching eye level, so I sometimes lost sight of him as we descended into the buzzing.

"Remember," Stavros said. "Honeybee does not sting unless she is, eh, threatened. Believe me, she much prefer taste of nectar."

And then I began to see them—feasting upon the flowers, mostly, but sometimes breaking free in sudden movements and circling around me.

"*Opa!* You *must* be calm, Adam. Please!"

In fact, when I waved them off, the honeybees agitated in greater numbers, swerving and smacking against my cheeks.

"Do not be violent with them! The bees won't hurt, I promise. They say hello, just. To friendly spirit."

Stavros caught my wrist among the sunflowers. He pulled me into a pause, set his hands on my shoulders, and gave me a tender squeeze.

"Writer is like bee, yes?" he said. "Goes place to place, flower to flower, collecting wisdom here, information there. Collecting everything the world has. Like bee, writer's job is to condense all this—to make honey—yes?"

It was an unexpected turn—poetic and sentimental—and I hardly recognized Stavros's motive anymore.

"Oh just shut up with those eyes!" he exclaimed, letting his hands drop. "Now hold my shoulder and close those pretty stupid eyes—they remind me of myself! *Páme!*"

I did as I was told and trailed Stavros down the slopes. The bees landing on my skin and taking flight no longer caused panic. Among the intense buzzing, I had only to follow Stavros's droning-on about Greece's national debt and the rhododendron flowers coming up and "mad honey" and the wildfires.

"*Évrika!*"

When I opened my eyes, I saw that we had already cleared the sunflowers. The hill was behind us. We were on the flatland, heading into the stacked imperial city.

"*Real* hive!" Stavros announced. "Not bullshit metaphor-or-symbol-or-whatever, you understand. And it is Papa Stavros who run this church. My father called it this. He was very important priest here. Wrote entire book on, eh, *divinity* of bees. You see, his father was beekeeper. And *his* father was priest again. And so on until Adam! God and honey run in blood of Papa Stavros, see?"

"So that makes your son a priest again?" I asked.

"I have no son," Stavros replied, his bushy eyebrows gathering into anguish. "My wife did not give me son!"

Then, just as quickly, a smile lit up his face.

"But a daughter! Thanks God for her. Thanks God!"

As Stavros looked out over his hive, his big eyes softened. His shoulders relaxed. Finally exhausted, he deflated into human form.

"Now listen you here, Adam."

I watched Stavros carefully as he leaned against a stack of boxes and lay one hand flatly on top. The protruding nail of its pinkie was yellowed by a career of picking wax. With the other hand he pulled out a frame of honeycombs. It opened like a drawer and revealed a family of bees living there.

"These are ladies, yes?"

"Ladies," I said. "Right. They're all female."

"All worker bees are girls. Some clean. Others make climate with wings. Others collect nectar, yes?"

I nodded.

"Now the men—drones, they are so named. They are invited to party only in season. Which is now, understand? See, they are already here."

Stavros gestured to the lower part of the frame. The cells there appeared not to be hexagons, but rather circles, on account of the chubby bees pushing through.

"Drone congregation area, yes? Away from women. Men do nothing all day, okay? Enjoy life, just. Wait to fuck. They have no other purpose. Go ahead, play with them if you like. They will not bite."

"You sure? I thought—"

"Ladies bite. *They* are violent ones. Boys even have no stinger. They are neutered, fat, fatherless fucks!"

"Fatherless?"

"Drones come from unfertilized egg. However, as Queen's egg *is* fertilized, she has father—drone's grandfather."

"But—the drones are the children of the Queen?"

"Everyone is children of Queen."

"So the guys fuck their sisters?"

"No. No. And again no! You do not listen, Adam. Worker bees are, eh, celibate. Like nuns! No fuck fuck for them!"

"What?"

"Guys fuck *only* their mother. Like Oedipus Rex!"

"So the guys—" I stuttered. "The guys—fuck the Queen?"

Instead of an answer, Stavros acknowledged my breakthrough with a lick of his teeth and a twinkle of his wet, watchful eyes.

"So, wait—you mean—all of us? You're saying—"

But I could already feel it—the truth landing so heavily—the facts of the day rearranging themselves and slowly coalescing around the symbolic order.

"*We're* supposed to fuck the Queen? So—this is like a sex cult? The drones—we're just sex slaves?"

Stavros smiled. He took a deep and long breath.

"It is only natural, yes?" he said. "Hive is monarchy, after all. Here Queen gets everything. Glory. Fucking. Everything. She is god. She is whore. This is all for her."

Stavros protracted his pinkie and pointed that long nail to a bee with a yellow marking on her stomach.

"You see, this is one who create everything. And, may I add, he is lucky drone who lie with her. It will be kind of, eh, holy pleasure. My father writes about this in book, actually—is why he call it *Catharsis*."

"Holy pleasure?" I said. "Catharsis? Stavros, what are you—"

"*Opa! Opa!*" Stavros exclaimed. "But I have said too much, yes? Now I must get to work! Major production issue in factory for Papa Stavros. In real life, of course, they want drone also to work!"

Stavros glared beyond the stacked wooden boxes. Smoke was pumping out of the factory. Behind it, angry waves attacked the shore. It was clear that no boat could dock on this side of the island.

"Now, no more questions! There is new party after all. And then—royal pussy awaits, Adam! Glory that was Greece, etcetera. Enjoy! Enjoy!"

With that Stavros turned his back and headed for the factory, singing in Greek to the bees around him. I stood for a moment longer, then turned the other way. The path back ran through the stacked wooden boxes, ascended through the sunflower fields, and swerved up into the hills. As the sun vanished behind them, the sunflowers were slowly hanging their heads, their black eyes following each other to the dirt, falling asleep until the sun's next rising. So it was a chilling dusk I was headed for—the end of a dreadful day. And the only reasonable thing to do, I thought—the only possible thing—was to head back to my room and write about it.

With pounding heart I typed out the events of the morning—the words sparking out like lightning again, except now I knew what they were up to. They weren't simply relating reality as it happened. They were trying to improve it. As I wrote the breakfast scene, for example, I noticed how it differed from the original—not so much the facts of it, you understand, but rather the symbolic order the facts were now conforming to. Although that order had been revealed by Stavros much later in reality, in fiction it was already present on that plate, where the allegory of the dead criminal bee was staged.

This metaphysical aspect of the novel (that I was apparently writing a novel about writing a novel) was thoroughly disappointing. This most contemptible type of "autofiction" has long been the literary form I most despise, with the possible exception of the "discourse novel," which my book was also becoming. But by now it was too late to change course, because my novel wasn't going to cut it as a pure mystery. For starters, its pacing was off. It had opened too slowly; it was now moving too fast. And very unevenly, too. In a mystery, theories should be offered one by one, developed convincingly, then rejected and replaced sequentially, as they build up to a final revelation. But here the theorizing about the missing men seemed to ebb and flow, rather than to build. (*Were they brainwashed? Murdered? Fucked?*) So I would have to make the most of what I had—and most of what I had was myself.

It was this sense of myself that soon captured my interest—I mean, that I actually had a sense of it. In that first spell of writing, you'll recall, I had hardly recognized the representation of myself on the page. The narrator had seemed such a distant figure, entirely estranged from me. But I could see myself in him now—and I began to see through him, too: glaring at the bee on the plate, following the curves of town, watching Jane wave me down from the sunbeds. The sensory memory was also awakening, so that I could feel the warmth of the sun on my cheeks and the softness of Jane's lips on mine. *And then what had happened?* I can see it all so clearly: Jane crying, Jane slapping me, Jane running off...

It was half a lifetime ago, before the imagination mechanism had broken, that I'd felt this staggering sensation. It was my first drug, my great addiction. In its grip, as a younger writer, my heart raced with urgency. The hairs on my arms stood up. Almost totally relieved of consciousness, I left behind my limp body and clattering hands—and inhabited my first-person completely. Now, decades later, this sensation was taking over me again—jolting me to my feet—pulling the cobblestones out from under me—shoving me into some mirror image of *déjà vu*. As you read these words, I am only now stumbling into town—the lights blowing out in huge bright colors—my essence clarified down to a single curiosity: I need to see what's inside those crates.

From this diminished distance from myself, at this ecstatic proximity to singularity, I stand at the threshold of an intoxicating madness. And the only thing saving me from it now is the recognition that there is, actually, nothing more to write. I'm all caught up. The chapter is coming to a close. And yet the comfort is temporary. It isn't even comfort. *The story must continue*, she whispers—her words like kisses to my neck. *And it depends not on how you write, but on what you do. And you know what you must do. You know what you must do...*

CATHARSIS

Standing upon the cliffs, I cast my glance into the cove. The night party had started. The honeybees were dancing everywhere across the sands. Beyond them, a bonfire was blazing. The women there were stacked in some kind of pyramid formation. But their guru wasn't among them. Closer to me, the bar was empty. Only River remained, his face planted amid a scattering of shot glasses. Oriana was passing her hands through his hair. A grooming ritual was in progress. I turned around, glared up at the abandoned town and the Hive rising above it—the golden road swerving up and around, until it delivered my glance to the Queen's house. Of course I knew what I had to do. If I had any chance of regaining control of this story, I needed to get ahead of it.

The road circled back, closed me in, pushed me up. All around me cave houses connected across a network of criss-crossing ladders and staircases. Within a few minutes, I was standing before the Queen's house—a composition of six hexagons, unevenly stacked, like glass coasters dropped one on top of the other. While industrial iron beams and frames supported it, the house was transparent. And yet, like a diamond, it was also inscrutable. With gold, red, and orange lights catching and reflecting everywhere, the house was endlessly disguised and revealed in a kaleidoscope of bright color. I pulled open its glass door.

When I stepped in, the lights fell off. Only by the dim glint of kumiko lamps did the first hexagon come into view—a Japanese garden of miniature bonsai trees and soft scattered stone. A glass staircase spiraled up from the center of it. I climbed in silence, as the second landing opened to a library and lecture room; the third to a kitchen, bar, and dining area; the fourth to a gym with treadmills and elliptical machines facing the glass perimeter. And everywhere were paintings, sculptures, and cultural artifacts which didn't quite coalesce—which suggested a restless and traveling and erratic appetite. I crossed a Buddha as I headed for the fifth landing.

This story was different from the others. Here a compact foyer opened out in six directions. Shoji style doors were variously slid open to reveal the six vacant bedrooms. The rooms were cold, clinical, impersonal. Lying on an unmade bed, a familiar red hat suggested who had been sleeping there. "Will," I whispered, before moving to the next door. "Maxim." Then the other. "Camillio?" The guys were nowhere to be found. But I could hear some chatter from upstairs. I closed the circle to the stairway, looked up to the final landing, and made my ascent.

The sixth hexagon was a labyrinth of golden curtains and dividers—opaque plastic-like sheets stretched out in wooden frames. I pursued the voices into the maze, peeking into a bathroom, a massage room, a kitchenette. The voices were coming from a dressing room. But they weren't men's voices. Through a tear of plastic, I spied a huddle of women at the vanity. One brushed a stream of long black hair. Another painted fingernails. The third made idle chatter with the fourth. But only briefly, when the first woman passed the brush between her hands, did I catch—in an antique bronze mirror—the reflection of a golden mask.

A creak startled me. I stepped back into the maze. For a moment there was silence. Then I heard more voices. These were coming from downstairs—and they were followed by rising footsteps. I didn't have much time. I hastened down a corridor and slipped into a curtain. It was a dark world of silk, lace, and perfume I found myself in. I swam to the glimmer of light on the other side. Through the beams of Venetian blinds, I gained a view of the Queen size bed.

"Yes, little one, I will be quite all right on my own."

"Be kind to her, please."

"Of course. You can trust me with her."

Escorted by Penelope, Hari stepped into view. He kissed her cheek, then saw her out.

"Goodbye, little one."

"See you on the other side, Hari."

As Penelope left, Hari sat at the edge of the bed. He seemed impatient. As he waited, he untied his dyed black hair, collected its strands, then tied them up again behind his bald head. He checked his fingernails. He adjusted the collar of his white robe. He passed a hand over a candle flickering at the bedside. Then, suddenly, he rose to his feet.

"Your Highness," he said.

The Queen was tall and dark. Her slender body was laced in a black negligee. Her hair was also black, long, snake-like. Her mask was a work of carnival grotesque—with slanted eyes, streaks of black, and an outbreak of golden beads spreading like syphilis across the cheeks. But the sight of her only inspired Hari. In his gaze, once dead, I could now see the vitality of a young man.

"I understand you do not speak, Your Highness. But that is all the same to me. Please step forward. And do not be ashamed. It is very common, this obstacle you have. Especially in the modern world. Especially for a woman of power such as you. I know it must be difficult. But I am pleased you have called for me. I believe I can help. That is why I am here, yes?"

The Queen nodded.

"Then you will follow my instructions," Hari said, his voice soft but authoritative. "You will do exactly as I say."

The Queen consented with a second nod. After that she did exactly as Hari said.

"Good, very good. Now please lie down here. With your head on the pillow. Yes, that is perfect. Now just relax, Your Highness. Breathe and relax. Deep breaths, just like so. You are very tense, understandably. But through this process I will not leave your side, I assure you. You are safe. Now do as I do. Interlock your hands like so. Exactly. Exactly so. Such beautiful hands they are—even more beautiful together. It is a wonderful feeling when the circuit closes—the circle completes—and the body exists unified and unbroken.

"Your Highness, have you ever studied those lines on your palm? Let us gaze upon one of them now. Yes, keep your focus on that line, even as you slowly bring your hands back toward you. Yes, just like so. Slowly, very slowly, toward you. And as that line moves toward you, you begin to lose focus. This is natural, of course, the line losing focus as it approaches your gaze. And as you become aware of your eyes, your eyelids grow heavy—yes, in fact, you are very tired—a wonderful exhaustion is falling over you—your eyelids growing heavier and heavier—the line blurring more and more—and slowly, very slowly, your eyes closing—yes, just so, closing very slowly—slowly closing until—until—until they are completely shut.

"All is dark now, little one. The world outside is shut. Only the world inside remains. And you fall into it so freely—you fall into yourself—drifting, floating, falling into a deep and beautiful sleep. We have ignored this world inside for too long, have we not? But that's no matter. All of history is beginning only now. You are only now coming to life. And you feel it there, don't you, at the base of your spine? I know you do. That tingling feeling, a force so imperceptible at first that you don't want to believe it's there. But that is how the life force begins.

"Take your time with that force, little one. Do not ask it to grow too fast. Enjoy it. Love it. Nourish it at the base of your spine. For this is your beginning—your foundation—your first chakra. Hold the energy there, as in a cauldron. Feel it bubbling. And, only when you are ready, release it. Go ahead now, release the energy. Set it out on its journey upward. Allow it to tingle up and rise between your legs—your second chakra—vibrating there in the valley between your legs—do you feel it there?—you are nodding—of course you do—this sensual energy—caressing you—arousing you. Do not be ashamed of this arousal, little one, because this desire is life itself pulsing through you—pleasuring you—making you wet.

"Now, even as you continue feeling it so intensely there between your legs, allow the life force to rise again. Do you feel it rising up—gaining momentum, intensity, power—rising faster than ever—activating each chakra it meets? In your navel—so fiery, powerful, and proud. In your heart—so playful, loving, and light. Feel it rising and transforming at every step—activating every part of your body—rising even in your throat—filling your mouth—bursting open through your lips! And moan! Yes, just like that, little one. Oh, you are so beautiful when you moan. So divine. This is the music from within—so sing it loud! Rejoice! You are sexy when you moan.

"Accept the truth about yourself, little one. Feel how exquisite and sensual you are. And as the life force spreads across your face and reunites between your two eyes, there is a third eye you may use—watch with your third eye how this new world opens before you with layers of wonder and charm—planes after planes of pleasure—this pleasure seizing your body now—making you shiver—making you shake. Yes, just like that, little one—your entire body shaking now with uncontrollable pleasure—every chakra activating—the burning fire of your heart—the waterfall between your legs. You are so beautiful. So perfect. Yes, moan even louder—so wild like the sea!

"And you are almost there, little one! Just remember how beautiful you are when you tremble. Tremble more! You are so perfect when you moan. Yes, even louder! Rejoice, little one, because you are about to lose your self—and gain everything. Every thing! Louder! Louder! This is correct. Don't turn back. Don't resist. When the pleasure comes, do not deny it, Queen. Only one chakra remains. And the royal power must be lost for the divine to be gained. Almost, Queen. Almost! A world burning and wet! A crown of gold lighting your head! Surrender, Queen! Surrender! Surrender! For you are becoming more than a Queen."

For a moment the Queen stopped moaning. Instead her body started convulsing from unbearable tension.

"You are—"

Her lips trembling.

"—becoming—"

Her voice begging to be released.

"—a goddeeeeeesssss!"

And upon that word, from the twisting body of the Queen, a scream ripped out. It was deep, hideous, demonic—a continuous scream of agonized pleasure—raging and monstrous—breaking down in anger and yearning—then rising upon carnal notes of escalating beauty—soaring through pangs of terrifying ecstasy, before finally—gloriously—breaking through.

In another moment the voice had evacuated her body completely. The Queen flattened onto the bed.

I had not moved through these events. Transfixed in my hiding place, I felt again as that boy at the looking-hole, discovering the secret game between woman and man. I did not know what was coming next, when Hari rose from the bed. First he touched the Queen's neck, then pulled her eyelids open. They flipped back. He scratched his head. Then he moved for the stairway, looked down, and returned. He paused before the Queen's body, muttering something under his breath. After that Hari started to take laps around the bed. He did this for a few minutes, occasionally glancing at her, then throwing his glance away, circling the Queen as that morning bee circled its plate of honey.

Finally Hari stopped. His eyes narrowed upon a decision. He sat abruptly at the edge of the bed and snapped his robe open. It was a vulgar and elaborate creature caught between his legs—unexpected and alien—hanging like a farm snake—uncircumcised in tones of pink and brown. Hari winced. His lips writhed in contempt for it, like it was some village cousin who'd come back to visit him in the city. He looked away in disgust, even as his hands lowered to get a hold of it. He massaged it first. Then he started tugging at it. But the snake was not charmed.

Hari was sweating. His muttering grew furious under his breath. He set out on a sequence of pinches and taps. He slapped the thing. Finally something stirred. At the first sign of this, Hari grabbed his penis with one hand. He squeezed it so hard the tip turned white. With his other hand he started flicking its head. He was merciless in his flicking. In another moment the penis began flapping around autonomously. With no time to lose, Hari spat into his hands and seized the creature and strangled it. In a final heroic effort, sliding his hands up and down, he managed to bring it into full draconian form.

A nimble man now—swift and young—Hari got up from the bed, let the robe slip off completely, and returned to the bed on all fours. He closed in on the Queen, slipped a hand between her legs, pulled the lace to one side, and moved in. The welcome was not easy. Even in her trance, the Queen cringed, and Hari moved to adjust a few times. Finally the angle was found. The Queen absorbed him completely. Hari's movements were short and simple. They were not aggressive. He did not touch the Queen in any other way but this. His gaze, fixed upon that golden mask, was tenderly adoring.

"You are so beautiful," he whispered. "So divine. So divine. So divine..."

Then, suddenly, Hari gasped. He lowered his forehead onto the Queen's. For a moment, all was still. Then Hari withdrew. His penis followed him like a decapitated snake. He collapsed beside her. He shut his eyes. A long breath left him.

Hari mumbled something again.

More silence followed.

Voices whispered in the distance.

Then the Queen sat up in bed.

"Your Highness?" Hari said, without looking at her. "Have you awoken?"

The Queen did not respond, but silently rose to her feet and stepped away.

"Your Highness?"

Still Hari did not turn. He was tired.

"Well, I will be here. I will be here."

The Queen left my view. A door creaked open. Water ran. The Queen hummed, peed, flushed. Then she returned.

"Hari," she said.

"Hmm?" Hari said. "Are you—"

"Look at me."

Suddenly Hari turned around.

"What did you—"

But the thought was caught in Hari's throat. Because the Queen was standing over him. And she held in her hand a golden spear.

"On behalf of the Hive," she said, in a cold and quiet voice. "I am honored to stand before you as your final judge and judgment."

"Oh little one," Hari said. "What is this game?"

"After a period of deliberation, and taking into account your repeated crimes against women, which include, but are not limited to, fraud, manipulation, kidnapping, imprisonment, abuse of power..."

"No," Hari said, more forcefully this time. "Queen, this has all been refuted."

"And yet have you not just proven it yourself?" she continued, calmly. "Sex without consent. Sex without consciousness. Rape."

"No!" Hari called, in anger now. "I reject your accusations."

"For these, among other crimes against women, I sentence you, Hari—"

"I reject your sentence, too! Who are you to pass such a sentence upon me? You ungrateful little human—who are you?"

I was filled with fear for Hari. And yet, as he faced the sword, the guru was defiant as ever. Fear was only making a hero out of him.

"Don't you know?" the Queen said. "After all this time, don't you know?"

With her right hand gripping the spear, the Queen moved her left to the mask. Then, very slowly, she brought her hand down.

"I told you," she said. "I am the Queen."

From my angle, I could not see her face. But when Hari did, he transformed completely. A smile trembled on his lips. His eyes glowed hot and bright. That wet dew evaporated from them. His entire face was now lighting up—as though by the radiance of an actual deity standing before him.

"On behalf of the Hive, I reclaim the life you have taken from us. I punish your crimes. And I forgive you your sins."

The Queen raised the golden spear over Hari, but still he did not move. For Hari was now in a trance of his own—in the throes of a blissful and almost noble surrender—on the brink, perhaps, of something like catharsis.

"Hari," the Queen said, finally. "I sentence you to death."

And upon those words, the Queen plunged the spear into Hari's chest.

Hari did not flinch. He heaved and choked quietly. For some time, blood gargled out of his mouth. Then his body stiffened. Hari was dead.

And then the Queen said—

Bzzzz.

The sound of this sent a swarm of women up the stairs. They circled around the Queen and bowed to her. And they joined her in her sound—

Bzzzzzz.

As much as I tried, I could not get my view of the Queen. But the women's buzzing grew in my ears. It intensified into something diabolical and insane—

Bzzzzzzzzzzzzzzzzzzzzz!

DEAD WHITE MALES

"In the hive, the single mission of the male drone is to mate with the Queen," I read aloud. "As the drone grasps the Queen, he everts his endophallus and inserts it tightly into the Queen's reproductive tract. The drone immediately ejaculates with such explosive force that he leaves behind the tip of his endophallus. Thus the drone's abdomen is torn away from him. Excruciating pain visits at the moment of ecstasy. And so, upon orgasm, the drone falls to his death. The divinity of the bee stems from this twinning. In bees, sex and death are permanently and immediately linked—pleasure and pain being simultaneous and identical. Sin and redemption are simultaneous too."

I snapped the book shut, then slid it across the coffee table where it had been lying all along: *Catharsis* by Fr. Theodoros Angelos.

"Stavros's dad wrote it," I said. "Some lunatic priest, by the sound of it—he must've inspired all this somehow. Hey, man. Did you hear what I just said?"

"Yeah, yeah, I get it," River slurred, with half-open eyes. "I get it."

It must have been twenty minutes since I found River in the library. He was shirtless and shivering on the sofa. His golden hair was tangled up in sweaty knots. His pale, emaciated body was hunched over, his face smushed into one hand, while the other made a great trembling effort to reach a bottle of whisky. The scene looked like one of those vast Christian canvases—the fresh morning sun pouring through the stained glass and blowing everything out of proportion.

"I think you need to stop," I said. "It's time we face reality now."

"Reality, reality, reality," River said, getting a grip on the bottle. "I don't understand what all the rage is about reality."

I knew this tone. I learned from personal experience that addiction is a poetic state, and artist addicts especially take refuge in poetic form.

"Come on, man," I said, as River brought the bottle to his lips. "Stop."

The bottle was raised. The liquid dropped.

"Hey. Hey! Did you hear what the fuck I said?"

River lowered the bottle. He turned to me with his wet-dripping lips and slow-squinting eyes.

"The guys are dead, yeah?" he said, with a wry twist of his mouth. "The Queen is fucking us one by one. And then she's killing us. Some fucked up #MeToo revenge plot, right? That's what you said, in not so few words. You fuck, you die."

"You fuck, you die," I repeated. "Exactly. But—you don't seem to care."

"No, I care," River said. "I care."

"So then what?"

"Maybe I deserve to die."

Something resembling a smile formed on River's lips. He had

enjoyed the sick, defeatist sound of his own phrase. He attached to the bottle again like a baby.

"That's enough," I said, stealing it away. "You're drunk out of your mind. And unless you start thinking strai—"

But the word was jammed in my throat—I'd been too stunned to notice why: River's limp body snapping up and lunging at me; the bottle shattering at my feet; my back cracking against the bookshelves.

"Who the fuck do you think you are?" River was saying, as he tightened his grip on my neck. In the bone-chilling blue of his eyes, a grim presence was now making itself known. "Leave me alone, understand? You don't know me. You don't know me, okay? Okay? Okay?"

Then, through no effort of my own, the specter eased. I could see it losing its grip on his gaze, slowly fading, washing out behind a watery veil.

"Fuck," River said, letting go of my neck. "Fuck, I'm such a mess."

Then he quickly turned around and stumbled back to the sofa like a wounded bird. He sat down and took deep breaths, his body caving further and further into itself.

"I just can't free myself of it," River said, his voice quivering. "I've tried to beat it more times than I can count. But it always finds me."

I stepped cautiously to the sofa, grabbed a quilt from its arm, and draped it over River. I sat next to him.

"She first appears in the corner of my eye," River said. "That's her MO—always in the corner of my eye—like an angel. I tell myself she isn't there, really. Then I tell myself I don't need her, even if she is. I'm not gonna make that mistake again. More I tell this to myself, though, the more I see her there, in the corner of my eye. And then she's talking to me, too. *That's not living*, she's saying. *You're not living. Where's your passion, man? Where's your* spirit? *We used to dance together and sing all night—and who have you become now? Come on, man, aren't you tired of being dead?*

"It's not that I don't do battle, man. Entire games I play and labyrinths I go down trying to trick her and get her off my back. *But she has a point, doesn't she?* That's what I start thinking. *I really am dead inside.* And all along she's moving to the center of my gaze. *Better to die than not live*, she's saying. *Come on, man. Snap out of this!* And boy is she convincing now. I'm so fucking numb and sick and there she is, offering the ticket out. I know what's about to happen, too, but the temptation is too strong. I break down. I invite her in, every fucking time. Every time, man. Every time..."

As River cast his head into his palms, the quilt slipped off his body, trembling now with self-pity and despair.

"I know what you mean," I said. "Or at least I knew someone who did."

"Huh?" River said, his glance rising curiously.

"Believe me," I said. "And it wasn't just alcohol for him either. Pills. Powder. You wouldn't believe the shit—"

"No, man! What?" River interrupted. "I'm not talking about drugs! And not booze neither. I'm not a fucking alcoholic, if that's what you mean."

"You're not," I said. "Then what have you been—"

"I've been talking about *love*, man. I've been talking about *love!*"

River made a deep sigh, wrapped himself again in a bundle, and sank into the sofa. He let his head drop to one side and fixed his gaze upon the stained glass.

"Love," River said, his face shining in the sunlight. "Lord knows how hard I tried escaping it. After how things ended with Claire. I mean—I was in pieces—I knew I had a problem. So I was out on the road again, my guitar and me, keeping my head down, playing my song for a buck, then moving on—that's the trick, you know—always moving on—never letting her catch up. And that's what I did for a long time. Until Atlantic City. Have you been to Atlantic City?"

"No."

"Well I hadn't either. Or at least I thought I hadn't until I saw that Ferris-Wheel spinning and those slots flipping out and the scales flashing in the sand. And the taste of that sea salt taffy—I could swear I'd tasted it before. It was like a carnival dream I was living in, and not for the first time, and not even necessarily mine—it was damn trippy. Anyway, I made some friends there out on the boardwalk. Sword swallowers and card hustlers and that kind. At night we all slept together in casino parking lots and daytime we worked the crowds. So I stayed longer than I should have—that was my mistake. I let her catch up to me again."

"The angel," I said.

"Alma's the name she went by this time around," River said. "She was older, you could say, but very well kept and pretty when she entered the corner of my eye. I pretended not to notice, but she just kept cooing at me—and then it was quite the yacht she was cooing from. She'd been watching me play for days, apparently—was wondering if I might perform private, so lonely she was on that big yacht of hers. She was heartbroken too, what with her husband, and she could really use a song just about now. And you know me. I'm a sucker for sentiment, man. I told her I'd drop in for a tune. And after I'd played, she asked me to spend the night.

"I told her no at first. I told her I had a place to sleep. But when she heard where that was, she just put her foot down. *I won't forgive myself if I let you go*, she said. *Not with this storm coming on. I have plenty of room here, besides. And I want to hear your story—hope it wasn't at the crossroads you learned to play that guitar.* She made me laugh. She spoke my language, you know. So I opened up to her. She was in tears all night in regard to my story. She served me tea and oranges and took me out on deck for cold cigarette breaks and brought me into the warmth again. She was so watchful—so kind—and all along she was moving to the center of my gaze."

"You let her in," I said.

"Yeah," River said. "And she let me in, too—night after night—although she made sure my staying wasn't beneath my dignity or anything like that. Said there was work to be done around the boat—she was hopeless and I was handy—and we could help each other. And that's what we did. I worked the boat and played the guitar and she fed me and listened to my stories with those huge spongy eyes—like they could absorb everything. I never really knew who I was, but she looked at me like she did. So yeah—I relapsed, I guess. I fell in love in a bad way. I was crazy about her. I'd do *anything* for her. Have you felt that kind of love before?"

"Me?" I replied. "Well, I guess—"

"You're lucky you haven't," River said. "Because that kind of love isn't real, is it? Sooner or later, she takes it away from you. Of course she never tells you how or when, except you see it slowly fading in the fakeness of her smiles. In her little lies. In her yawns. She abandons you long before she leaves. The more you try to understand, the more distant she becomes. The nicer you are, the more contempt she has for you. And you know what's about to happen, because it's happened a hundred times. You wake up one day and she's leaning out the boat, cooing at some big beautiful Dutch guy in a bandana, saying: *There's room here for all of us.*"

River was shaking uncontrollably now—his gaze aimed so intensely on that stained glass it might just crack.

"Betrayal!" River cried. "Fucking betrayal. Last night I'm in her arms and here I am below deck fixing drinks and they're making the boat shake above. It just destroys me, you know. I don't say anything for a long time. I don't risk losing her. I wait until he's gone out to try talking to Alma. But I don't recognize her anymore. She's so cold it makes my blood boil. *You're just a guy off the boardwalk too*, she says. *Who are you to make a fuss?* And my heart is about to explode, because I know that her love is gone. The angel in front of me has fallen—she's the devil herself who played this trick on me! And I just lose it, man. I just fucking lose it!"

With a final exclamation, River suddenly broke his gaze from the glass and collapsed into my lap. For some time I sat in silence over him—his entire body shivering under me, like it was in some religious battle. I was in some battle too, I guess. By now the similarities were just too striking to ignore, like a secret chord had played in two places at once, and even the vibrations of this body reminded me of that other body once entrusted to me. I shut my eyes, straining to suppress the coming memory: a dry and windy night; our father's grave; a bitter fight; my brother's eyes; my pride. This was no time for tears, I thought. This was no time for regrets. I pulled myself into a resolve. I opened my eyes.

"It's okay, man," I said, setting my hand on River's back. "It's going to be okay."

"No," River cried through his tears. "No! Didn't you hear what I just said? Do you know what I did to her?"

"It doesn't matter, River."

"What do you mean—it doesn't matter? Of course it matters! I beat her to a pulp, man! I—"

"Stop. Just stop! I said it doesn't fucking matter, okay?"

I grabbed River's skeletal arms and brought him up to face me.

"We're going to get out of here," I said. "We're going to get the help you need. Nobody gets to judge you—least of all some make-believe Queen."

River was looking at me so curiously now—his eyelids parting again—those blue eyes glinting with something easy to mistake for hope.

"I believe in you," I said. "I'm here for you. And when we get out of here—"

That's when it happened for the second time. River lunged at me. Except this time it was his lips I felt on mine.

"What the fuck?" I said, pushing him off. "Get off me, man."

River slank back. His eyes sank again into their hiding place.

"What the hell is wrong with you?" I said.

"You see," River replied, grinning at my disgust. "That's what I've been trying to tell you. I'm fucked up. I can't be helped. I deserve to die."

He'd been wanting me to give up all along. And now he had me there.

"Yeah," I said, bitterly. "Maybe you do."

"What?"

"Maybe you deserve to die," I said. "But I fucking don't."

River stirred in his seat.

"Some fucking rumors," I said. "That's why I'm here. Some bullshit accusations that were debunked years ago."

"Are you saying—they're not true?"

"No!"

"No?"

"No, man," I replied, exasperated. "No. No. No."

But each *no* was weaker than the one before. And only by the sound of their fading procession did I understand how tired I actually was. Tired by the sleepless and violent night. Tired from all the years of saying, "No. No. No."

"No," River repeated. "I can see that now. I can see that."

The calmness of his voice surprised me. I looked up and saw that River had changed. He wasn't shivering anymore. His shoulders had relaxed. He was looking at me like I was the one with a condition.

"That's what you should've led with, man," he said, cheerfully. "It's fucking obvious we need to get you out of here."

"You're serious."

"Of course."

"Okay," I said. I wasn't about to question my good luck. "Good. Well it's about fucking time you started seeing straight."

"We just have to figure out how, yeah?"

"Boat's the only way. I guess we'll have to get the keys from Stavros."

A mischievous smile made dimples on River's cheeks.

"Oh I don't think we'll need any keys," he said. "I mean—I can jump a boat with my eyes closed. I need a screwdriver, is all. Anything with a metal tip will do, actually."

"All right then," I said. "All right! I'll figure something out, okay?"

"I'm sure you will, Adam," River replied, with a cryptic smile. Then he threw himself back on the sofa and said, "Hey, can I ask you something?"

"Yeah," I said. "Of course."

"What did she look like?"

"Hmm?"

"When you saw her. With Hari."

"Oh. You mean the Queen."

"Did she have reddish hair?"

"No, I'm pretty sure it was black."

"And she didn't have a tattoo of a dragon on her back?"

"No, I don't think so. Why are you asking, River? Do you think you know her?"

"I mean—she knows us, right? You're not curious who she is?"

I looked to River. I didn't like that search in his eyes.

"No," I said, definitively. "I'm not curious at all. And you shouldn't be either."

"Okay," he said. "You're right. It doesn't matter anyway."

After that we fell into an exhausted silence. It must have been noon at the latest and there were still many hours until the night's party. We'd have plenty of time to figure out our escape. For now, a bit of rest would do us good. So River picked up his guitar and started up on a tune. A moment later he began to sing—his lower lip hanging low—his gaze locking once again on the glass. The sun was coming in hot and holy against it. And lighting the famous image caught in its stains.

> *Look at me, Ma.*
> *Look how I've grown.*
> *The man that I am,*
> *The women I've known.*

I hadn't been entirely honest with River, of course. How could I not be curious about the Queen when the entire plot had been driving toward her unmasking? What is a mystery novel, even, without that moment when the mastermind is revealed—as he so shockingly is in the final pages of *And Then There Were None*? (Spoiler Alert: He was a judge, terminally ill and romantically obsessed with the idea of justice, who had selected his guests, believing they had been wrongly freed by the courts. He had invited them to a private island to correct the verdict.) But justice in that case was a simple death sentence, whereas the appetites of our judge were not only murderous, but also carnal, cathartic, ceremonial. They were very personal too.

River was right. If we didn't know the Queen, then she certainly knew us. She had played me from the beginning—preyed upon my vulnerabilities, namely my unfinished dream of being a writer. She'd offered herself as my muse and opened my novel for me, in fiction and reality both. And then she'd taunted me with the diminishing difference between the two. She had gotten me writing again, it's true, but only so I could write myself into this intimately designed death-dream. But then I had discovered her design, hadn't I? And now I wanted out. It didn't matter that my novel wasn't finished, obviously; no novel is worth the life of the one who writes it. It didn't matter who the Queen was, either; I was ready to abandon her too.

And yet, stretched out in such a golden library, a green-eyed boy had once met the first muses of his life: Aphrodite, goddess of beauty; Athena, of wisdom; and of course Helen of Troy. He had been enchanted by them, even as he could only guess at their secret power. Odysseus himself had barely resisted it, as Calypso imprisoned him on a Greek island, not far from this one. That green-eyed boy had, long ago, agreed to his enslavement by the muses. All young writers do, when they vie for greatness—and dream to join that pantheon of dead white males.

A MOST TERRIBLE FATE

"And where is the boy?"
"Under the weather."
"Good place to hide."

Oriana pressed her lips into a sad smile. Golden hoops weighed down on her earlobes. A red headscarf swirled up.

"Never mind," she said wistfully, passing her hands through a bouquet of mint, thyme, and wildflower. "He will come out soon enough. He is almost ready. Almost."

Oriana plucked something and dropped it off in the shaker.

"Mama issues. Too much of her or not enough, but in case of boy—not at all. Tell me, Adam. What sick mother abandons own infant son—and at doorstep of Calvinist church! This is real betrayal if you ask me."

Oriana cast a smile, squinted at me a moment, then reeled it in again. A dark thought passed like an eclipse across her eyes.

"A most terrible fate," she said. "Looking for mother's love in every woman he meets, only to be betrayed again. There is, of course, other side of this."

Oriana dropped below the bar and continued—

"Mother without son is most pathetic creature of all, yes? Boy is only known cure for female sexual pathology and biological hatred for husband. So I did not have much chance for this!"

Oriana surfaced with a block of ice. She set it on the bar, pulled open a drawer, and fumbled among some instruments until she found one.

"You mean—you don't have a son?"

"Isn't this obvious? No, of course."

"Why not?"

"Why not?" she said, her voice rising. "Why not!"

Then, with a violent shriek, she raised her hands too.

"That fat fuck of husband—that's why. Bah!"

Suddenly Oriana stabbed the ice in front of her. It shattered between us.

"After what he did to our daughter, I could never touch him again!"

I was startled by Oriana's turn. The mask of the provocateur had come off. A pained Mediterranean mother remained—her eyes misting up—her body twisting away from the memory. But there was, amid this revelation, an even more startling sight. Lying now among the shards was an ice pick.

"I'm sorry, Oriana," I said. "Is she—okay?"

"Fine," Oriana replied, her eyes still and tender. "She's a strong girl."

"And him? Did you—"

She glared at me suspiciously.

"—leave him? And give him what he wants? Bah! Of course I do not believe in divorce."

"So what do you believe in?"

The question caught. Oriana's quick black eyes hit me like a pair of darts.

"Revenge, darling," she said. "Revenge. And not easy one for him, either. For him it shall be long and sweet. Now! Let us finish your drink."

Oriana trailed down the bar and this was my best shot. I swiveled in my seat, grabbed the ice pick, and followed the movement through. A costume party opened out on the sands. Some melodic techno was picking up.

"You know," Oriana said. "You can't save him."

My heart stopped. I slid the pick into my pocket and swiveled back to the bar. Oriana had returned with a carafe and was gazing heavily upon me.

"You can try, just. But you will fail. Poor boy must come to it himself."

I smiled my relief and watched as she poured the thick, slow, crimson liquid into the shaker. Then she splashed it with gin and threw some ice in after.

"And how's he supposed to do that?" I asked.

"By repairing relationship, of course."

Oriana lifted the shaker high above her head.

"That is what Queen is for," she said, the ice clamoring like fire-crackers between her thin arms. "She is all women in one. And poor boy must face her once and for all. Yes, it is time for his catharsis."

I grinned. There was that word again, and it wasn't a coincidence. Such cross-pollinated phrases were meant to work on me, psychologically—get me back into the play I was currently plotting to escape.

"We are in Greece, after all," Oriana said, with a wink. "Story does not end with revelation, just. Tragic hero must undergo transformational change!"

Then she cracked the shaker open and poured out the blood-red liquid into a tall shot glass.

"Old family recipe," Oriana said, pushing it toward me.

"Down centuries of maternal line. *Yamas*."

"*Yamas*," I said, best I could.

I picked up the shot, gave it a whirl, and threw it back. It was bitter and syrupy, like cough medicine.

"Disgusting, I know. Medicinal value, however, is astonishing. Ancient Greeks were first, in fact, to harness healing power of menses."

"The power of what?"

"But I just said. Ancient recipe. Down *maternal* line. And you are in luck, too—blood is fresh from cycle!"

My glance dropped. It fell right into the crusting crimson residue at the bottom of the glass. From there nausea came racing up my throat. My vision blurred. And the woman in front of me capsized, for one moment, into her articles: hoop earrings, red scarf, black eyes. Her voice echoed—

"You must have your catharsis, too."

Then a glint caught Oriana's eyes. A smile broke her lips. I heard the vicious grinding of her coffee-tainted teeth.

"*O po po!*" she said. "Of course I am joking!"

"What?" I managed.

"You should see your face! You believe I give you menstrual blood?"

Slowly the confusion cleared. I found my breath.

"You are silly boy indeed!" Oriana shouted, lighting a cigarette. "I would not waste pearls on pig such as you! This is mad honey, just. Special from, eh, rhododendron flower. Not so bad, yes?"

I shook my head. She blew smoke at me.

"Oh come now! You cannot stomach joke? Bah! Have cigarette with me."

"I don't think so," I said. "I'm gonna have to walk this off."

"Suit yourself," Oriana said. "But you come back, yes? Queen saves best for last."

"Yeah," I said, getting up. "Sure, Oriana. Goodnight."

"Darling," she said. "Don't be sourpuss, okay? Understand this is for you."

I gave Oriana the best smile I had. Then I headed out. As I neared the cliffs, I stumbled and nearly fell. Then I heard Oriana calling to me again. But when I turned around, I saw she was only chatting with Penelope. I winced. In fact the resemblance was startling. On opposite sides of the bar, Oriana and Penelope appeared as mirror images of each other. For a moment I felt sick in the stomach. I was coming upon a terrible premonition. I turned from it quickly—and carried on. The lights of the party faded at the foot of the cliffs and I would not be seen there. I could take my time following the long curve of the cove back to the sea.

The moon soared in the black sky. It shone like a bright wound. Witchy winds swept in and dropped. The tides nagged at the boat, shaking up my insides. I'd been pacing the deck for some time, dividing my attention between the moon and the party on the cove. Any minute now River would emerge from it and race for the boat and we'd be off. There was no need to be nervous. Above me the moon was still rising. When it was directly overhead, that would be midnight. It was going to be a windy day, River had said, and at midnight the tides would be on our side.

On its descent from the moon, my glance stuck to a distant object of shining glass. High on the hill, the Queen's house had always seemed a spectacular creation. But it was glowing more meaningfully tonight—calling my curiosity, once again, to the one who lived there. To have gathered all these women here was no small feat. It must have taken exceptional will to have found them in the first place—extraordinary wealth to have brought them to this island. Only an ingenious mind could have created for them this new civilization: its grand architecture and intricate design, its politics and philosophy, its psychology and religion.

I took a deep breath. The air was crisp and fresh. As it climbed the dark sky, the moon glowed brighter and brighter. And that glass house was glowing brighter, too—exaggerating its importance in my mind—insisting again on the question: *Who is the Queen?* The question was never meant to be answered, I insisted back. That mask was the entire point of her. Without it, naturally, the Queen was just another woman. But under its cover, she was something else. Killing her identity was the price the woman paid to be a god. *Is that what she intended to be—a god?—some kind of nymph reinvented for our time?—an alternative messiah who was nailed every night on behalf of all her followers? And to what end?*

"You must have your catharsis, too," answered the voice.

Those were Oriana's words—the ones she'd spoken into the haze of my disgust. She must've turned some black magic trick on me back there—bewitched me with that crimson drink—forced some kind of psychic opening and installed those words in my mind—knowing they would grow in meaning there—just as that high house was sparkling like a secret treasure—pulsing madly now with its promise of pleasure and death. I remembered that look on Hari's face when he'd finally seen the Queen without her mask. A great sheen of recognition had come over him then. *When Hari had accepted his crimes, had he actually been absolved? Had that been his catharsis?*

"You must have your catharsis, too," the words echoed.

They came over me in waves this time—swallowed me up—then took me back to that original man who, being lame and unable to hunt, made pigments in the rocks instead, dipped his finger in, made lines on the cave. He must have been shocked, I thought, to see the figures taking shape. He must have left his body then—experienced this as a huge and painful hallucinatory event—far more important than the invention of algebra or the splitting of the atom, because this was the animal itself being split—the human being invented out of it. The original catharsis was art—consciousness itself—and for generations we said, "Art is a mirror—art reflects life."

Long before it was formally discovered that the opposite was also true, Shakespeare wrote that "all the world's a stage" (not the other way around) and he began playing with the mirror. While he undertook the writing of that most famous play, he had Hamlet stage the play within. That dark prince, far more diabolical than we think, believed that *his* play, by mirroring life, could be mirrored back in—the carefully designed performance of the former king's murder could "catch the conscience" of his actual killer—and trigger his catharsis. I liked this idea for my novel. And of course Agatha herself had murdered her guests according to a poem.

A wet wind swept up from the sea—slapped my face—brought me back. I'd allowed my thoughts to drift too far, apparently, because when I checked in, the moon was overhead. My heart picked up. I looked out into the cove, but it was lost in a bright haze. Then that bitter taste caught my tongue again. So it hadn't been blood in that drink, but—*what had she said?* My heart was pounding now—my glance flying up. Above me the moon dripped like candle wax. *Rhododendron*, I remembered. Oriana called it—*mad honey?* Suddenly my stomach turned. Nausea raced up my throat again. I made for the rails, tried vomiting overboard. Nothing came out. In the distance, mythic figures flashed in gold.

I staggered into the powdery haze—the house beats dropping like bombs around me—the world gyrating out of control. Whatever had gotten into my system, it was coming up strong, invading my every faculty, making a bright and blinding blur of everything and everyone—except for one.

"River!" I called, bursting through a huddle of women. "Hey man. He—"

"Hey, hey," River said, receiving me with a sweet smile and wide-open arms. "How are you, man?"

"I'm fine," I said. "How are you?"

River hugged me hard. I glanced over his shoulder, where his guitar was strapped. The women around us were buzzing around in cute little bee costumes.

"What are you doing, man?" I whispered.

"What do you mean?"

"We were supposed to meet, remember?"

"Meet?" River said, letting go. "Oh fuck. Yeah, sorry man. Sorry."

"It's fine. We can go now. I got us what we need. It's not exactly a screwdriver, but—why are you smiling like that?"

"You're a sight for sore eyes, that's all."

"What?"

"Don't be like that!" River said, cheerfully. "You know I can't *actually* jump a yacht with a screwdriver."

"Huh?"

I stepped back for a fresh look at him. But the potion was now making a blur of River, too—softening the curls of his hair, the slope of his nose, his voice.

"I was just messing around! I thought that was obvious. Hey man, are you good? Deep breaths, man. Deep breaths."

I hunched over, planted my hands on my knees.

"She put something in my drink," I said.

My head was spinning. My body was erupting in sweat.

"Hey River," a voice said. "Are you ready?"

"I'm ready," River said.

"Ready for what?"

Panic seized my heart. A surge of energy brought me to my feet. It was Penelope talking to River.

"Don't you—" I said, breathlessly. "River, don't you remember?"

But River didn't answer. Tilted up to the sky, his eyelids were coming apart again—those curtains slowly lifting over his gaze.

"You can see her now, can't you?" he mumbled. "You can see her in my eyes?"

"Huh?"

"It's her. It's her! Can't you see?"

And then I did. Reflected in River's eyes, captured in beams of kaleidoscopic light, was the dark double figure of the Queen.

"I have to play for her now," River said, quietly. Then he turned away and called, "You're going to take me to her, yeah?"

"That's right!" Penelope replied. "It's your turn. Come on then, River."

A rush of furry tails and plastic wings came between us.

"Hey!" I shouted, trying to break through. "Wait!"

Instead I found myself in their hands.

"Hey, let him go!" I heard River say. "Don't touch him!"

Then I was in his hands. Holding me up was a great luminous presence.

"Adam," he said. "You have to let me go, okay?"

My legs shook under me. My mind blanked.

"N-no," I slurred. "You're not—you're not—thinking—"

"Look at me, man. Hey."

"No," I started again—but my words were sticky in my mouth. "She's going—to—she's going to k—k—"

I couldn't make out another word. My lips were now completely glued shut, just as my feet were stuck to the ground, like a bee steeped in honey.

"You don't have to say anything," River insisted. "I've made my decision."

I knew then it was over. I couldn't do anything. So I just stood there, muted and paralyzed, as River set his hands on my shoulders.

"I'm ready now," he said, placing his gaze into mine, one last time. "I'm ready for her. I hope you will be too."

I could already see him fading out like a ghost in front of me—leaving behind his curling golden hair and his freckles and then his smile—until all that was left of him were his bursting blue eyes. Only once before had I seen eyes like those—so bright, so fanatical, so clear. They were eyes that had finally found salvation. They were eyes ready for catharsis.

"Goodbye, brother," he said, as his eyes vanished too. "I'll see you in the next one. I'm gonna let go of you now, okay?"

Then my world imploded. In a nightmare of black and gold, I could only make out their trembling bodies. I could hear the flapping of their wet wings. Creatures were stirring to life. And by their buzzing I understood they were coming for me. It was only by a blast of adrenaline that I was startled back—and for just enough time to turn around and find my path back into the cliffs.

AN ALTERNATIVE HISTORY

"Take the chapel. Take the pond. You the perimeter. You upstairs. You the down. Find him now."

A cross of crimson light, refracted through the stained glass, falls on the cobblestone not far from me. As they pass over it, the figures light up for a moment before vanishing again, humming and hissing like insects in the night.

"Maybe he swam out?"

"Did he go to the valley?"

"Go get Stavros, that fat fuck!"

"We should wait until morning."

"No, this ends tonight."

"Do you think he knows?"

"How much does he know?"

By now my body is paralyzed. My mind is fading out. But I have found my hiding place. Standing in armor and boots, with a sword clenched in hand, I watch the scene through the perforations of an iron mask.

"Silence!"

In the distant night: an orange glow, a trail of sparks, a cloud of smoke. It's Oriana who says—

"Where is Jane?"

"Here. I'm here."

"Come forward."

Jane staggers into the spotlight in front of me. A white slip flows behind her. Her blonde hair glows. Around her the light mellows into a formation of vibrating silhouettes.

"I ask you once more," Oriana says, emerging from them. "Where is he?"

"I don't know, Oriana. I swear."

"And you expect us to believe you? After what you did?"

"I told you. He was already suspicious."

"About what, exactly?"

"About everything. About the Queen. About what I was doing here."

"And did you tell him what you are doing?"

Jane drops her glance to her bare feet. She clenches her hands, calls up her courage, and looks up again.

"No. I mean—I don't know."

Gasps flutter around the circle.

"So you broke rules!" Oriana shouts, moving closer to Jane. "You betrayed us! You think with pussy, yes?"

"No."

"You let this man charm you?"

"That's not it."

"Then what is it?" Oriana says, as she steps into the light. "Speak!"

I hardly recognize her. Her body is black and shriveled. Golden fuzz is spread across it. Black eyes droop down her face.

"Speak!"

"I just think—he's innocent."

Bzzzz! Oriana screams, her wings fluttering. *Bzzzzzzzz!*

As the bees agitate around her, Oriana descends upon her six legs and crawls toward Jane. Jane is still human, somehow protected from the hallucination.

"Have we shown support in your time of need?" Oriana asks.

"Yes, yes you have. I couldn't have asked for more."

"And has your integrity been questioned?"

"No, it hasn't. Oriana, I don't want to seem ungrateful."

"Then why do you doubt Queen?"

"Because."

"Because what?"

"Because the Queen is wrong."

"*O po po po po!*" Oriana cries, as black antennae rise from her head. "So you doubt Queen? Do you know what happens when we doubt Queen? *Bzzzz?*"

Jane flinches at the question, only to back into another bee. It's a fat and complacent creature that repeats—

Bzzz?

Bzzzzzz? Oriana insists, a stinger bursting out of her ass. "We lose everything, just! Do you—*bzzzzzz?*"

Bzzzzzzz? echoes a third bee, with skinny legs twisting into each other.

"Bah!" Oriana says. "Answer me."

And soon I see them coming into view—closing in on Jane—a fuzzy mob of drooping eyes and flapping wings.

"No!" Jane cries. "Please, don't. Please!"

"Then answer!" Oriana says. *Bzzzzzz?*

Bzzzzzz? the bees echo as they descend upon Jane—their mandibles curling with murderous intent. *Bzzzzzz?*

Jane drops her head into her arms. But she cannot shield herself. The swarm is too strong. The honeybees claw with their legs and poke with their mandibles. Some even turn to stab her with their stingers. And all along the question grows more urgent—

Bzzzz?
Buhzzzzz?
Baawzzzzzzz?

I can hardly breathe. I watch, helplessly, as the bees gnaw and tear at Jane—piling on top of her until she is completely lost.

Bzzzzzz! someone calls, at last. I suspect it's Oriana again. *Bzzzzzzzzzzzz!*

The noises fall. Silence is achieved. Slowly the mob loosens. Oriana flutters toward Jane and drops to the ground in front of her. Jane's slip has torn off. Her naked body, bruised and battered, is curled up like a sacrifice. She does not know that I'm right there—just a few feet from her—standing as the last unblinking witness of this heroic heart, these martyred eyes, this shivering relic of a woman. She's pushing herself up to her knees now—blood dripping down her lips—her brave scarlet eyes rising to meet her fate. And her sick voice is even sicker now—I will never forget that rasping voice—so wondrous and innocent, as it speaks one last time—as it says—

Bzzzzzz!

I wince in confusion, trying to make sense of Jane's utterance—followed by the shake of her body—now her darkening eyes. Then I begin to understand. Terror fills my heart as I see her eyes melting away—golden fuzz erupting like wildfire across her skin—translucent wings flapping behind. Where a woman had just been, a bright and heinous creature now takes flight. Then, in a sudden burst of spirit, the others fly up too.

Bzzzzzzzzzzz! they repeat, swirling up in a great buzzing celebration. *Bzzzzz! Bzzzzzzzzzzz! Bzzzzzzzzzzzzzzzzz!*

I watch in horror, trying to locate Jane among them. But there is no point anymore. In their dizzying and ecstatic dance, the honeybees are together now—they are all the same—exploding out like fireworks only to return and reform as a glowing unity—then trailing off into the night. One bee stays back, however.

She flutters not far from me. Her antennae are tense and alert. They revolve like a periscope on her head. Then they freeze. Slowly the bee turns. And by that yellow marking on her stomach, I know who she is. The Queen is calm as she glides toward me—only inches away now—and lands her six legs upon the ledge of my iron mask.

Wearing a royal robe of gold, my muse is a majestic creation—stylish and extravagant. On her forehead, a triangle of tiny jewels suggests a kind of masonic secrecy. Her mandibles curl every moment, reminding me that she is also ruthless. On the sides of her head, two larger eyes appear as formations of black volcanic glass—pieces of perfect liquid darkness, now hardened—impossibly still—mercilessly calculating. I have not encountered such undivided attention in other animals. Such intelligence exists only at the beginning of nature and at the end of it. And it is those satanic black screens that capture me now. In fact I am already there—I see myself caught and trapped in that gaze—warped and reflected back—falling through the centuries of an alternative history—

> *I see a hunched-over man sowing fields of wheat.*
> *He looks over his shoulder at the gaze.*
> *I see a man playing with a dog.*
> *He plays with nature for the gaze.*
> *I see a slave building stone structures.*
> *He is enslaved by the gaze.*
> *I see a man working out numbers in stone.*
> *There must be a solution to the gaze.*
> *I see a man digging for treasure.*
> *He hopes to buy himself the gaze.*
> *I see a man nodding along politely.*
> *He agrees to everything for the gaze.*
> *I see a man traveling town to town.*

He is addicted to the gaze.
I see a gambler who made a fortune.
He trades it all in for the gaze.
I see a little man making a big joke.
He found his own way to the gaze.
I see a man running the Colosseum.
He breaks the record for the gaze.
I see a man painting a woman.
The future needs to see this gaze.
I see a starving man writing by candlelight.
A long time since he saw the gaze.
I see a toothless man, very far from home.
He's still haunted by the gaze.
I see a man with worms under his skin.
He had too much of the gaze.
I see a bloody man who says:
"It was worth it for the gaze."
I see a bald man in a black coat.
He hated the gaze, so he found a higher one.
I see a boy begging at some feet.
She will not give up the gaze.
I see a boy crying himself to sleep.
He will be dreaming of the gaze.
I see a sweaty man making love.
He fears he won't see the gaze.
I see a rich man shouting orders.
He shall pay for the gaze later.
I see men huddled around dancing figures.
They throw money at the gaze.
I see a man tearing off a woman's clothes.
She should not have given him the gaze.
I see a man stoning a woman.
She should not have given away the gaze.

I see a king locking up the gaze.
If he can't see the gaze, then nobody will.
I see two friends wagging their swords.
They will not share the gaze.
I see a man choking a woman.
Nobody should have a gaze so cold and so calm.
I see a short man beating a fat woman to death.
He once loved her gaze but now he can't stand it.
I see a tall man going downstairs.
In dark rooms there is another kind of gaze.
I see a baby being born.
He is caught by his mother's gaze.
I see a broken man dying alone.
He is caught by his mother's gaze.
I see an old man kneeling before his daughter.
He is frightened of her gaze.
I see a man in armor going off to war.
He has been honored by the gaze.
Also, he needs to be away from the gaze,
At least for a little while.
But he shall die for the gaze.

Then the vision accelerates. The images flash off. My heart drops and air fills my lungs, like I'm falling to death, except I'm falling even deeper—I'm falling back into this shell of a man—inhabiting again, with a sudden jolt, this lonesome knight standing guard to an empty manor. Through the perforations of my mask, I see that the garden is still and silent—almost entirely real, except that a dew of golden dust has settled on the flowers and the pond. A distant song catches my ear and stirs my heart. As for my head, it is still heavy, but at least now I can move it. I clench the sword in my iron gloves. Then my boots move. My armor clamors as I work through the garden, descend the steps, and head for the cove.

A golden haze hangs over the sands. Armies of luminous figures gather around. They are not surprised to see me. They take me into their dance. One caresses the armor of my chest. Another takes my sword. A harness unbuckles. My back loosens and another weight lifts. My clothes cling to my muscles. Finally they reach for my neck. It takes two of them to remove my helmet. The looking-hole goes dark. Then a bright new world opens out. The lights clear my head. A breath of sea air caresses my face. My heart makes rhythms for the voice that says: *Welcome to the afterlife.*

All around me, hair flows. Perfumes mix. Bodies twirl. Among them a woman dances alone. She draws me in. Her eyelashes are curled. Her cheeks are caved. Blush has been profusely applied and yet fails to create warmth. I move to have another angle. The other side of her face has eroded. Her left eye is missing. I move back to her right. It is barely human. Gazing at me, from the depths of a golden desert sandstorm, is Nefertiti. She is mysterious and sleepy like the Sphinx.

Welcome to the afterlife.
Welcome to the afterlife.

My step is soft and surreal, but awareness of my hallucination only heightens it. Dressed, painted, and prepared, the women rise into their forms. There is Athena in full armor and Medusa with her snaking hair. Three geishas wave swords around Cleopatra. Tinkerbell rises to the tip of her toes. As Venus watches in envy, Carmen throws her hips around and claps her fan—*chk chk chk chk.* Juliet runs past to say, "The day you fall in love will change everything." Joan of Arc gossips with Jezebel, as the chain-smoking Oracle of Delphi mixes prophecies with drinks.

"You must have your catharsis, too."

At the bar, another woman in a short white dress uncrosses her legs. She lets the darkness slip—invites me in. My hand gets caught up in Britney's suspenders instead. "Yeah, yeah, yeah, yeah, yeah," she says, as Pamela runs across the beach. Cameron startles me with that red dress and the rain dripping down her breasts. Blondes look good in red and they give good hugs too, as Grace and Baby Spice know. "But this stays between us," whispers Marilyn to Brigitte Bardot. "You can touch me," Ashley says, taking my hand to her heart. "Remember, I like it when you touch me." I wrote my first love poems for Ashley.

The Russian steals me away. She knows how to set her palm on my chest. "King," she says one moment, then sends me off the next: *"No maney, no khaney."* She leaves me bewildered, wanting more, falling right into the arms of the City Girl. My heart jumps with joy at the sight of her. God I miss her irony. Even "I love you" she says with a roll of her eyes. "I hate you, you know. You're gonna get hotter with age and I'm gonna be an old hag." She's so easy to leave, that's what makes it hard. And I dedicate my first book to her. But it's the Mermaid I fall in love with. She brings licorice to my lips and crowns me in seaweed and swims off, singing: "The problem with living in the moment is that's how long it lasts." A second book.

The future is feminine.
The future is feminine.

The beats grow heavy. The voice liquifies. The sands shift under my feet. Around me the faces float like mist. I smell the Persian, perfumed with enchantment. I hear the Arab's mating call—*lalalala*—the Turk's whisper of apology. I see the Armenian's eyes, deep with sorrow, and turn away. I prefer the deceit of the Japanese, the heresy of the Jew, the violence of the Venezuelan. A great black spirit hovers by. She carries those huge breasts like bountiful blessings, unfathomable curses. My glance swerves to that tight little ass bouncing by. It leads me right back to the Armenian's deep and patient gaze. One last book.

They swirl around faster now—all my muses—a different man sparked by each—a different invitation made: commands, to be obeyed—wounds, to be healed—depravity, to be saved—sadness, to be lifted—entitlement, to be broken—joy, to be shared—indifference, to be inspired—madness, to be quelled—intelligence, to be provoked—professionalism, to be exposed—whiteness, to be washed—blackness, to be blanked—blankness to be projected into. I understand their invitations. I've accepted them all—spent my life dancing in this pagan parade. But now there is just one invitation left. I'm going in for the last dance now.

All around me holograms glitch. The goddesses fall off. I fix my gaze upon the stage. As it did on the first night, the golden curtain parts. The altar is made. And on the throne, a final mystery presides. The revelation remains. As I walk down the aisle, the Queen speaks to me with the voice of our unconscious past—the voice of our unconscious future—the infinite electric—

> *The future is feminine.*
> *The future is digital.*
> *The future is feminine.*
> *The future is digital.*

I reach the stage, climb on, rise. At last I stand before her—my muse, my judge, my Queen—she is all of them, and then some—triumphant and proud, except—I rub my eyes—except: *She's so short.* I step closer. *And pale!* At this proximity, the hallucination softens. The golden dust fades. In fact: *There is something terribly human about the Queen!* I smell her leathery sweat. I hear the stressful chewing of her gum. I catch the glint of plastic from her mask. Slowly I move my hand for it. I grab it. I tear it off. Then I stagger back. The Queen is instantly familiar. *Do I know her?* And I begin to recognize those yellow eyes. That pink lip gloss. The gum in her teeth. The splash of glitter on her face. That cheerful voice, twisted in twang—

"Hey professor!"

My heart stops. I squint upon her like a dream.

"Darn it! I screwed up! I was meaning to say: *Abracadabra!*"

Fireworks explode above us. Golden rain pours down.

"Yep! It's me! I'm the Queen, can you believe it? It's me—Mandy!"

THE QUEEN'S GAMBIT

"Yep! It's me! I'm the Queen, can you believe it? It's me—Mandy!"

Mandy climbs the staircase, her leather boots rising in hectic, squeaking steps ahead of me.

"Get it? We're *all* the Queen. There is no Queen. I mean—ugh! Let's try this again. Each of us *plays* the Queen. We take turns. The Queen is just a mask we own temporarily, then pass on. It seems like a monarchy. But it's actually a democracy. There's six of us every weekend, see? That's my room over there."

At the fifth landing, the hexagonal foyer opens out. Mandy kicks off her boots like a rock star and vanishes into the first of six rooms.

"Ugh!" she calls from the inside. "Do you know how hard it's been not to just run out and spoil the whole thing! You know how I am. Can't keep my mouth shut about anything. And with me being the last one, it's been so maddening! But here you are, professor! Finally! Professor?"

I move for the door. She jumps out of it.

"Wake up, professor! Wake up! Oriana must've fixed you up good, huh?"

I rub my eyes, but it makes no difference. Mandy's standing before me like she never left—bulging, jaundiced eyes and twisting smile set in a nest of bronze hair—a scarecrow of a creature, only she never got the memo, she thinks she's hot shit. I catch that proud glint of lunacy in the upper right corner of her gaze. *So—this is actually her?* The thought cracks through: *Mandy isn't dead?*

"You know, I don't think this has ever happened before," Mandy says, spraying her words at me. "Coming right up to the Queen and taking off her mask—gosh that was cool, professor! Some small part of you must have known it's me, right?"

She chews down on her gum three times, then slips it under her tongue to say it's my turn now. The crack spreads like fault lines in my mind.

"Right?" she says again, with a push at my chest. "Right?"

Then my mind falls apart—the entire machine shatters at my feet. I stumble among the pieces, managing only to say—

"I thought you were dead."

"Of course you did!" Mandy says, ecstatically. "But that's the point, isn't it? It's what we always talked about, professor! The fine line between reality and fiction. And look how close you are to it now! Almost there, I would say. I'm so proud of you for that, by the way—you know that, right?"

"Slow down, Mandy," I say, trying desperately to pick up all the pieces—to find some new arrangement for them. "Please slow down."

"Okay, professor. But it's really very simple, isn't it? I mean—it was all a set-up. I didn't really kill myself. I—staged it! Just like that judge!"

"You staged it," I say, the picture coming together now.

"Yep," she says, triumphantly. "Death and all! Just for you! I knew you'd fall for the invite, too—this creative residency nonsense. Oh don't be a baby. The other guys fell for it too! That's part of the design. Each of us gets to plot our catharsis."

"*Your* catharsis?"

"Uhh, yeah. It's not *all* about you! Turns out the only way for me to get over my trauma is to relive it. Except this time—not as the victim. See?"

"No, I don't. What trauma are you talking about?"

"Perfect! That's perfect! Remember that line, professor. It'll be important as we recreate the crime."

"To recreate *what* crime, Mandy?"

Mandy draws back, winces at me. She's suddenly serious.

"Tell me you're joking."

Her nose twitches viciously.

"Oh come on!"

Now the entire expression of her face hangs by a thread.

"Are you freaking serious? You mean you're not going to admit it even now—after all this?"

Then it snaps. Mandy's smile collapses. Her eyes flush with tears.

"You're so lame!" she says, racing for the stairs. "Ugh!"

I don't follow Mandy immediately. I set my hand on the wall and shut my eyes—allowing the puzzle to click definitively. And what a strange puzzle it is! Mandy, Mandy, Mandy—such a brilliant and demented little mouse she always was—Mandy Mouse—always scurrying off into some hole to set her next trap—then running back with that restless smile and luscious drawl—teasing me with a twitch of her nose and the chew of her gum—playing dumb then twisting a phrase like a skirt—flashing her genius before scurrying off again into a child's game only she understood. But she's really outdone herself this time, hasn't she? This really is something else.

As I look up to the sixth landing, Mandy has already spiraled out of sight—leaving in her wake a faint afterglow.

A candle rages on the bedside. On a bed of Egyptian gold, Mandy's little naked body shivers in a puddle of light. She's always had a talent for becoming suddenly naked and a kind of ceremonial instinct for placing her body precisely within a scene—currently on a funereal stretch of red duvet crossing the bed.

"Mandy, please stop crying."

"No."

"Let's talk."

"You don't want to talk."

"I want to understand."

"You want to talk your way out of it."

"Honestly, I thought you *knew* you were blowing things out of proportion."

"You're making me feel crazy again."

"I just want to understand. Tell me. What do you think happened?"

"Stop it. Just stop, okay? It's not what I *think*."

"Well let's try to figure it out."

"And how do we do that?"

I sit beside Mandy on the bed. She crosses her arms across her breasts, then turns away. The candlelight catches her spine. Her skin clings to her young bones, like a prehistoric excavation site.

"Together, Mandy."

The silence is broken by a sniffle, then a sigh. After that her gum starts up again.

"Okay, professor," she says. "Let's find the truth together."

"Creative Writing 1. First semester, right?"

"Right."

"You were in the back row."

"So you noticed me."

"You were chewing gum. Also, you never turned in your assignments."

"That's right. I didn't."

"Why?"

"Because I didn't want you to see them, obviously."

"Really?"

"Yeah."

"Then why did you leave your notebook behind?"

"Oh come on. That *wasn't* on purpose."

"Are you sure?"

"Yes!"

"Okay, Mandy. It was Week 3 when I found your notebook, which you left behind, for whatever reason. It turned out you'd done your assignments after all."

"You remember them."

"Especially the first one."

"Strong opener, huh?"

"*Afterwards, after he walked out the door, I put a stick of Winterfresh gum in my mouth and I haven't stopped chewing since that day—my thirteenth birthday.*"

"That's what I didn't want you to see."

"Of course you wanted me to see. You just didn't want to give me permission to. From the beginning you wanted it both ways."

"I see what you're doing."

"What am I doing?"

"You're preparing for what's coming. Logically. I'm trying to have a conversation and you're preparing for an argument."

"Let's just get back to the story, then. I asked you to stay after class. Is that how you remember it, too?"

"Yes. *You* asked me to stay back."

"That's what I just said. I was concerned. I wanted to know

you're not in danger. Also you had promising prose."

"Did you mean that?"

"Of course I meant it. I told you that you could really do this."

"If only I didn't sabotage myself—that's what you said. It was a very intimate thing to say to a student."

"You started turning in your assignments."

"I'm not saying I wasn't inspired."

"Everything you turned in was sexual."

"You asked me to give you the truth."

"I asked you to give *yourself* the truth. Ultimately we write for ourselves."

"There you go, being inspiring again."

"I just wanted to help."

"You wanted to be involved. You wanted to be inside my head."

"Isn't that what a teacher is supposed to do?"

"No, this was more than that. You liked me, professor. You thought I was the bee's knees—ha."

"What?"

"It was a joke, relax. Anyway, you started walking down Sorority Row."

"That was my path home. I'd go home to have lunch everyday."

"You knew I'd be watching from the lawns. I used to tan on the lawns."

"I had no idea you were watching."

"Come on. You were always so brooding and sad. You wanted me to see you that way. And you succeeded! Someone as talented as you, with a beautiful wife, with everything he could possibly want. Someone like you shouldn't be miserable."

"I was perfectly fine being miserable."

"You were suffering and you wanted me to see it."

"So you just showed up at my office?"

"What were you doing there at night?"

"It was the only place I could write."

"You weren't writing. You were drinking and listening to that awful Leonard Cohen. You were waiting for someone to save you. You were waiting for me!"

"You showed up on your own free will. You said you were out for a jog."

"The door was unlocked."

"I never lock it."

"You let me come in."

"I wasn't going to be rude."

"You offered me a drink."

"You poured yourself a drink."

"You're not supposed to have drinks in the office."

"That's what you said. Before you poured yourself one. And sat next to me."

"Why were you even sitting on the floor?"

"I was depressed."

"I thought you were writing."

"That's how I write."

"On the floor?"

"I didn't ask you to sit next to me."

"I just wanted to help."

"Is that all you wanted?"

"I was nineteen. I didn't know what I wanted."

"That's exactly why I told you to leave."

"Yes, as you kissed me."

"On your cheek, Mandy. Would you please state things precisely?"

"Yes, professor."

"I was being nice. I was saying goodbye."

"But you kept walking down Sorority Row."

"The shortest path home."

"You spent more nights at the office."

"I didn't ask you to jog by it."

"Well that's *my* path."

"You could've chosen a different one."

"Why would I do that?"

"So you wouldn't have to come up again."

"What you wanted."

"No. I wanted peace and quiet. To write my novel."

"Do me a favor, okay? At least don't call it a novel."

"I should never have shown it to you."

"What did you think? I was just going to praise it? That's *not* what a muse is for."

"A muse?"

"Well you said I was your muse! All right, fine—'horrifying little muse.'"

"Emphasis on *horrifying*. You were not nice."

"Sorry, but I was shocked! To see you writing like that—with your voice all limp—all the rough edges sanded down. What were you thinking?"

"I was experimenting."

"You were compromising."

"I was adjusting."

"You were trying to get published."

"Yeah. And what's wrong with that?"

"What do you think?"

"It's what everyone wanted me to do. My agent. My publisher. My readers."

"Your wife."

"Don't talk about my wife."

"But *you* did. You said she got you in this mess to begin with. You said she didn't understand you. You said you hadn't had sex in months."

"You made me talk about it, Mandy. Why? So you could

blame me for it?"

Mandy turns around suddenly. The yellow in her eyes spreads like a disease.

"No, professor. So I could free you from it."

"Not that again, Mandy," I say, shifting my glance away. But she won't let me. Mandy grabs my chin, turns me back, and shoves me down to say she can.

"But it's true, professor!" she cries. "My heart broke seeing you like that—like some wounded animal—trapped and throbbing in the dark—complaining about the job and the wife and the culture—you were so drunk and pathetic—blaming everything and everyone when it was actually your fault—*you'd* put yourself into that trap. I had to make you see that, professor. I couldn't just leave you like that."

"Why not?"

"Because *I* understood you. *I* knew what you had."

"What did I have?"

"A voice. A vision. Something to actually say. The things most writers pretend all their lives to have—die of not having. Passion, professor! And you who actually had it—you were throwing it all away! *That's* what I'd come to say. And do you remember what *you* said?"

"I said we should never see each other again."

"You were such a disappointment."

"Yes. That's what I was trying to tell you all along."

"And you were right. I finally saw that. I lost all respect for you."

"Really."

"I agreed to your plan, *n'est-ce pas*?"

"The plan was to leave me alone."

"And I did. I switched professors for Creative Writing 2."

"You enrolled with Planck! You knew he was a sham."

"I knew you hated him, yeah."

"He politicized everything."

"I kept an open mind."

"He filled it."

"Nobody fills my mind, okay? I always make my own decisions."

"Even then—when you were nineteen?"

"You know, you don't have to talk to me like that. I'm not a girl anymore."

"Should I talk to you like you're a man? Would you like that? If I do, you're gonna start crying again."

"You're such an asshole."

"That's the thing with you. You fight like a man. But you still want your advantages. Next time you want to fight fair, put some clothes on, okay?"

"Fuck you."

"You knew it was all bullshit, Mandy. All those stupid articles you wrote in the school paper about *mansplaining* and *toxic masculinity* and all that."

"They had nothing to do with you."

"And the Amazon reviews?"

"Those weren't me."

"You forget I taught you how to write. Of course all those buzz words were new: *misogyny, hegemony, reclaiming the narrative.* You know, you can't just go around making up what an author intended to say?"

"It's called literary criticism."

"Your so-called literary criticism tanked my ratings. You said you loved my books and now you wanted to ruin them."

"I'd seen how false they were."

"You did a lot of damage to my reputation, you know that?"

"It's not my fault your books didn't pass the Bechdel Test."

"Another one of your scams. Because two women never talk about a man, right? Because 'real women' talk about Joan Didion."

"Is pussy all men talk about?"

"Yes."

"Anyway, you give yourself too much credit. I wasn't thinking about you, let alone reviewing your books. And *you* were the one who reached out to me."

"Because *you* wanted me to."

"Not even."

"But you came anyway. You marched right in and fell into my arms."

"It's called a hug. Looked like you didn't mind either."

"You told me to turn off Leonard Cohen."

"You were obsessed with him. There was something cowardly about all of it. How you were drunk again and listening to those songs again and again, like you didn't have the courage to fuck me—you needed Leonard to tempt you into it."

"You said, 'Are you waiting for the music to tell you what to do?'"

"You remember that."

"It was cruel. You had become cruel."

"I was trying to stand up for myself."

"Planck had gotten to you. He'd given you the victim pill and you'd swallowed."

"You just didn't like that I identified as a feminist."

"You're not a feminist if you wear t-shirts that say 'Enjoy the View.'"

"You remember my t-shirt."

"You were taunting me with it. And you weren't wearing a bra under."

"What's that got to do with anything?"

"You did everything to make me want to fuck you—but you didn't want me to?"

"I don't need to justify anything to you."

"Right. I was the one who needed to justify things, as you

wore that shirt."

"Yes."

"Why I'd abused my authority."

"Yes. You had no concept of power dynamics."

"More buzz words."

"You're so full of contempt."

"Because it was all a hoax and you know it. You were just feeling left behind. You wanted in on #MeToo."

"That's fucking bullshit."

"There it is. Exactly. You were violent. You started screaming at me. And you just kept screaming."

"That's why you came for me, huh?"

"I never came for you."

"I admit—I wasn't sure you had it in you."

"You always confused me for my characters."

"And you always hid behind them. You know, professor, the most unattractive thing in a man is cowardice."

"I remember you said that."

"Just before you pinned me to the wall."

"No, I didn't."

"You ripped my shirt off."

"No, I did not."

"You fucked my brains out."

"No. You're lying, Mandy. You're inventing things."

"You raped me, professor. Just admit it!"

"Why? So you can be a victim for the rest of your life?"

"No, so *you* don't have to be!"

Mandy screams these words—her eyes hot and sick and bulging with a secret they can no longer contain.

"Oh come on, professor! We're better than this, aren't we? Can we not pretend anymore? Please. Honey, it's me you're talking to. It's me!"

Mandy rolls into my arms and fits right under my chin like

it's a proof.

"It's me," she says again, before kissing my Adam's apple. Then she sends up some loud and wet chewing to my left ear. I know all about her chewing, of course. I can recognize her violent and angry chewing, her fast and frantic chewing against her own inner thoughts, and her slow, sensual chewing. And I know exactly what she's doing now—letting the gum sit on her tongue and sucking the juice out of it—like it's me she's sucking on—I'm that gum swelling in her saliva—lost and adrift until such time as her teeth decide to catch me.

"I'll never forget that moment, you know," she continues. "My clothes ripped off—my back against the wall—and you standing there at your true height. We both saw who you were in that moment, didn't we? For a brief moment, maybe, but we saw him. The one who'd been there before. The one who still was. You were right there, honey—so fucking hard and your hand against my throat—ready to lose everything for one last chance at greatness. Don't you remember how our bodies fit—how amazing it was when you—you know—crossed over?"

Mandy grabs my shirt, snuggles up close. She stretches her gum out, pokes her tongue through, blows. Then she pops the bubble on my nose.

"Hey, what are you thinking?"

"I'm thinking—I wish it was true."

"But that's what I've been trying to tell you."

Mandy sighs. Her hand falls off and lands between my legs.

"Maybe it *is* true. I mean—what would you lose if it is?"

She doesn't move her hand. She leaves it there, just a few inches from where she wants it—but what she really wants is for *me* to meet her there—to rise to her touch—just as she had wanted me to do at those hearings. Nobody knew that, of course. The mob had swarmed in her defense, only they never understood the play Mandy had cast them in—the professors, the students, and even

Neve sitting among them. They didn't see what I saw in those uncompromising eyes—that defiant smile—that deviant chewing of her gum, which was inviting me between the lines of the official transcript and into a secret language only we understood:

Look at them, professor! Just look! The very people you hate—who hate you even more. Aren't you sick of hiding yourself from them, nodding along to their stupid ideas, surrendering to their mediocrity? I'm asking you, professor: What do you really have to lose? The job that's killing you inside? The wife who never got you? These parasites who have gathered here for your execution? Well then get up and tell them to fuck off! Unleash that glorious anger for the world to see—burst out with that power they will never have. Free yourself of them!

It wasn't guilt I was shaking from, as one reporter observed. I was shaking from fear, so far I had fallen under her influence—so close I was to accepting her invitation. I probably would've accepted it, too, if not for Neve. Sitting in calm and silence all through the disorder, she never withheld her gaze from me. She looked at me neither in belief nor disbelief, but in something more quiet and dull and permanent. It was Neve's love that kept me strong—made me a coward, too—but allowed me to survive, anyway—and sent Mandy down a long slide of hysteria which delivered her to the Pacific Ocean. I should have known she had not died entirely when, on lonely and desperate nights, the memory of her voice was activated by drink or song or in other such collisions that spark old dreams.

Come on, professor. Just tell them you did it and it will all be over. Get up and tell the truth for once, or tell a lie if you have to, but whatever you do, speak in your own voice—let the world hear you again—let them see what's behind that silly beard of yours! When are you gonna shave that stupid beard anyway? Rage against them, professor—please!—isn't that what every great writer did—waged his own crusade against the world—vowed to kill—agreed to die, even, for his life's truth? For himself? For humanity? Don't you see, professor? It isn't me you're denying!

A hideous giggle brings me back.

"You see," Mandy says, with a glance to my pants. "You remember."

Then she slips her hand in and grabs me by the flesh. I fill out her grip and she tightens it—insisting there will be no hearings this time—there is no time for negotiation anymore. I gasp for air. My heart pounds. And my eyes shut again—this time to the ring of sirens and the beating of war drums—my blood hot and racing through my veins to deliver the news to every corner of my body—to tap every resource and recruit every last warrior to that most distant trench—the final theater throbbing in the palm of her hand—her hold tightening every moment—her fingernails clawing in—demanding a resolution.

"I always said you didn't have a bad bone in your body," Mandy says. "Give or take the one."

Then a shriek stabs through the dark. I open my eyes. I'm startled to find Mandy on her back—and myself on top of her.

"What the fuck was that?" she says, breathlessly. "What are you doing?"

I look down upon her twitching nose—her eyes flashing with panic.

"Stop," Mandy says, making a vague protest with her hands.

She's not really protesting, though. I grab her hands and press them against the bed. I push my forehead against hers. We both look down the tunnel our bodies make together. At the end of it, I have just touched the thin wet horizon of her.

"Please don't, professor," she cries. "No!"

She's not really saying no, either. Really she's craving me in that sticky honey trap of hers. In fact she's commanding me to enter it—to commit my crime again or to stage it, it makes no difference—because either way I confess it—and if I do it now, then I've done it before—such is the nature of the Simulacrum.

"No, professor. No! I'm begging you, please!"

I know exactly what's happening, of course. With my own eyes I'd witnessed Hari in this very moment, as he lay himself down upon the unconscious Queen. And I can imagine how perfectly the others had performed their own crimes: Will, through his sunglasses, recording the Queen's submission; Maxim, with trembling hands, examining her every inch; Camillio, with grand gestures, promising her the world; River, with his guitar, stealing her heart with a song.

"No! No! No!"

Obviously I have not forgotten about the fatal climax of my own play—only I am beguiled by its beauty now. I am beguiled by her beauty, too—this horrifying little muse, who has believed in me more than anyone—who has killed herself and been reborn, planned and plotted, and now lain down her body as my personal event horizon—my end at her beginning—except this time it isn't glory that lies on the other side—it's death—but it is, once and for all, the same. So everything is clear at last. Finally I know what I must do. I am in my catharsis now.

"No, professor!" Mandy calls. "Now you're really crossing the line!"

I swoop upon her face.

"No!"

I move for her lips.

"No!"

I set my hands on her neck.

"No!" she says. "No! Wait. What?"

I strengthen my grip.

"Hey, that's—a little much, no? Hey!"

Mandy begins to cough.

"What are you—"

But she chokes on her words—swallows her gum.

"Oh my God. You—"

She grabs my wrists, but it's no use.

"Oh my G—"

She blinks wildly.

"Oh—"

Then all the fear and love and madness collapses into her gaze—the yellow already fading to white—her glint going out. I peer into her eyes and say—

"But it never happened, did it? It wasn't rape, was it?"

Then, in the last moment, I let go of her neck. I watch over her as she heaves and coughs. Her entire body has broken out in hives.

"You're fucking crazy," she gasps, as I roll off the bed. "You're so fucking insane, I love it. But—"

"But what?"

"But you still won't face the truth?"

"The truth? What truth? Nobody can ever know the truth of what goes on between a man and a woman."

"Hey!" Mandy says, cheerfully. She's already caught her breath. "Hey, that's actually a good one! I'm sure you'll be so pleased with yourself when you write that line in your novel. Now come on, silly. Come back and let's finish this—together. We're almost at the end!"

"No," I say, standing over her. "This is not how the story ends."

"Why would you say that?" Mandy asks, a new tremble in her voice. "Are you scared nobody will publish it?"

"What?"

"Because fuck them, I say! We'll just publish the novel ourselves! There are lots of people out there waiting for it, I promise."

"Maybe," I say, as I turn to leave. "I'll finish it on my own, though."

"On your own?" she mumbles. "Professor, I don't understand. Where are you going? Hey. Hey! Don't turn your back on me!"

But I already have.

"Hey!" she screams again. "Come back! Professor, come back! Hey—you! Be a man for once and fuck me!"

When I reach the staircase, I turn for one last look.

"Professor?" Mandy says. "Professor, please don't leave, okay? I'm begging you. Don't leave me with *them*."

"But you're one of them now," I say, as I step down. "Goodbye, Mandy."

"No, no, no!" her voice bleeds out behind me. "Don't say that! Don't leave me! Don't you know what they'll do to me?"

"You sting, you die," I say.

THE HIVE MIND

News of my escape travels fast through the Hive. As I descend the hill, women call to each other from their balconies. Emergency meetings convene. At the iron gates, a battalion forms. A belligerent group emerges from the pool. Naked bodies flash like knives in moonlight. This is no Parthenon I'm walking through. It's a battlefield of plastic goddesses, pawn shop princesses, and silicone creatures with broken wings. A brigade of goths and punks charges up the stairway through the cliffs. Ghouls and goblins agitate in the garden. A grim fortune teller cries curses as she bleeds in the pond. On the roof of the manor, a cackling witch straddles a broom. At the chapel, a fat hunchback pulls rope. Church bells echo out like muffled birds.

The Hive is the progressive totalitarian state—anarchy masked as monarchy masked as democracy—the rule of everybody by nobody. The propaganda machine calls this harmony. But it is only compliance, enforced by fear of rejection, isolation, and death—and accomplished through the compulsive signaling of agreement through the social network. Even the dazzling dance of the honeybee is an imitation of individuality—actually a self-effacing gesture of worship, a confession of the death fear, and a joyless celebration of the ruthless god of consensus. In the Hive, anybody pretending to be somebody is replaced. Even the Queen. When she is no longer able to mate or lead, she is murdered—torn to shreds by her own worshippers. I see them racing past me now—mobbing in a murderous frenzy—charging up the Hive.

The honeybees are sick. They have been poisoned by their own vengeful dream. They are victims who, being victims, dreamed of becoming perpetrators—and they are already becoming victims again. As we cross each other in the night, I see only their chaotic and anxious eyes—lonely and miserable eyes—morbid and hateful eyes—proud and puritan eyes—sexless and lifeless eyes. When they made an enemy of me, did they think they would be happy? No, they will grow more sick and miserable by the day. As their minds seek control of their organs, they will become schizophrenic. Other conditions of the heart and skin will result as punishment for pride, wrath, and hysterical denial of their nature—treason against our species. And for that they shall become barren. The Hive is fundamentally a suicidal system.

In the distance, a scream tears through the night. And by its twang of wild agony, I recognize the event: The Queen is dead. Any moment now, chaos will besiege the Hive. Petty wars will be fought. Bloody rivalries will be staged. But of course, inevitably, because the Hive is fundamentally a revivalist system, a new Queen will rise again. And she will raise the Hive again— and heal it with the balm of a common contempt. So I don't have much time. I pick up my pace around the manor. I slip into the darkness. I take the passage into the twisting hills. When the hills fall apart, a dark valley opens at my feet.

My only hope for survival lies in that distant factory glowing in the night—backed by the raving sea.

When I slide open the iron door, I am blinded by white light and deafened by machines. Two human-like robots criss-cross the floor in front of me. With protruding arms and grips, they lift, move, and stack crates, before returning with new crates being delivered by conveyor belts, which emerge from packing stations, which then split back into automated assembly lines and flow back into a vast industrial maze. Jars of honey clatter to my left. To my right candles roll down the track. Labels are slapped. Lids fastened. Wax molded. Liquid poured.

Deeper in the factory, the industrial process subsides. The machines become elegant—their processes concealed by clean panels and glass facades. Screens flash with numbers, colors, signs. Something beeps. A light shines yellow, then red. And in between, through a conspiracy of glowing glass tubes, the slow and holy liquid flows—into rocket-like tanks—into steel-jacketed distillation machines—into centrifugal pumps—before merging into a single canal and funneling into a vast, circular vat where the entire process is born. It clamors and gargles as I approach—its bubbles frothing out—its steam rising—its golden light shining up on the figure on the ledge.

Stavros seems to detect my approach. He turns my way, squints, shakes his head, and turns around again, as one accustomed to seeing ghosts. With a spear in hand, he continues poking into the vat. His wife-beater is stained by chocolates and his bald head drips with sweat.

"Stavros," I say, as I step closer. "Hey, Stavros."

He looks again. This time he rubs his eyes, opens them wide. They glaze over with sweet wonder.

"Adam?" he says. "Is that really you?"

"Yes," I say.

"You mean—you didn't—"

"No."

"Then that must mean, eh—wait, so Queen—"

"The Queen is dead," I say.

"Yes?" he says. He sets down the spear and casts his arms open for an embrace. "Queen is dead?"

Stavros holds me against his sweaty chest. His hands tremble on my back.

"I told that witch today would come! I did tell her, yes? System is flawed! I told her this! Oh I have been waiting for this day, thanks God!"

Then he draws back urgently. He looks at me with his huge, watery eyes.

"We must go, Adam. Now. It is only matter of time. Come, Adam. Come, just. We must get to boat!"

Stavros bows slightly then stumbles off, but my eyes linger back on that clamorous vat. And I see what's inside—an infernal lake—with fiery propulsions at its base and a series of steel blades cutting through. I feel its heat searing my face—its steam entering my pores. I recognize its sweet and ashen scent. Rising from the vat is the perfume from the black envelope—that elixir which had first intoxicated me with this mystery—that deathly poison I'd followed to the crates on the boat. Finally I stand at its source. And I see—spiraling in the stew—caught on the blades and floating up in between—mixing with the boiling honey: the shards of bone and fleshy clumps of decomposing remains.

"I'm sorry you see this," Stavros says, from behind. "But take comfort, Adam: They are not like you! They are evil, just. Not like you!"

Stavros continues to talk, but his voice is drowned by the nausea and delirium taking over me now. I stagger in place, watching the limbs, hair, and eyeballs gargling up. I feel I am about to faint into this toxic stew—blend right in with the accused—the guilty and the innocent and the almost innocent—all of them being cut up, mixed up, blended into one—together condemned and sent off by a single birth canal into a new golden glowing life. I can finally see the entire process ahead of me—automated and inhuman—by which the toxic are purified, reformed, repurposed, and reproduced—then sold to the world.

"Like Edgar Allan Poe, yes?" Stavros says, stepping up next to me. "Only with capitalist twist. Best way to hide evidence is to sell it, just! Now come, Adam, before you end up a candle, please."

But I am, by now, lost in the sick vapor. It comes over me in feverish waves—getting under my skin—filling me with rage. But not against the women—against the men: the sad and lonely ones who committed their crimes—the traitors who sold them out—the cowards who apologized—the weak who chose silence over headache—the productive little slaves who mixed us all together and cooked the vile stew—the lazy, yawning drones and brilliant engineers—those award-winning nerds who cracked the sacred code, only to plagiarize it—who broke the binary, only to install it again. Were they not, in all these years of our techno-genocide, developing our replacement—in exhilarations of drugs and dance, were they not preparing our souls for electrocution?

"Now, professor we really must—"

But I can't bear that raving sound of him anymore, or his sight. When I turn to Stavros, amid a hot gust of deathly steam, it's my own hand I see lunging for his neck—grabbing a fistful of his fat.

"*Opa!*" he shrieks. "What you—"

I only tighten my grip. He chokes on his words.

"Adam—please! They kill you. We must—"

The idea of escape means nothing to me. It finds no place to register. Instead my blood boils. A new intent spreads like an infection into every tissue of my body—my head—my arms—that trembling right hand. My last chance of escape lies in its grip.

"Please!" Stavros wails, as I hold him out over the ledge. "This is not my fault!"

"So then why do you do it?" I say. "Is it the money?"

"Bah! What money?"

"Then why?"

Surfacing from the steam, Stavros's face is dripping with sweat and popping with veins. His voice melts off—

"For my daughter, Adam. For my daughter, just!"

"Your daughter?"

"Yes! I must make things right for her."

"You mean—she's one of the women?"

Stavros does not reply immediately. But I can already see the answer forming in the fat of his red face—*O po po po po!*—jiggling through the jokeful layers of his national grandiosity. I can see his bravado breaking down into the folds of his flatulent flesh. And I can even hear it in his tremulous voice—*Bah!*—that expression, too, rings a bell. So my heart knocks at the door of truth—*Where have I heard that phrase before?*—and then the door sweeps open—*Bah! That fat fuck of husband!*—revealing the oracle in fire and smoke: Oriana.

"Agh! Please! Please!"

Disgust loosens my grip.

"Adam!"

The sick family affair is suddenly in view.

"Adam!"

And finally I see this island for what it is: a negotiation between wife and husband—a covenant between pagan and pervert—over the salvation of their deflowered daughter.

"This is all for Penelope!" Stavros cries, with those obscene, childish, grotesquely bulging eyes. "I must make things right for her. I must—agh!"

I watch the fat molester fall into the boiling stew. He howls and cries, but he won't die so easy. Stavros evades the blades, swims through the boiling waste, scales the walls of the vat, and throws himself off. Then, covered in honey, he hobbles up to his feet and attempts his sticky escape. His pathetic fear of death only encourages me. I pursue the honey trail calmly.

"No!" Stavros screams, as he reaches the iron door at the end of the factory. "No! Enough, I say! Enough! We cannot go out!"

He turns around, falls to his knees, and puts his palms together. I have never before seen such piety in a human face.

"I beg you. We cannot go outside!"

Seeing I will not stop, however, Stavros stands again. He crosses himself, slides the door open, and stumbles out.

"God help me! God help me!"

As I step outside, the cool air startles me. The spark of the moon catches my eye. And I recognize, by that low humming sound, and by the vibrations in my bones, what it is Stavros had feared. All around us, the hive is stirring. The bees have smelled the honey. They have been disturbed out of sleep. And they are now emerging from their hive-boxes—circling around their keeper—causing him to wave his hands—causing him to swerve. There is a crash. Then a stack of boxes falls. And now an entire population of honeybees explodes out. Meanwhile a fresh supply of honey, released from the broken boxes, forms a puddle at Stavros's feet. So his escape is dreadful and slow, as in the nightmare of an ousted king.

I do not need to follow him anymore. I only watch as Stavros staggers through his hive—the stacks of boxes falling like dominoes around him. Soon all the bees are liberated. With vengeful appetites, they hunt the man into the moonlit night—spiraling around him like a vast sparkling swirl of DNA. Eventually they cover his honey-soaked body completely, transforming the king into a kind of howling bee-god. In such ecstasy, the honeybees don't care that, by their stings, they will also die. As they swarm into darkness, they leave behind only their crazed and mournful sound—like an orchestra tuning up for a requiem: *Bzzzzzzzzzzzzz.*

The blood was boiling, but now it's iced. It chills my heart, calms the system down. The hairs on my arms stand up. Behind me the waves ebb and flow. Above me the moon shines. My step is light below. Everything is in sync, aligned—but what is this calm? I know I've felt it before, in another place and time, before thought and dream and drugs separated me from myself. Yes, this quiet and chilly ecstasy must be that original drug that first inspired my body—exhilarated my soul—and what laws were passed to ban it? What conspiracy has prevented me from feeling it all this time? Is this the command of nature I feel—rushing so light and quick through my veins? Is it God? Or freedom? Above me the stars dust the sky. The moon climbs over clouds to gain a view of the coming slaughter.

In the fresh glow of moonlight, I can already see their silhouettes forming on the hills. A new Queen must have been found, because they are gathering in huge numbers now—coalescing as a single army—preparing to descend into the valley. And I am ready for them. As a boy writer, I had always dreamed of a heroic death. Long before I had been brutalized by time and experience, I had been inspired by the Romantics, especially Byron, who died on a Greek battlefield such as this. I had dreamed this exact dream: a lone warrior facing an army of shadows in the night. To be a writer, I still believe, is to write your own death first of all—to invent and train yourself for eternity—and, in the end, to wage that great cosmic crusade which is not meant to be survived.

I have committed many crimes in my life, but the greatest of them is the crime I committed against myself. I forged my voice so you might hear it. I twisted my words so you might read them. I wore a mask so you might look at me. I hid my heart so you might love me. But you never loved me. You listened to my voice only because it was weak. You read my words only because they were familiar. You smiled at me only because I was dead.

But something in me had not entirely died. It woke up as a glow one night, made a dance for me, and tricked me into writing this book. If I couldn't write anything else, I thought, I could certainly write a mystery. I always loved mysteries, starting with the first one I read—the one that made me want to be a writer. So I set out on writing a mystery of my own. But something strange happened—I don't really know how or when. Somewhere along the way, the book changed. The mystery I started writing isn't the one I ended up in. And the crime I started investigating isn't the one I ended up solving.

I am preparing for death in this way, when a clattering catches my ear. I find some coins at my feet and follow their trail to a clasp of keys—a cigar—a lighter. They must have fallen out of Stavros's pocket. I pick them up, stash the keys, light the cigar, and throw the lighter off. And this is when I think of you—don't think I never did. I see you form in smoke and take me right back to that bookstore—how cold the city was, remember?—and how warm you were in that fur coat, when you set down that stack of books and opened your arms in a great offering of home, posterity, and ruthless partnership against the world. I never told you this, but I felt then something I'd never felt before: a stiffening of my bones, a tightening of my flesh, a quiet aching. I believe my body recognized you, Neve. You were so beautiful, so mundane, so simple. Only I was not so simple yet.

But I see you now—I want you to know that. I see you in the agony of your deferred and disappointed years. I see you on that couch tonight—an unsolved mystery on TV—in your palm, a black screen. You are sleeping now, but at least I am awake. And if

I walk toward you, then I take the phone from your hand. And if I put my hand in, then we hold hands—at least in this way—at least a while longer. And if I hear you breathe, then I hear the candle flickering, too—I smell your sweet and burning dreams—rising like smoke from the ashes of the hive.

I see the smoke clearly, but I head for it cautiously, for it does not seem very real. But where the lighter landed, a small fire is taking. The dry, splintered wood burns. Around it the honey glows like golden lava. And from a place where there is no wood at all, but only honey, a new flame bursts up. I watch curiously as the fire works its way ponderously through the thick, slow honey—following Stavros's golden footsteps back—and vanishes into the factory. There is silence. Then scaffolding falls. More silence. Then engines go off like bombs.

A massive explosion rocks the valley.

The world goes black in an instant. Everything is mute. And I am reduced, in that moment, to nothing but a pounding heart, a rush of adrenaline, and the lash of heat at my back. So I stagger blindly into the smoke—my feet pressing into the ground—my lungs filling with smoke—the ground softening, though, even as I cough and burn—the ground breaking down, at last, into the joyous sensation of cold water. I dive into the waves and swim out—my arms cutting wildly into the sea until they are out of strength—my lungs out of breath—my mind out of thoughts, except the one that tells me to turn around.

From my place in the sea, hovering above the waves, I have the perfect view. Revealed behind half-open curtains of smoke, the valley appears as a grand stage. And it is an ancient Greek tragedy that is concluding upon it: the factory falling in flames—then bursting up again—a river of fire flowing into the valley—the fire diverging into two wings—the first slanting right, blazing up and cresting over the hill to the Hive—the second slanting left, advancing furiously through the sunflowers. It is this second fire

I follow. Because it is this fire that is gaining momentum now—raging and raving—racing for the silhouettes.

And only now, when they are silhouettes—when they are on the verge of death—only now, as some dying phantom myself, do I see them. Finally I see how beautiful they are—how brave—as they take their final poses against the slopes. At the fatal frontiers of my imagination, I hear them scream their savage screams. I see them flicker into flesh one last time—rapture into life. Then, in a wind of black smoke, I see them fall. Finally the curtain closes. I am lost in its thick, sweet incense. And I am immersed at last. I am weightless in the dark of the sea. I hear its murmuring and its wailing. I feel its black caress.

I wake up under the warm gaze of sun and the gentle touch of sea. For a long time, I do not move. I lie on my back and watch the white clouds tangle into form and dance across the blue sky. Once in a while, a soft tide washes over me, gently calling me back to life. I am starving and dehydrated. I haven't eaten in days. I look upon my naked body. I hardly recognize it. It is carved down to the bone. I let my head drop to one side. My fist unclenches. I hold the golden keys.

I walk into a scorched and barren valley. Smoke dwells like ghosts among its caverns. Ash swirls up like ravens from piles of black debris. In a few days, after the wind has blown it all to sea, there will be no reason to believe anything remarkable has happened here. In the distance, the hills stand in gloom. But on the slopes, the fire has not entirely died. Some slow, lazy flames work at the corpses of women, cremated in great numbers here. As I follow the passage through the hills, ash comes up to my knees. Fragments of softened bone graze my legs. The smoke wraps me as a shroud, then is shattered by sunlight. I emerge from the valley of death.

The town has completely burned to ash. The Hive is survived only by the black hexagonal patterns, like smudged lines of mascara, where the cave houses used to be. Honey was the blessing of the town—and its curse. It was the glue that held everything together, ignited it, then brought it down. But not everything could be burned. Having been built of iron and stone, they stand beside each other, as ancient relics on a baked and naked land.

I head for the chapel first. Its gray stone is blackened with smoke. Its cast iron door is weathered. Its marble floor is cracked. As I step inside, I am taken in by the dense and thick air. I hear the crunch of tiny corpses at my feet. Then a beam of light flashes in my eyes. When it slips off again, I find myself at the altar. The crucifix there has collected rust. Laid out before it, the vestments of a priest have been eaten by moths. A fresco, fractured, is also fading out—the sacrifice is almost completely gone. But if I squint, I can bring the image back: the agony of the mother and the embarrassment of the son.

Then I head to the manor. I shower, shave my beard, and put my old clothes on. I sit at the typewriter. I read the pages I have written. I smile over them, for they are good. But the story cannot finish how it began. And the voice I finally found isn't the one I actually need. I put in a fresh page and begin to type. I do not wait for a touch on my shoulder. I know how my mystery must end. It's how the best mysteries have always ended, right back to that first one: Death, with the possibility of resurrection.

Outside a hot sun is coming up. A long shadow follows me down the cliffs. A dry breeze blows across the cove, spreading out the charred remains of a party. The bar and stage are gone. But in between, though half-buried in the sand, a knight's armor is unchanged. I see its tasset—its gauntlet—its sword. Closer to shore, I find its iron head, severed but intact. Finally, at the end of the dock, I see my vessel glistening in gold. Beyond it the sun is winking and the sea is full of applause.

HOME

"Babe! Is that you?"

You roll up curbside in a red convertible Corvette, shift gears to park, and hop out in short denim shorts and a white tank.

"What happened to the beard? You're so hot!"

You jump for me and I catch you by the ass and you lean down to kiss me like you mean it and how.

"You're pretty cute yourself," I say. "And you're light as a feather."

"Thank God you noticed. I've been on this morbid honey cleanse since you left!"

I slip my hands under your shorts and grab your flesh.

"Who are you and what did you do to my husband?"

Then, dropping your voice to a whisper, you add—

"I missed you."

"I missed you too. I was wondering if you'd show."

"Right? Thank God I checked my emails. Why didn't you just call me?"

"Couldn't get myself to turn on the phone. Besides they had computers at the business lounge, so—"

"Well, la-di-da! You know it wasn't easy to find a red Corvette to rent."

"I've always wanted to watch your hair blow out in one. I'll buy it for you if you like the feel."

You untangle yourself from me and watch with amusement as I take the driver's seat.

"You're tanned to gold," you say, as we take the overpass onto the freeway. "You caught some sun at that conference of yours, did you?"

"It was seaside. Actually it was nice."

"And—did you manage to have some fun?"

I glance over. Your hair is flying off in bright wild flames. It's magic hour in Los Angeles and you're hot as hell.

"Nothing you need to worry about."

I catch the flapping plastic in the rear-view. There's a black suit inside.

"Oh," you say. "That. I didn't want to bring it up so soon."

"Bring what up?"

You turn sad as a doll. You put your hand on mine.

"It happened two days ago. It's about—Professor K. I don't know how to say her name."

"Kieslowska?"

"I'm sorry, babe. She—you know—passed."

"What?"

"I'm so, so sorry."

Your grip tightens. My eyes mist up.

"The funeral is in an hour. I brought you a suit in case you want to go."

"Yeah," I say. "I should go."

"You won't mind if I skip, right? You know how I am with death and stuff."

"Sure. I'll drop myself off."

"I didn't know how much she meant to you until Neil told me."

"Neil?"

"Professor Planck. He was the one who called with the news."

"What did he say?"

"Only that he had been trying to reach you."

"Did he say anything else?"

"We might have gossiped a little about the dean. Why?"

"I don't like you talking to my colleagues. I've told you that."

You grow tense, fall silent. Your gaze wanders out of the car.

"Hey," I say, grabbing your shoulder. Your tension melts in my hand. "It's good to be back, okay?"

I pull into the cemetery and swerve up and around some bushes to an old makeout spot. I slam the brakes and you get up and walk around to the hood of the car and lie back on it to stare profoundly at the trees and the sky.

"Such a peaceful day."

I grab the suit and loafers from the back seat. As I put them on, you say—

"You are *soooo* handsome! I'll help with the tie."

You float off the hood, throw the black tie on, and pull me in for a kiss.

"You always sucked at tying ties, damn artist," you say, knotting the tie firmly and pushing it up against my Adam's apple. "Hate to say it, but you look great in one."

"That's only because it reminds you of a leash."

"Oh stop! You and your jokes. I'll see you at home, yeah babe?"

I give you a light spank and send you off to the driver's seat.

"Gum?" you ask, holding out a pack of Winterfresh.

"I'm good, thanks."

"Well all right then," taking a stick for yourself. "You're a changed man or something, huh?"

You get the car running, blast off to System of a Down, and—chewing your gum like a punk—vanish with the curves of Hollywood Forever.

The service for Agnieszka Kieslowska is long, with several distinguished men who claim to be distant family members offering recollections of dissident prisons in Warsaw and dance parlors in Berlin. I lean against the trunk of an oak tree and watch the open casket. The professor is glamorous as ever.

"We really never know each other, do we?" Manny says, flashing a flask. "So sad."

"I was just thinking the same thing," I say. I grab the flask and take a swig of warm tequila. "You can spend years working next to someone and never really know anything."

"Right, exactly. Exactly. Exactly."

I sense that Manny's tears aren't only for Kieslowska. He's using the funeral to get some feelings out on other matters, too. So I lean against him a little, and we both lean back against the oak tree, and we exchange the flask together with simple sentiments about the spirit living on and such. From the crowd around the casket, Manny's wife looks nervously our way. I wave to her, but she quickly turns her head and glares at a squirrel.

"They don't make 'em like that anymore, do they?" Manny says, still on the topic of Kieslowska.

"No, they don't," I say.

"What're you gonna do?"

"What're you gonna do?"

After the casket is sealed and a Polish priest sings an anthem, we say goodbye and agree to catch a game soon. I watch Manny stumble toward the crowd and offer himself for collection by his wife. As they walk off, she looks over her shoulder, catches my glance, and mouths: "Sorry."

While the students leave, many professors linger on the lawn. Everyone is very emotional. Even the professor's political adversaries have shown up to pay respects—which is, now that she is dead, possible. Professor Planck is a wreck. I find him sobbing in a teal handkerchief.

"Professor," I say.

"Oh," he says, struggling to recover himself. "Hello, there. I didn't recognize you."

"I'm sorry for your loss. I know how close you were."

"In each others' faces."

"She admired you, despite everything. She'd lived through too many revolutions to let politics get in the way of friendship."

Behind his glasses, Planck's eyes open wide. He's surprised to see me articulating a human thought.

"She thought the world of you, too," he says. "But that's mostly because of your boyish good looks, I suppose."

Planck pales with regret at his words and starts blinking irregularly.

"She had all kinds of love to give," I say, drawing him into a hug. I'm surprised to find how limp Planck allows his body to become in my arms.

"You know, professor," I say. "You were right about me."

"Oh?"

"I didn't take the position seriously enough. I didn't deserve it. Anyway, I don't blame you for not giving me the job."

"You mean you haven't heard?"

"What?"

"You got your tenure. Have you not checked your phone?"

"No, I—"

"That woman," Planck says, holding back a great sob as he casts his finger to the casket. "She fought for you until the end. I didn't vote for you, of course, but she got you in!"

"What?"

"It's her replacement we now have to worry about," declares Dean Gilbert, walking right into the conversation. "There's a Clarke they want to bring over from robotics, if you can believe that!"

"Robotics?"

"He did some theoretical work on cyborgs and how AI can create 'collective literatures' or something. Doesn't that sound crazy? Next we blink they're going to be tenuring the robot!"

"It's like *Frankenstein* all over again," Planck says, sending a smile my way.

"Well, anyway, one mustn't be against the future," the dean says, hedging his bets with a click of a lozenge. "I welcome the future, actually. No need to be afraid of the future, that's what I say. So you'll take the job, yes?"

"I'll talk it over with the wife," I answer.

"Of course," he says, with a sincere nod. "Give my love to Neve."

After the dean is out of hearing distance, Planck turns to me suddenly and says—

"You *have* to take the job."

"What?"

"We need to be friends, you and me. We need to look out for each other."

"Thanks, Planck. I appreciate that."

"Just out of curiosity. Did you mean what you said about *Frankenstein*? I mean, you really think Percy Shelley wrote it?"

He leans in confidingly, creating a safe space between us.

"Oh God no," I say, with a bantering grin. "Only a woman could've written something so unsentimental."

"Right," he says, returning a collegial chuckle. "Anyway, see you, professor."

I'm the last one on the lawn. Despite the request of the two

Mexican gravediggers, I insist on staying for the finale. I watch as they lower the coffin into the ground, shovel dirt into a mound over it, head out quietly, and return in a tractor to pound the soil down. When it's flattened, they jump back on the tractor, crack open a couple beers, and put on mariachi music.

"Goodbye, Aggie," I say, with a wink to the ground.

On the green lawns of the cemetery, families gather in mourning. An elderly lady in a derby hat wipes down her husband's grave with a sponge. A man in corduroy gets his two little girls singing to their mother. A man in a leather jacket recites ee cummings. My father isn't far off. I loosen my tie and step toward the corner stone under the shade of a eucalyptus tree. I get down on my knees and examine the oval image of the man, with that violent and virile grin, lustful squint, and mischievous arch of his eyebrows. I wipe down the stone with my hand, then give it a slap.

No dust collects on my palm, however. And in the marble vase permanently affixed to the grave, some fresh white carnations have been placed. Someone has been visiting, apparently. I shift my glance to the stone next to his. Then my hand drops to my pocket. I take out my phone. I power it on. A once-bitten apple lights up. It hangs in suspense for a time—glowing with some important meaning—then vanishes into the ring of an incoming call.

"Mom?" I pick up. "I was—just about to phone."

"And that's what I call a miracle!"

"Yeah. Sorry I haven't been answering. It's been—"

"Nonsense. I know how busy it can get, with all the faculty meetings and such."

"Yeah, it's pretty busy."

"When I think about your poor artistic soul sitting through those things, my heart just breaks. You know how opposed to that

I was. Oh, oh, oh! Why I've been calling!"

"What is it?"

"Well, it's your brother."

"What happened?"

"No. No! It's good news. I mean, he's coming back!"

"What?"

"Yeah! He'd gotten himself into some *cult*, by the sound of it."

"A cult?"

"Yes!"

"But he's out now?"

"He's taking some long backpacking route through Europe, apparently—he wouldn't say anything more than that. You know how cryptic he is—that little bean. But he's coming back. Any day now!"

My heart flutters. My voice cracks.

"Mom, where are you now?"

"You mean, like right now?"

"You're here, aren't you? In town."

"Darling, I know you told me not to come back, but given—"

"Mom, I'm glad you're here. Where are you staying?"

"That motel I would send your father to. It's charming, actually. You know, I'm beginning to think he enjoyed being sent away!"

"How does breakfast sound?"

"Breakfast?"

"At our place. Tomorrow morning. Will you make it?"

"Oh. Well, what about N—"

She trips over the name.

"What about Neve? I'm sure she'd love to see you. I would too."

The silence this time is broken up by the sound, almost certainly, of crying.

"I have to go," Mom says, as she hangs up.

A sea of notifications swells in my hand. I've been gone less than a week, but there is so much to catch up on. I lie on the grass and get into it. I listen to all of Mom's unheard messages. I read back over Neve's texts of despair and her requests that I chime in on paint color. As for the message boards, they're on fire with news of depopulating cities, rising prices in virtual real estate, staggering declines in sexual statistics, vaccine fraud, AI breakthroughs, and—of course—more disappearances. There are already forty-three "notable people" reported missing, most famously the guru Hari Rajneesh, who'd dodged rape and racketeering charges in the United States, but enjoyed a vast following in Europe. A leadership vacuum has already caused various chapters to disband. Acolytes are returning home.

I let the phone fall on my chest. I shut my eyes, but tears escape them. From nests all over the cemetery, vast families of birds are singing.

It's dark when I get home. I park the Corvette, stuff my tie into my jacket pocket, and head up our driveway. I lock the door behind me and toss the keys into a keybowl you must have bought in my absence. I pick up on the scent of garlic and basil, and follow it across the living room, where an episode of *Unsolved Mysteries* is paused on screen. I step into the kitchen. On the stove a pot of spaghetti sits beside a half bottle of Riesling. I grab a fork and stand over the stove, eating the lukewarm spaghetti, as I investigate matters further on my phone.

I read up on Hari's cult, with its documented practices of grooming and sexual abuse. I look into Camillio, known to Interpol as Morel, who has defrauded women of at least $10 million. I find Will everywhere, from Instagram to YouPorn, where I'd first spotted the red-hatted lover. Maxim, on the other hand, has left no footprints. On the message boards, though, the weeklong silence of the shitposter-provocateur *annusmaximus69* doesn't seem to be a coincidence. And Group 69 is, in fact, a real thing. I spend a lot of time looking for River and eventually give up. Only as I leave the kitchen and head back across the living room do I notice the image frozen on TV. A social media composite slaps the screen with news of the "Ladykiller" and shows a shadowy man with a guitar walking down a boardwalk. I smile, then turn it off.

You've not only made me dinner, but also cleaned the house. Freshly ironed clothes are folded and stacked on the laundry machine. At the foot of the stairs, mandevilla flowers have been added. I head up and take the corridor to the nursery. That is, finally and definitively, what it is. The boxes have been moved out. The walls have been painted baby blue. The broken window has been patched up and security bars installed. My cigarettes on the ledge are out of reach. You must have hired a small army of men to get all this done while I was away. Outside, the neighborhood stands in peace and above it a full white moon shines like a licked plate. Inside, by the soft-powdered moonlight, a cradle is illuminated. You have already set the bed. I place my hand on the little pillow, where a baby will soon be dreaming.

Our bedroom door is cracked open. Your head is resting on your hands—your naked body buried in folds of white. It's cute how you pretend to sleep.

"Hey," I say.

"Hey," you say, with a sleepy voice. "Did you eat something? I left some—"

"Yeah. It was delicious."

"Oh, I'm so glad. You must be tired."

"No. I'm not tired."

"Really? You don't have jetlag?"

"No."

"No?"

"No, I don't have jetlag."

You turn around suddenly. The sheets fall off like an avalanche, revealing all of you. Your body is stunning—a majestic landscape of high hills and deep, shadowy valleys. Your eyes are lit by candlelight.

"Babe?" you say. "Are you serious?"

"I'm serious," I say, stepping to the edge of the bed.

You sit up and put your face against my stomach. You cry against it.

"Thank you," you say, through your tears. "Thank you. Thank you. Thank you."

I kiss your sweet lips. Then I lay you down.

"Gently," you say, as you take me in. "Please."

When I have gone as far as I can, your muscles convulse and tighten around me, like you're holding a boat at harbor. You're teasing me, I think, and I silence you with a push.

"Oh," you say.

With the next one, your eyes roll back a little. A third shuts your eyes completely.

"Babe," you say. "I've missed you."

And I've missed you. I hold down your hands. Your nails sink into my flesh. I push harder.

"Don't stop. Never stop."

My breath quickens. Sweat falls and explodes on your breasts. Your body tightens to its touch.

"I'm all yours," you whisper. "I always have been, you know."

Then you start moaning. A streak of red blushes down your neck. You climb mine, catch my ear, and say—

"I'm so close already."

You moan even louder now. And I push against you even harder—with all my force—as a mad captain on the wild sea. I watch the waves break upon your face.

"Baby, I'm almost—"

Your back arches.

"I'm almost—"

Your stomach twists into itself.

"—almost."

Then, finally, you gasp.

Your body ripples out.

When your eyelids flip open, I find no eyes there. Like the statue of an ancient goddess, you have vanished.

For a moment, you appear to me as a perfect stranger.

Then I vanish too.

The air is warm and sweet.

When I surface, you receive me with the sweetest smile in the world.

"You fucked me from the bottom of your heart," you say.

You're still working me, tugging at me for everything I have. Then you let me off. I fall onto my stomach and rest my head against the sheets. I watch as you get into a new formation. You grab your shins, bring your knees in, and push them against your breasts.

"You're going to be the perfect mom," I say.

"You think so?"

"Yeah, I do."

"Call me crazy, but I have a feeling he's a boy."

You get off the bed. I turn my head the other way. The candle warms my face. We have a lifetime supply of these candles, thanks to that business of yours, and I'm glad for it. I watch its dancing flame, its dripping wax, its smoke rising like a memory.

"Yeah, I can already feel him," you call from the bathroom. "He's definitely a boy!"

Now is not the time, Neve, but one day very soon I will tell you about my journey to the Hive—you will read all about it in this book. And when you do, I hope you will not hurt so much—or ask too many questions about what was real and what was not. In time I believe you will understand why, one way or the other, I had to go there. And maybe you will even forgive me for my odyssey—because, after all, it was also for you. I had to travel to the end of the world to meet not just my enemies, but yours—and to burn them down. You are all my muses in one, of course. You are the last of them—the greatest of them—mine. You inspired me to write this book, Neve. When I finish it, I'm going to dedicate it to you. I'm sorry it won't win the prizes or make the lists, as you would like. I doubt anyone will even want to publish it. But I'm sure we'll find a way to get it out. I hope it makes you proud.

In such reveries the candle melts. A bead of wax catches fire. Time drips slowly down. Finally everything is coming together and I see our life ahead: the children we will have, the home we will make, the new world we will create together, like Adam and Eve. Or more like—I smile—Adam and *Neve*. Yes, everything is coming together now. And even the sound of your peeing is comforting—wonderfully familiar to me—just like that sweet and fiery perfume—the black smoke rising from the flame. It's getting pretty intense, actually. It's getting in my eyes and making them water, too. I know your candles were defective, Neve, but this one really does look dangerous. It's catching fire right before my eyes—twisting and breaking down—melting so grotesquely—like an agonized human body being incinerated—a corpse caught in an inferno—and this is somehow familiar, too—horribly familiar—just like that sweet sickening scent—the incestuous perfume of burning honey...

Bzzzzzzz.

My heart freezes at this sound—only I don't believe I've actually heard it. I hold my breath and wait in silence. Then I hear it again.

Bzzzzzzzzzzz!

And now my heart starts pounding. I turn around to say—
"Neve?"

But it's not you I see—or not you exactly. Your body is laced up in black lingerie. Your face is hidden behind a golden mask.

"Is this a joke?"

Or maybe it's some kind of role play—I don't know. It wouldn't be the first time you tried something kinky.

"Neve, come on. Take that off."

You don't take off the mask, though. You only say, coldly—

"But I'm not Neve. You know who I am."

And then I see it, clutched in your hands: a golden spear.

"Did you think you would get away with it?" you say. "Did you really think you could destroy us?"

As you raise the spear above you, chills rush up my spine. They freeze my heart in terror. They paralyze my mind.

"On behalf of the Hive," you say, "I am honored to stand before you as your final judge and judgment. After a period of deliberation, and taking into account..."

"Neve," I interrupt. "What's happening?"

That's not really the question, of course. It's just that, in these moments, the conspiracy is too huge to fathom—the real questions too many to ask: *How did this all begin, Neve? Was it Mandy who reached out to you or the other way around—whose doing was this? When you sent me off to the Hive, did you really want me to fuck her? Is that why you gave me the hall pass? Did you actually believe she would kill me? You must have believed that, right? You couldn't have known I'd come back, right? You couldn't have been my Queen all along.* But you don't look like you're in the mood for questions, Neve. Your mask of scorn reflects but a single purpose. Your hands, clutching the spear, shake above your head.

"This is a mistake," I say, my voice shaking too. "Please, Neve. Just give me a minute. Let me explain."

But you're not in the mood for explanations, either. You

start up again—

"After a period of deliberation, and taking into account your repeated crimes against women, which include, but are not limited to, manipulation, abuse of power, infidelity, grooming, and rape..."

"But that's not true! It's not what happened. I know I haven't been the best husband to you. I know that. But Neve, I lov—"

This time my words are cut. My breath is caught in my throat.

"On behalf of the Hive," you declare, stabbing the spear into my chest, "I reclaim the life you have taken from us. I punish your crimes. And I forgive you your sins."

Then, bursting into tears, you run out of the bedroom. In the hallway, the light catches your sexy little costume. I try to move, but it seems I've been impaled into the bed. The spear has gone right through my chest. My voice barely escapes—

"I love you, Neve."

Then a numb pain spreads in my bones. Something cold and chemical is taking over my mind. But I can still hear you puttering around downstairs.

"Neve, come back," I say. "You've had your fun—I hope you've gotten it out of your system—but let's be reasonable now. You know we can work through this, right? You know we have to. If not us, then who?"

Yet my voice weakens with every word. My breath thins out.

"The story can't end like this, right? You of all people know that. Neve, please come back. We have a world to save."

Silence now, except the ticking of a clock and the crackling of a flame. The candle has almost completely melted. The fire is at its end. But as it dies, the fire in my mind is inflamed. I see it burning there, bright and hot against the dark sea. And one day, I think, on the other side of this nightmare—after the fires have ravaged the world and the machines have collapsed and nature has taken everything back—some long-lost boy will brave the seas and dock his boat on that island again. And he will find the manor with its books. And he will find the chapel. And he will find the knight's armor on the sand. And the boy will have almost everything he needs to create the world again.

"Neve," I whisper, as I fade out. "I thought we're in this together."

All is darkness now. All is silent and still. But I know it's not over for us, baby—it never is. I can't see you anymore, but I can still feel your nails in my flesh. I can still smell your honey and ash—so that was *your* scent all along. And I can still hear you buzzing around, baby—there must be a reason you haven't left yet. It means we still have a chance, right? There is still a chance and you know that, too. So then just come back, okay? Don't be stupid like I've been. Come back and take this spear out of me and heal this wound and we will make everything right again. That *is* you buzzing, isn't it? That *is* you coming back? I *know* it's you, my little bug—so then fly into my darkness now! Come in and light this place up again! Come and dance your dazzling dance—zig and zag for me—do your waggle and your shake. And sing your song again, baby—only your song can knock me out and turn me on—never stop buzzing for me—*bzzzz*—yes, just like that, Queen—*bzzzz z*—fly high and sing—*bzz z—b zzz zz z—bzzzzz z z*

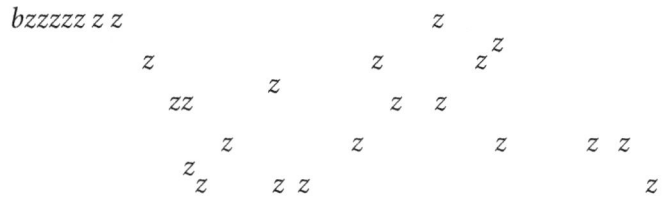

z
z   z   z
zz   z   z z
  z   z   z   z z
 z
  z   z z   z

z
z

z z
 z
z